Reviewers can't resist the Buchanans!

"Mallery is at her addictive best in the charming second installment of her Buchanan family saga... the bestselling author crafts vivid characters and a winning story about the risk and joy of second love, studded with warm, alluring sex scenes."
—*Publishers Weekly* on *Irresistible*

"*Irresistible* is a lot of fun....
I can say I've found my summer beach read!"
—*All About Romance*

"Mallery has written an emotionally charged story of two people who are perfect for each other but need to get past their personal demons before they can forge a relationship. This is one book that lives up to its title."
—*Booklist* on *Irresistible*

"Using her patented blend of wit and humor, Mallery explores deeply complicated family relationships that are laced with love and loss. Outstanding!"
—*RT Book Reviews* on *Delicious* (4½ stars)

"Seasoned with humor, the start to Mallery's new Buchanan series has a wonderful cast of characters.... Readers who can't get enough of Nora Roberts' family series will latch on to Mallery's, which is sure to be a hit."
—*Booklist* on *Delicious* (starred review)

"An outstanding book...Susan Mallery has written a winner with *Delicious*, and the series looks to be a knockout group of books you won't want to miss."
—*Romance Reviews Today*

**Also available from
Susan Mallery and HQN Books**

**And don't miss Susan's new Fools Gold series,
beginning in summer 2010!**

SUSAN
MALLERY
Sizzling

HQN™

ISBN-13: 978-0-373-77519-4

SIZZLING

CHAPTER ONE

UNTIL 6:45 ON THAT Thursday morning, women had always loved Reid Buchanan.

They'd started leaving notes in his locker long before he'd figured out the opposite sex could be anything but annoying. During his sophomore year of high school, his hormones had kicked in and he'd become aware of all the possibilities. Over spring break of that year, Misty O'Connell, a senior, seduced him in her parents' basement on a rainy Seattle afternoon, during an MTV *Real World* marathon.

He'd adored women from that moment on and they had returned his affection. Until today, when he casually opened the morning paper to see his picture next to an article with the headline: Fame, absolutely. Fortune, you bet. But good in bed? Not so much.

Reid nearly spit out his coffee as he jerked to his feet and stared at the page. He blinked, then rubbed his eyes and read the headline again.

Not good in bed? NOT GOOD IN BED?

"She's crazy," he muttered, knowing the author had to be a woman he'd dated and dumped. This was about revenge. About getting back at him by humiliating him in public. Because he *was* good in bed, dammit. Better than good.

He made women scream on a regular basis. They clawed his back—he had the scars to prove it. They stole into his hotel room at night when he was on the road, they begged, they followed him home and offered him anything if he would just sleep with them again.

He was better than good, he was a god!

He was also completely and totally screwed, he thought as he sank back into his chair and scanned the article. Sure enough, the author had gone out with him. It had been one night of what she described as nearly charming conversation, almost funny stories from his past and a so-so couple of hours naked. It was all couched in "don't sue me" language. Things like "Just one reporter's opinion" and "Maybe it's just me, but…"

She'd also claimed he regularly blew off charity events and kids in need—neither of which was true. He couldn't blow off what he never agreed to do. And that was his standard rule—not to get personally involved in anything, including benefits.

He studied the name of the reporter, but it meant nothing. Not even a whisper of a memory. There wasn't a picture, so he grabbed his laptop and went online to the paper's Web site. Under the bio section he found a photo.

He studied the average-looking brunette and had a vague recollection of something. Okay, yeah, so maybe he'd slept with her, but just because he couldn't remember what had happened didn't mean it hadn't been incredible.

But along with the fuzzy memories was the idea that he'd gone out with her during the playoffs, when his former team had been fighting for a chance to make the World Series and he'd been back in Seattle, in his first year of retirement. He'd been bitter and angry about being out of the game. He might also have been drunk.

"I was thinking about baseball instead of her. So sue me," he muttered as he read the article again.

Deep, soul-shriveling embarrassment chilled him. Instead of calling him a bastard to all of her friends, this woman had chosen to humiliate him in public. How the hell was he supposed to fight back? In the courts? He'd been around long enough to know he didn't have a case, and even if he did, how was he supposed to win? Parade a bunch of women around who would swear he made the earth move just by kissing them?

While he kind of liked that idea, he knew it wouldn't make a difference. He'd been a famous baseball player once, and there was nothing the public liked more than to see the mighty fall.

His friends would read this. His family would read this. Everyone he knew in Seattle would read it. He could only imagine what would happen when he walked into his restaurant, the Downtown Sports Bar today.

At least it was local, he thought grimly. Contained. He wouldn't have to deal with hearing from his old baseball buddies.

The phone rang. He grabbed it.

"Hello?"

"Mr. Buchanan? Reid? Hi. I'm a producer here at *Access Hollywood.* I was wondering if you'd like to make a comment on the article in the Seattle paper this morning. The one about—"

"I know what it's about," he growled.

"Oh, good." The young woman on the other end of the phone giggled. "How about an interview? I could have a crew there this morning. I'm sure you want to tell your side of things."

He hung up with a curse. *Access Hollywood?* Already?

The phone rang again. He pulled the plug and thought about throwing it against the wall, but the damn phone wasn't responsible for this disaster.

His cell rang. He hesitated before picking it up. The caller ID showed a familiar number. A friend from Atlanta. He exhaled with relief. Okay, this call he could take.

"Hey, Tommy. How's it going?"

"Reid, buddy. Have you seen it? The article? It's everywhere. Total bummer. And for the record, dude—too much information."

IF LORI JOHNSTON HAD believed in reincarnation, she would have wondered if she'd been a general, or some other kind of tactical expert in one of her past lives. There was nothing she liked more than taking a few unrelated elements, mixing them together and creating the perfect solution to a problem.

This morning she had to deal with hospital equipment arriving the day *after* it was supposed to and a catering service delivery with every single entrée wrong. In her free time, she had her new patient to meet and safely deliver home, assuming the ambulance driver wasn't late. Where other people would be screaming and making threats, Lori felt energized. She would meet this challenge as she met all others and she would be victorious.

The delivery men finished assembling the state-of-the-art hospital bed and stepped back for her inspection. She stretched out on the mattress to check for bumps and low spots. What might just be annoying to someone healthy could be impossible to endure when one had a broken hip.

When the mattress passed inspection, she worked the controls.

"There's a squeak when I raise the bed," she said. "Can you fix that?"

The men shared an exasperated glance, but she didn't care. Trying to get comfortable while in pain was bad enough, but an annoying noise could make things worse.

Next she checked out the bedside table on wheels, which was fine, as were the wheelchair and the walker.

While the workmen dealt with the squeak, Lori hurried into the massive kitchen where the catering staff sorted through the meals they'd brought.

"The chili?" a woman in a white uniform asked.

"Has to go." Lori pointed to the list she'd posted on the refrigerator. "This is a woman in her seventies. She's had a heart attack and surgery on a broken hip. She's on medication. I said tasty, but not spicy. We want to encourage her to eat, but she may still have stomach issues from all the medication. She doesn't need to lose weight, so that's not a problem. Healthy, tempting dishes. Not chili, not sushi, nothing fancy."

She'd been so specific on the phone, too, she thought with minor exasperation.

Still, she would prevail and when the details were handled, she would stop at Dilettante Chocolates for a little something. Chocolate always brightened her day.

"You could beat them. That would get their attention."

That voice. Lori didn't have to turn around to know who was standing in the doorway of the kitchen. They'd only met once, at her interview.

During the twenty-minute session, she discovered it was possible to be desperately attracted to someone she despised. Everything about him was burned into her brain, including the sound of his voice. For a moment, it made her consider a lobotomy.

She braced herself for the impact of the dark, knowing eyes, the handsome-but-just-shy-of-too-handsome face and the casual slouch that should have annoyed the heck out of her, but instead made her want to melt like a twelve-year-old at a Jesse McCartney concert.

Reid Buchanan was everything she disliked in a man. He'd always had it easy, so nothing had value. Women threw themselves at him. He'd had a brilliant career playing baseball, although she'd never followed sports and didn't know any details. And he'd never once in his entire life bothered with a woman as ordinary as her.

"Don't you have something better to do than just show up and annoy me?" she asked as she turned toward him.

Her reaction to his physical presence was immediate. She found it difficult to breathe, let alone think.

"Annoying you is an unexpected bonus," he said, "but not the reason I'm here. My grandmother's coming home today."

"I know that. I arranged it."

"I thought I'd stop by to visit her."

"I'm sure knowing you stopped by four hours before she was due home will brighten her day so much that the healing process will be cut in half."

She pushed past him, ignoring the quick brush of her arm against his and the humiliating burst of heat that ignited inside her. She was pathetic. No, she was worse than pathetic—one day she would grow enough to achieve pathetic and that would be a victory.

"She won't be here until this afternoon?" he asked as he followed her back into the library.

"Unfortunately, no. But it was thrilling to see you. So sorry you can't stay."

He leaned against the door frame. He did that a lot. He must know how good he looked doing it, Lori thought grimly. No doubt he practiced at home.

She knew Reid was shallow and selfish and only interested in women as perfect as himself, so why was she attracted to him? She was intelligent. She should know better. And she did…in her head. It was the rest of her that was the problem.

She was a total and complete cliché—a smart, average-looking woman pining after the unobtainable. The bookstores probably contained an entire shelf of self-help books dedicated to her condition. If she believed in self-help books, she could go get herself healed.

As it was, she was stuck with enduring.

"Don't you have to go away?" she asked.

"For now, but I'll be back."

"I'll count the hours."

"You do that." He stayed where he was, apparently unmovable.

"What?" she asked. "Are we waiting for something?"

He smiled, a slow, sexy smile that caused her heart to actually skip a beat. It was a new low.

"You don't read the paper, do you?" he asked.

"No. I go running in the morning and I listen to music."

The smile brightened. "Good. I'll see you later."

"You could wait until the evening nurse shows up and visit then. Wouldn't that be a great plan?"

"But then you'd miss me. Snarling at me is the best part of your day. 'Bye, Lori."

And then he was gone.

"YOU'RE GLORIA BUCHANAN'S home-care nurse?" the woman at the main nurses' station asked. "Oh, honey, you have my sympathy."

Lori was far more interested in getting her patient home and settled than chatting with the rehab facility staff, but she knew the importance of getting as much information as she could up front. The more she knew, the better plan she could develop.

"Cranky from the pain?" Lori asked as she glanced at the name tag on the other woman's scrubs top. "That's fairly typical. As she heals, her mood will improve."

"I don't think so. She's more than cranky," Vicki said. "Miserable. She complains constantly. She hates her room, the food, her treatments, the staff, the sheets, the temperature, the weather. Let me tell you, we're all so grateful to get her out of here." Vicki leaned close. "If you have another job offer, take it. Even if it pays less. Trust me, whatever you're making, it's not enough."

Lori was used to patients who were frustrated by their condition. "I'll be fine."

"You've already met her?"

"Ah, no."

It was Lori's practice to visit her patients before bringing them home. Establishing a good working relationship ahead of time often smoothed the transition process. However both times she'd stopped by the rehab facility to meet Gloria, she'd been told that Mrs. Buchanan was refusing all visitors. Calling ahead to make an appointment hadn't changed the fact.

Vicki shook her head. "It's your funeral, hon. You haven't met anyone like this woman before. But that's for you to decide. I've made copies of her chart. She's already signed out by the doctor. He was as happy to get rid of her as the rest of us. She had her lawyer call and threaten to pull his license— twice. I hope they're paying you a lot."

They were, which was why Lori had taken the job. She was saving up so that she could take a few months off next year. But even without the high pay, she would have kept the job—just to prove everyone wrong about Gloria Buchanan.

Lori took the thick folder. "She's making progress with her physical therapy?"

"If the screaming is anything to go by." Vicki sighed. "Yes, she's healing. We took x-rays of the broken hip yesterday and she looks good. The heart attack was minor, the blockage is gone and with her new medication, she should live another twenty years…God help us."

Lori knew very little about Gloria personally. Researching her, she'd discovered that the woman had been widowed at a young age. She'd taken a single restaurant and, during a time when women were more likely to either stay home or be schoolteachers, created an empire. Gloria's only son had died in his early thirties and his wife had been killed in a car accident a few years later.

Despite what must have been overwhelming grief, Gloria had taken in her four grandchildren and raised them herself, all the while managing four restaurants. Anyone who had suffered that much had earned the right to be a little difficult.

"I'll go introduce myself, then," Lori said. "The ambulance is already here to transport her home. I'll pick up the paperwork on the way out."

Vicki nodded. "Sure thing. I'll be right here. Good luck."

Lori waved and walked toward Gloria's room.

The poor woman. Everyone was determined to see her as difficult. But from what Lori had been able to find out, no one in her family wanted anything to do with her. Gloria was injured, lonely and probably feeling frail. Isolation was never good under any circumstances.

She found the right room and knocked once before entering.

"Mrs. Buchanan," she said as she smiled at the small, white-haired woman lying in the hospital bed. "I'm Lori Johnston. I'll be your day nurse while you're convalescing."

Gloria put down the book she'd been reading and glanced at Lori over her glasses. "I doubt that. Reid was going to be choosing the nurses who would care for me. I'm sure he found the idea hilarious. He only likes beautiful women with large breasts. Unfortunately they have IQs smaller than their waist. You're neither attractive nor well-endowed. You have the wrong room."

Lori opened her mouth, then closed it. She was too surprised to be insulted, which was probably a good thing. "I don't doubt your grandson's taste in women. In fact it fits everything I already know about him. I may not be his ideal, but I'm still your nurse. At least during the day. You'll have an evening and a night nurse."

"You're not anyone I want to work with."

"How do you know?"

"I have a sense about people. I don't like the look of you. Go away."

Now this was a level of crabby Lori could relate to. She smiled as she crossed the room to the bed. "Here's the thing. I have an ambulance waiting right outside. There are a couple of burly guys who are going to drive you home. At your house, there's a bed waiting downstairs, food and privacy you never get in a place like this. Why don't you wait until we're there before firing me?"

"You're humoring me. I loathe that."

"I'm not thrilled about being insulted, but I'm going to go with it. What about you?"

Gloria narrowed her gaze. "You're not one of those perpetually cheerful people, are you?"

"No. I'm sarcastic and demanding."

"Have you had sex with my grandson?"

Lori laughed. In her dreams, perhaps, but never in real life. After all, she was neither attractive nor well-endowed. Talk about being dismissed. "There hasn't been time. Is it a requirement?"

Gloria sighed. "The man has no Off switch. If it has a vagina, he's probably been in it."

"Not mine. I'll agree he's shallow but pretty. Isn't that always the way? So are you packed?"

Gloria's expression tightened. "I do not pack my own belongings. Even if I did, my condition would prevent any such activity."

So the momentary rapport was gone. Well, it had been good while it lasted.

"No problem. I'll collect everything. Do you have a suitcase? If not, I'm sure there are some shopping bags in the staff's lunch room."

The older woman practically crackled with outrage. "You will not put anything of mine in a shopping bag. Do you know who I am?"

Lori was careful to keep her back to her patient as she pulled a suitcase out of the closet by the bathroom. Gloria knowing she found this conversation kind of funny wouldn't help things. "Sure. You're Gloria Buchanan. Speaking of which, I think I'm going to call you Gloria. Mrs. Buchanan is so formal and we're going to be getting really close."

"Not after I have you fired."

Lori set the suitcase on the only chair in the room and opened it. "You don't want to fire me, Gloria. I'm really good at my job. I have experience with both heart and orthopedic patients. I'm tough enough to bully you into doing everything you should be doing. That's going to get you on your feet faster. Because here's the thing. Old ladies who break their hips have one of two outcomes. They get better or they die. *My* patients don't die."

Gloria glared at her. "You're not a very nice person."

"Neither are you."

Gloria stiffened. "How dare you? I am incredibly polite and thoughtful."

"Really? Want to hear what the staff here has to say about you?"

"They're a group of incompetent fools. Everything about this place is substandard."

"Then you're going to love my standards." She leaned close and lowered her voice. "I'm a real bitch about getting it right. You should respect that."

"You will not swear in my presence, young woman. I won't tolerate it."

"Fair enough. I won't swear and you won't act annoying."

"I'm never annoying."

"Should we take a vote of your peers?"

"I have no peers."

Which, Lori remembered a little too late, was sadly correct. From what Reid had told her when he'd hired her, Gloria didn't have any friends at all and her grandchildren rarely had anything to do with her. No wonder she was so difficult. It was heartbreaking.

Lori finished packing Gloria's belongings. There had been a few nightgowns, some undergarments, the clothes she'd been wearing when they'd brought her in, two books and a few cosmetics. Nothing else. No flowers, no get-well teddy bear, nothing personal. Nothing from family.

It was one thing if the elderly were alone, Lori thought, getting really annoyed with the Buchanan grandchildren. But when there was plenty of family hanging around and they were all just too busy with their own precious lives, it really pissed her off.

Lori pushed aside her feelings and moved next to the bed.

"So here's the plan," she said, lightly touching Gloria's arm. Physical contact helped with healing. "I'm going to get the nurse to give you something for the pain. The trip home is going to jar you and that will hurt. The stuff she's using is pretty strong, so expect to be a little out of it for a while."

Gloria's eyes narrowed as she jerked her hand free of Lori's touch. "There is no need to speak to me as if I'm eight. I'm completely capable of understanding without a lengthy and moronic explanation. Fine. Get the nurse in here. She'll be delighted to indulge her sadomasochistic tendencies on my person one last time."

"Okay, then. Be right back."

Lori walked to the nurses' station where Vicki was ready. "We're good to go. If you want to give her the shot, we'll head out."

Vicki stepped from around the counter. "So? What did you think?"

"I like her."

Vicki stopped in midstride and stared. "You're kidding. You like her? Gloria Buchanan? She's mean."

"She's alone and in pain and scared."

"You're giving her way too much credit, but, hey, if it gets her gone, I'm all for it."

REID SAT in his houseboat and wished he'd bought a condo in a security building instead. Here, on the water, he was too exposed, too accessible. He'd closed all the blinds and pulled all the shades, but that hadn't kept the press away, dammit. They were everywhere—setting up cameras on his dock, crawling up to his balcony. Speedboats kept zipping by outside.

They wanted a story and they wanted it now. No one cared that he was totally humiliated. His manager had told him the interest would die down in a few days and to just lay low until then. Great advice, but where was Reid supposed to go? This was his town. Everyone in Seattle knew who he was.

His cell phone rang. He glanced at the screen before answering it, then frowned when he saw his grandmother's name and number. If she'd read the morning paper, he was going to be verbally beaten and left for dead.

"Yes?" he said, his voice clipped.

"It's Lori Johnston. Your grandmother's day nurse. Your grandmother is leaving the rehab facility now and should be home within the hour."

He grinned. "Let me guess. You want me to stop by and cheer her up." So much for Miss Priss's disdain. She needed him. Eventually they all did.

"Not exactly. She's been given some medication and is pretty out of it."

"You're drugging my grandmother?" he asked in outrage.

Lori sighed. "My God, don't be such a girl. Of course I'm not drugging her. I asked the doctor to prescribe some pain medication. In her condition a car ride can be excruciating. Not that you would care."

He ignored that. "How did you get her phone?"

"I took it from her purse and before you start squealing in protest, I did it because I need to get in touch with you. No one sent the woman flowers or anything. There wasn't a get-well card or note in her room. I find that astonishing. I'm surprised any of you could bring yourself to actually give her medical care. Why didn't you just put her on an ice floe and push her out to sea?"

Reid opened his mouth, then closed it. To anyone who didn't really know Gloria, the lack of attention was pretty horrible.

"She's not a flower kind of person," he said at last.

"Is that the best you can do? Claiming an allergy would have been a lot smarter. So you're the rich baseball player, right?"

"Ex-baseball player. I was a pitcher."

"Whatever. Order your grandmother some flowers. A lot of flowers. Have them delivered at regular intervals. Do you hear me? Throw in a few stuffed animals. Bears, cats, giraffes, I don't care. Something to give this poor woman the illusion that her family cares if she lives or dies. If you don't, you'll be answering to me and you won't like that."

Her concern was misplaced, but he respected her enthusiasm. "You don't scare me."

"Not yet, but I will."

CHAPTER TWO

LORI GOT GLORIA SETTLED at home with a minimum of fuss. Of course, the fact that her patient was practically unconscious really helped things along.

Lori unpacked Gloria's suitcase, confirmed her physical therapy appointment for the next morning and picked out something light for her evening meal. While the older woman was getting better, she'd lost a little too much weight in the past few weeks. Lori intended to put some meat back on her fashionably thin bones.

She was on her way to look in on her patient when the doorbell rang. She answered it and found two delivery men, each holding several vases of fresh flowers. One had a giant giraffe tucked under his arm.

"Perfect," she said as she motioned for them to leave the flowers on the floor of the foyer. Lori had already picked out several strategic spots for floral displays in Gloria's room. "I appreciate the fast service."

"The guy who ordered these wanted us to ask if you're satisfied now."

She grinned. "Tell him not even close."

The man shrugged, then he and his partner left.

Lori grabbed two of the larger vases and headed for the study. She'd just finished with the last arrangement when Gloria opened her eyes.

"What are you doing?" she asked, her voice surprisingly strong for someone who had, until this second, been zonked on pain medication.

"Putting out flowers. Your grandchildren sent them. Aren't they beautiful?"

"No. I hate flowers. And I see no reason for my grandchildren to send me anything. They're far too selfish."

Lori agreed with that, but kept her smile cheery. "I love the smell. Don't you?"

"Absolutely not. Cut flowers die quickly and that depresses me. Take them away."

"Sorry, no." Unfazed by Gloria's complaints, Lori made one last trip to grab the giraffe and returned with it.

Gloria actually raised her bed slightly and glared at the stuffed animal. "What is that? It's awful."

Lori hugged the cuddly creature. "It's here to make you smile. I think it's adorable."

"You have very low standards."

"I don't think so." She propped up the giraffe in a corner. "Okay, that's all done. Let's get you something to eat. You must be starved."

"I'm not hungry at all. Go away."

Lori did as she requested, but only went as far as the kitchen. She popped the entrée into the microwave and checked the rest of the tray. Everything seemed to be in place.

After the microwave dinged, she collected the steaming food and carried it back into the study.

Gloria might claim to not want dinner, but she'd raised her bed in anticipation of eating. A good sign.

"Here you go," Lori said, setting the tray on the table in front of her.

Gloria stared at the food, then pushed at the table. As it was on wheels, it slid away.

"This is disgusting. I will not eat it. Take it away. I'm not hungry."

Lori put her hands on her hips. Most of her crabby patients at least started out being pleasant. It usually took a couple of days for the anger and fear to come out. She had to respect that Gloria started as she meant to go on.

"You're too thin," she said calmly. "There are one of two ways to fix that. You can eat and gain back a couple of pounds, or we can hook you up to a feeding tube. I have to tell you, based on professional observation, you're going to want to eat. The feeding tube route is pretty unpleasant. However, it's an option. After all, you're rich, right? Nothing but the best for you."

"Then why are you here?"

Lori blinked. Okay—so there was nothing wrong

with Gloria's mental reasoning skills. "I'm the best. And really expensive. You should respect that."

Gloria looked her up and down, then sniffed. "You're shabby and poor. I can smell the poverty on you."

"Is that from personal experience? After all, you started out poor. Wasn't your first job working as a maid in a hotel?"

Gloria glared at her. "I will not discuss my past with you."

"Why not? I'm actually interested in how you got from there to here. You were running an empire at a time when most women were afraid to dream that big. You're a pioneer. I respect that."

"You think I care about your opinion on anything?"

Lori thought for a second, then smiled. "Yeah, I do. Not enough people respect you, which is their loss." She pushed the table back over the bed and nudged the tray a tiny bit closer to Gloria. "I picked out the meals for the first few days, but the catering service left a menu. I'm happy to let you look it over and choose your own food. Or if you'd prefer to hire a cook, that's fine, too."

Gloria kept her expression neutral, but Lori thought she saw a flash of emotion. She just couldn't tell which one.

"You're very free with my money," Gloria muttered.

Lori laughed, even though she knew the other

woman wasn't trying to be funny. "One of the perks of the job. Do you want me to cut up your chicken?"

Gloria's gaze narrowed. "Only if you want me to stab you with my fork."

"I'm pretty spry. You'd have to move quickly."

"I would be motivated."

At last—a flash of something very close to humor. A good sign. "Okay—I'll let you eat in peace. Do you want the television on?" She opened the cabinet doors, exposing the television and DVD player, then left the remote on the bed. "Call if you need anything."

By FOUR-THIRTY that afternoon, Lori felt as if she'd been the victim of a hit-and-run. Her momentary breakthrough with Gloria was nothing more than a distant memory once the older woman finished complaining that her bed was too hard, her pillows too soft, that her sheets had an odd smell and that the television buzzed.

"I'll get a serviceman in here as soon as possible," Lori said, doing her best to be patient. She also had to keep herself from looking at her watch. This had been the longest afternoon of her life. And to think it had only been a half day with Gloria.

She kept telling herself that Gloria was unhappy for a reason and that things would get better.

A little after five she headed for the kitchen and found a tall, pretty, large-breasted woman unpacking a giant tote bag. Her uniform marked her as a nurse. Her physical description told Lori who had done the hiring.

"Hi," the woman said, smiling brightly. "I'm Sandy Larson, twilight nurse. Which is a first. Usually I'm the night nurse. On call when it's dark. Hey, that sounds like the title of a book. Or a porn movie." Sandy grinned. "Not sure which I'd rather be in. On a good day…"

Lori did her best to greet the woman pleasantly, despite the sudden knot in her stomach. What on earth was wrong with her? So Reid had gone true to type with the other nurse. What did Lori care?

Lori brought Sandy up to speed on Gloria's care. "She's tired so she's a little difficult, but not awful."

"I can handle her," Sandy said. "If my patients give me any trouble, I start talking about my favorite soap opera. That usually bores them into falling asleep. It's why I love the night shift. You day girls work too hard." She leaned toward Lori. "Gotta love this job, though. Twelve hours of pay for an eight hour shift."

"It's great. I'll just go and tell Gloria goodbye."

"Sure thing. See you tomorrow."

Lori nodded and returned to the study. "I'm heading out," she told Gloria. "I'll be back in the morning."

Gloria looked up from the magazine she'd been reading and stared at Lori over her glasses. "I can't imagine why you would think I would care about your comings and goings. Stay or go. It doesn't matter the least to me."

Lori grinned. "I had a good day, too, Gloria. You're more than welcome."

REID PARKED his Corvette behind the Downtown Sports Bar and climbed out. He stood staring at the rear door for a full minute, then told himself it wouldn't be so bad.

Ever since he'd blown out his arm and had to retire from baseball, he'd been working at the family sports bar. "Working" being a loose definition of what he did. In theory he was the general manager. In reality he came and went as he wanted, occasionally worked behind the bar, entertained customers with stories about his baseball career and life and hired the female staff. He'd always thought of the sports bar as a refuge—a place to hang where he was known and admired. Today it was nothing more than a house of shame.

Everyone inside knew him and he was willing to bet his impressive bank account that each one of them had read the morning paper.

"Goddamn it all to hell," he grumbled, then used his key to let himself in the back door.

Figuring he might as well get it over with as quickly as possible, he bypassed the relative safety of his office and walked into the bar.

Instantly the low rumble of conversation stilled and all eyes focused on him. Reid kept moving.

"Hey, hon," one of the waitresses called, her

mouth twisted in some weird almost-normal smile. "Good to see you."

He nodded and continued walking through the happy hour crowd.

"Reid!" one guy yelled. "How's it hanging?"

Reid ignored that, scanned the clusters of patrons and saw two familiar faces in a corner. He headed directly for them.

"Reid." Maddie, one of the waitresses, grabbed his arm. "She's full of shit, okay? That night we were together was great. Let me know if you want me to sign a letter or something."

He nodded at the busty brunette, knowing that they *had* spent the night in bed and unable to remember anything specific in the blur that was his sexual past.

He hurried over to greet his two brothers and sank gratefully into the chair they'd pulled up for him.

They'd positioned their table just right, tucking his chair next to a display case of sports crap. It meant he wasn't in anyone's direct line of sight.

Cal, his older brother, pushed a full mug of beer in his direction. "How you holding up?" he asked.

"How do you think?" Reid took a long swallow. "It's a little slice of hell."

Walker, his younger brother, grimaced sympathetically. "Sucks the big one."

Reid eyed the nachos on the table, but he wasn't hungry. "The worst part is I don't even remember her. It was the week my team was in the playoffs. I'm sure I was drunk." He shook his head. "What does it matter? She wanted revenge and she sure as hell got it. Reporters are everywhere. They're crawling all over the houseboat."

"It's not a defensible position," Walker told him.

Cal looked at Reid. "So speaks our brother, the former marine."

"He knows what he's talking about," Reid grumbled. "I've got to get out of there. I thought about a hotel, but they'll find me there. Someone on the staff will sell me out."

"Come stay with Penny and me," Cal said. "We have room."

Reid hesitated. Their house was big enough, but Cal and Penny had a new baby. They were focused on other things.

"I appreciate the offer, but I'd be in the way."

"You wouldn't," Cal told him.

Walker shrugged. "You can bunk with me, but it would be on a sofa."

"Tempting," Reid said with a grin. "But, no."

"You could always move in with Gloria," Cal said. "No one would think to look for you there. Didn't you say one of her nurses had set up a room for her downstairs?"

"In the study," Reid said slowly, considering the possibility.

"You would have the whole upstairs," Walker told him.

"There's plenty of room," Reid murmured. His moving in would also annoy the hell out of Lori, and that would be a plus.

A woman walked toward the table. She was tall, built and cover-model gorgeous. She smiled at him.

"Darlin', I just wanted to let you know that the night we had together was incredible. I still remember everything about it and I'm willing to swear to it. Want my phone number?"

Reid studied her face and realized he had absolutely no recollection of ever having seen her before. What did that say about him?

"I appreciate the offer," he said. "I'll let you know if I need a signed statement."

"You do that. I'm always willing."

She turned and walked away. He watched her swaying hips and felt absolutely nothing. Given the day he'd had, it would probably be months before he could think about having sex again, and how grim was that?

He leaned back in his chair and looked at his brothers. "That reporter has me by the balls. I can't sue. There's no way to win. It would be a circus. I don't want that. My manager says to lay low and it will blow over."

"He's right," Walker said. "People will get interested in someone else's life."

"When?" Reid asked, knowing it couldn't be soon enough. "I talked to him about the other stuff in the article. Where that bitch of a reporter said I'd blown off kids and charity events. I wouldn't do that."

He hadn't. He hated that kind of stuff, so he made it a point to never accept any kind of invitation where he had to show up and speak. He sent checks…or his manager did.

"Just because some kid sent a letter inviting me to some charity thing doesn't mean I have to go. But that's not how the reporter saw it."

"You have to let it go," Cal said. "You can't do anything about it now."

Reid knew that was the truth, but he hated being painted in asshole colors. "I talked to Seth about the other stuff in the article, that baseball team that went to the state championships. He said that was just a mix-up with the travel agent. I didn't know anything about it."

His brothers looked sympathetic, but that wasn't helping. Maybe because sympathy wasn't enough. Not when he'd been accused of offering to sponsor a baseball team and send them to their state championships, only to have the travel agent forget to include a return ticket. All those kids and their families had been stranded hundreds of miles from home with no way to get back.

"I didn't do anything wrong," he mumbled, knowing in truth, he hadn't done anything at all. "I told Seth to send me everything. The fan mail, the charity requests. I'm going to read them myself."

"And then what?" Cal asked.

"Hell if I know. I'll do something. I have to. It's one thing for that reporter to say I'm lousy in bed, but it's another for her to claim I disappoint kids. I'd never do that."

Not messing up was one of the main reasons he preferred not to get involved at all.

"This sucks," he said, as he reached for his beer. "My life is at a new low point."

"Worse than when you blew out your shoulder?" Walker asked.

"No," Reid said quietly. "Not worse than that."

Walker shrugged. "Just trying to put things in perspective."

No, this wasn't worse, Reid thought, but it was close. A little too close.

REID WAITED until close to ten to drive to his houseboat. He'd borrowed Walker's SUV so he could load up his stuff and transport it to Gloria's house. Despite the late hour, there were two photographers waiting on the dock. They snapped pictures of him going into the houseboat and he heard one of them making a call, saying he'd been found. He also caught a suggestion about him taking an Internet class on how to please women.

Twenty minutes later, he'd packed two suitcases and was backing out of his parking space. The tow truck he'd hired pulled behind the photographers' cars in the guest parking section of the lot, preventing Reid from being followed. The guy would stay there a few more minutes, then leave. All Reid wanted was a clean getaway.

When he reached Gloria's place, Walker was waiting there to help him unload. They traded car keys and Walker left with the SUV. Reid's Corvette was already hidden in the garage.

"Hell of a way to live," he muttered as he walked inside.

He started up the stairs only to stop when he saw a somewhat familiar, tall blonde heading down. She smiled.

"Hey, Reid. How's it going?"

"Good," he lied, as he tried to remember where he knew the woman from. Then he focused on the scrub shirt and realized she was one of Gloria's nurses.

"Sandy," the woman said when they were on the same step. "Sandy Larson. You interviewed me for the job."

Right. And her beaming smile said the interview had gone well. He remembered now—Sandy had been eager to sleep with her favorite player. They'd had a hell of a time on his big desk at the Downtown Sports Bar.

"I heard you're moving in here," Sandy said.

"Temporarily."

"Sure. Makes sense." She touched his arm.

"Listen—I had a great afternoon with you, but I wanted to let you know I'm with someone now. It's exclusive. So I'm not going to be interested in a repeat performance. Please don't take it personally, okay?"

"Of course not," he said, careful to keep his expression politely interested.

He couldn't care less about sleeping with Sandy again, but that wasn't the point. She should be all over him, because hey, he was Reid Buchanan.

But given how his day had gone, why was he even surprised?

LORI ARRIVED a few minutes early for her shift. She put her jacket and purse in the hall closet and found yet another tall, well-built beauty in the kitchen.

She hated that she instantly felt short and curveless. Even worse was the cause. She refused to let a womanizing, brainless twit of a man ruin her day.

"Hi," she said cheerfully. "I'm Lori Johnston."

"Kristie Ellsworth," the stunning brunette said with a smile. "Gloria slept most of the night and woke up asking for you. I guess you made an impression."

"Hopefully a good one."

"I was going to take in her breakfast," Kristie said.

"I can do that if you want to head out."

"That would be great."

Five minutes later Lori walked in with Gloria's breakfast.

"You're back," the older woman said. "How unfortunate."

"I heard you were asking about me, so don't pretend you're not happy to see me."

"I'm not happy. I was asking in the hopes that you'd quit."

"No such luck." She set the tray on the table. "We're going to have to get you a hobby. Something other than being crabby. Maybe knitting. Everyone's doing it."

Gloria ignored that and poked at her pancakes. "I don't eat breakfast. I'll have some coffee and nothing else."

Lori leaned close and lowered her voice. "I have just two words for you, young lady. *Feeding tube.* Don't make me get ugly. Eat and be happy."

"You're a most annoying person."

"I've heard that. It's kind of a point of pride with me."

Gloria stared at her for several seconds, then passed over a section of the newspaper. "Did you read this yesterday?"

"I don't read the paper."

"You should. Women should be aware of what's going on in the world. Which is not the point. Reid has moved in temporarily. Obviously he's taking advantage of my weakened condition. You'd think he was old enough to clean up his own mess, but apparently not. Now he's dragged the family name through the mud. He's a constant disappointment and embarrassment."

Lori glanced at the headline and blinked. "*Good in bed...not so much?* That's kind of cold."

"Apparently he didn't please the reporter and she decided to tell the world. It's disgusting. She's nothing but a slut, but heaven forbid we should say *that*." She tapped the paper. "Read it. Learn from it. My grandson has a way with women. Don't be one of the idiots who falls for him and then gets her heart broken. I have no patience for stupid women."

"You're warning me off," Lori said, suddenly getting it. She grinned. "You're worried about me."

"Go away."

For once, Lori did as she asked, mostly because she wanted to read the article.

She settled at the kitchen table and spread out the paper, then scanned the first couple of paragraphs and winced. No guy wants to be told he's not good in bed, especially in public and in print. That had to hurt.

She almost felt sorry for Reid. While she had no sense of his sexual skill, he had to have learned something with all his experience. Didn't he?

The object of her speculation walked into the kitchen, looking rumpled and exhausted. He'd pulled on jeans and nothing else, his hair was mussed and he needed a shave.

He was fifteen kinds of gorgeous.

Lori watched him as he crossed the kitchen and poured himself a cup of coffee. His impressive muscles flexed and rippled with each movement. He looked warm and sexy and deep inside her stomach she felt the beginnings of a quiver.

He glanced up and saw her.

"Morning," he mumbled, then left.

She didn't exist to him. Never had, never would. Being attracted to him put her so far in the idiot camp that she would never find her way out.

She was an embarrassment to intelligent women everywhere. Worse, there wasn't a damn thing she could do about it.

CHAPTER THREE

LORI PULLED INTO her driveway a little after five. Her neighborhood was light-years away from Gloria's street of gated mansions, but Lori didn't mind. She loved everything about her house.

Its two-bedroom, two-bath size suited her perfectly. She loved the details of the Craftsman style, the built-ins, the moldings. She loved that she'd painted every wall herself and had done most of the remodeling without help. She loved the colors, the garden, the porch, the way the house looked solid…and made her feel safe.

She walked inside and breathed in the scent of garlic. "You're cooking," she yelled by way of greeting. "You're not supposed to be cooking."

Madeline stepped out of the kitchen and grinned. "I don't believe that was in the contract I signed, but I'll have to go check. Besides, I'm having a good day. On good days I want to cook."

Lori studied her sister's face, searching for lines of fatigue or paleness in her coloring. Neither was there. Instead Madeline looked serenely beautiful, as she always had.

In Lori's mind, the family gene pool had a killer sense of humor. Lori was average height, Madeline a few inches taller. Lori had inherited awful orange curls that had thankfully faded to a more muted reddish-gold. Madeline had auburn waves. She woke up looking like a 1940s movie star. With a little effort and some mascara, she looked like a goddess. It had taken Lori most of her life, but she'd finally learned not to be bitter.

"How was day two?" Madeline asked. "Gloria still a challenge?"

"She defines the term. This morning she nearly hinted that she liked having me around and then spent the rest of the day insulting me. I have to say there's nothing wrong with her brain. She's really good at the one-line put-down."

Madeline folded her arms across her University of Washington sweatshirt. "You still like her?"

"I do. I know I shouldn't. There's a power struggle in our future and I'm going to win, but still, there's something about her. She's trying too hard to be a bitch and I can't figure out why. Is it a defense mechanism? A way of coping? Did she have to be a bitch to get ahead all those years ago and forget to turn it off? One of her grandsons called. This guy named Cal. He wanted to come by and check on her. Gloria wouldn't take the call and told me to tell him that she would be dead soon and then he could be happy."

Madeline shook her head. "You didn't tell him that, did you?"

"No, but it made me wonder."

"Not every sick person is a saint. Aren't most of them exactly like they were in their regular life?"

"Yes, in theory. But I just don't want that to be true in Gloria's case. I keep thinking something's there. Maybe it's because Reid was so insistent that she was awful. When I interviewed for the job, he made her sound like the devil."

Madeline grinned. "Oh, so we're back to talking about Reid. You do have him on the brain."

Lori willed herself not to blush. "I have no idea what you're talking about." She sniffed. "I smell garlic but nothing else. What's for dinner?"

"Don't try to change the subject. Admit it. You have a thing for Reid Buchanan. My practical sister has totally fallen for a sports hero."

"Not exactly fallen," Lori muttered. "I have a stupid crush on him, okay? It's chemical, which means it's not my fault. I react to him. But it doesn't mean anything. I'll get over it. I'm smarter than him."

"Being smart doesn't have anything to do with it."

"So my hormones keep telling me."

"Maybe you should go out with him," Madeline told her. "Maybe he's better than you think."

Madeline was possibly one of the nicest people on the planet. She saw good in everyone and believed in miracles. But Lori had never been a believer, and most people got on her nerves.

In Madeline's fairy-tale universe, men like Reid Buchanan would absolutely date women like Lori. They would probably find them fascinating. Unfortunately, Lori didn't live in that universe.

She pushed up her glasses. "I don't think I'm his type. I get on his nerves. I'm not deferential enough." All excuses for the real thing—Reid would never see her as a sexual being. She was his grandmother's nurse. Sort of a living appliance. No matter how much she wanted that to be different, it wasn't.

"You're funny and pretty and smart. Of course you're his type."

Lori avoided mirrors whenever possible, but she couldn't escape them. Pretty? Not so much. She was average. Nothing more, nothing less.

"You're an optimist," she said. "Sometimes that's annoying."

Madeline laughed. "You can't be mad at me. I made spaghetti with garlic bread."

Lori's mouth watered. "A carb fest for dinner?"

"Absolutely. I was in the mood." Her sister linked arms with her and led her into the kitchen. "While we're eating, we can strategize about Reid. What you can do to get his attention."

"I don't want his attention. He's not anyone I would ever want to be with."

It was an old pattern, but one that had always served Lori well. She found it really helpful to put down that which she couldn't ever have. It made the doing without so much easier.

"I'VE MISSED EVERYTHING about this kitchen," Penny Buchanan said as she ran her hands across The Waterfronts countertops, then lightly touched the control knobs on the stove. "It's bigger than I remember. Is that possible?"

Dani Buchanan grinned at her sister-in-law. "No. You're remembering the kitchen filled with people and now it's empty."

"But it will be full soon," Penny said dreamily. "We'll be cooking delicious food and it will be like I was never gone."

She leaned against the counter, then stared at Dani. "Oh, God. Am I a horrible mother for being thrilled to be back at work? I am, aren't I?"

Dani laughed. "Not at all."

Penny shook her head. "No. It's not natural. I shouldn't have any interests other than the baby. What if Allison knew I loved my work more than her? She would be devastated."

Dani grabbed Penny by the arm. "Hey, slow down. Take a breath. You're fine. Loving your work is allowed, even encouraged. You need to be back in the kitchen because being a chef is part of who you are. As for the baby, Allison is incredibly spoiled and totally loved. Just be grateful you love your job."

"You mean be rational," Penny said with a slight smile. "Hard to do these days, when I'm living in a sea of hormones. But I'll try. You're right. I love Ally, but cooking will always be my passion."

"See, I think you have a much bigger problem with Cal than with the baby. He's not going to appreciate knowing he comes second to a bunch of pots and pans."

Penny's smile softened. "He knows I love him."

Dani had liked Penny the first time Penny had married Cal. The second time was even better.

"So you're back, you're excited about being back," Dani said. "This is a good thing."

Penny eyed her. "I think I can guess why. You want to leave."

Dani glanced around at the restaurant kitchen. Penny had given her a job when she'd desperately needed to do something with her life, but this wasn't where she wanted to be in five years, or even five weeks.

"Let's just say the thrill of sticking it to Gloria has faded," Dani admitted. "You were great to give me a chance here, but I have to move on."

"I understand," Penny told her. "I don't like it, but I understand. Do you have any idea what you're going to do?"

"Try to make up for all the time I wasted trying to please Gloria."

Penny touched her shoulder. "Maybe if you think about it as a growth experience…"

"So far, that's not working. As mean as Gloria is, I still can't believe she let me work for her all those years, let me believe I had a chance of moving up in the company, when she was never going to let it happen."

Dani closed her eyes and drew in a deep breath. If she continued to let Gloria upset her, then she continued to let the old bat win.

But it was hard to let it all go—and impossible to forget Gloria's bombshell. That the reason Dani would never make it in the Buchanan empire was that she, Dani, wasn't a real Buchanan.

"Look at the bright side," Penny said, affection obvious in her voice. "You have a great résumé and fabulous letters of recommendation from me and Edouard."

At the mention of the cook who had been left in charge of the kitchen while Penny had been out on maternity leave, Dani grinned. "Edouard said he wasn't going to write me a letter of recommendation. He said I hadn't been deferential enough while he was in charge. That I hadn't supported his pain."

"Oh, really? Then perhaps I'll tell Edouard I'm not feeling ready to come back. I can leave him in charge a little longer."

As Edouard had spent the last eight weeks whining about the extra work of covering for Penny, Dani knew it was the perfect threat.

"I'll let you tell him," she said.

"I can't wait."

LORI WAS STARTLED to find a woman lurking on Gloria's front porch. In this upscale part of Seattle, the houses were mansion size, the lawns perfect and no one lurked.

"Can I help you?" Lori asked as she slipped her key in her pocket and crossed her arms over her chest. While the woman was perfectly well dressed and seemed normal, Lori had a bad feeling she couldn't explain.

The woman smiled at her. "Hi, I'm Cassandra. Cassie to my friends. I'm a reporter. I recently wrote an article on Reid Buchanan."

No need to define which article. In recent weeks there had only been one anyone would remember. "An article, huh? Is that what you're calling it?"

Cassie smirked. "Oh, so you're one of his little fans."

Lori might have a stupid crush on Reid, but she wasn't about to admit it. Besides, this wasn't about her feelings, it was about using one's position to try to destroy an almost innocent—well, innocent—person.

"Do I look like one of his little fans?" she asked bluntly. "I'm actually just a person who wonders about today's standards of journalism. There's a difference between reporting and being mean. You got away with what you wrote because you're a woman. If the situation had been reversed, the article wouldn't exist."

Cassie shrugged. "Maybe, but I'm getting great play out of the story. It's all true. He was lousy in bed, but as I said, that's just my opinion. Others don't seem to agree. Is he home?"

"I have no idea what you're talking about," Lori said, staring at the woman and refusing to even glance at the door.

"I can't find him anywhere and I don't think he left Seattle. There aren't that many places he could go to hide."

"What about with one of his fans?"

Cassie laughed. "Reid commit to one woman? I don't think so."

Which was kind of how Lori saw him, but she was going to ignore that for now.

"You're trespassing on private property," she said. "Please leave."

"Sure. No problem. Oh, by the way, do you spend much time on the Internet?"

"What? Not really."

"Then you probably haven't seen these."

Cassie passed her several photos. Lori glanced down automatically, then wished she hadn't.

There were about a half-dozen glossy images of

Reid having sex. Each picture showed him with the same woman. The pictures were crude, explicit and grainy. But they made the point—he was a man who loved women.

Doing her best not to react, Lori passed them back. She felt like she needed to wash her hands or something. "Thanks, but not before breakfast."

"These are online. Even a ten-year-old could download them. Are you sure you want to protect him? We should stand together against men like Reid Buchanan."

Despite the sick feeling in her stomach, Lori shook her head. "I'm not interested in standing with you on anything."

She waited until the woman left before she headed inside. The sick feeling didn't go away. What horrible pictures. Did Reid know about them? Had he posed for them? She wanted to believe the pictures had been taken without his knowledge, but how could she be sure? She knew almost nothing about him. Wanting him to be one of the good guys meant absolutely nothing. Based on how he lived his life, he was most likely the guilty party.

That should take care of her little crush. It wouldn't, of course, but it should.

"You need to walk," Lori said, hanging on to her patience with both hands. "Just across the room and then we can be done."

"I'm done now," Gloria snapped. "It's enough that damn physical therapist pushes me. At least he knows what he's doing."

"You either do your physical therapy and get better, or crawl back in bed and die."

"You keep threatening me with death," Gloria snapped, "and I'm still standing."

Lori stared at the old woman hunched over a walker. "Barely. Don't you want to get strong enough to kick my ass?"

"What I want is to be rid of you. Get out. Get out now!"

The last couple of words were nearly a scream. Lori ignored them and patted the bed. "Eight steps," she said cheerfully. "Seven if you don't shuffle."

"I don't shuffle," Gloria told her icily.

"Looks like shuffling to me."

"I loathe you with every fiber of my being," the old woman said.

"I'm sure you do. Now walk."

Gloria slowly, painfully, made her way across the study. When she reached the bed, Lori steadied her as she lowered herself onto the mattress and slowly lay down.

"Great job," she said, careful to keep her voice neutral. She wasn't gloating and didn't want Gloria to think she was. At least their workout together was a distraction. Lori wanted to stay busy enough to forget the photos she'd seen earlier. Speaking of busy...

She opened the tote bag she'd brought with her and set several catalogs on the table.

"You have a lot of choices," she said, fanning out the pages. "DVDs, books on tape, your basic shopping, although all my catalogs are discount, which I'm guessing you don't do."

Gloria looked from the shiny pages to her and frowned. "What *are* you talking about?"

"Something to fill your day. Currently you're staring at these four walls, being cranky and, frankly, getting on my nerves. You need to do something else. Get interested in a soap, read, listen to a book, watch a movie. I would normally add 'visit with family' but you seem to be avoiding them."

Gloria stared at the window. "I have no idea what you're talking about."

"Interesting. Kristie told me that one of your grandsons stopped by early yesterday evening. Walker. That he'd called first and you'd told him not to come, but he'd shown up anyway."

The information had stunned Lori. After all, in her mind, Gloria had been the abandoned elder of the family. But first the old woman had refused to see Cal and now she'd told Walker to go away. As much as Lori hated to admit it, Reid might have had a point when he'd said his grandmother was a little difficult.

Gloria narrowed her eyes. "This is none of your

business. You mention my family again and you're fired."

Lori pretended to yawn. "I'm sorry. What? Did you say something?"

"Don't think I can't," Gloria told her. "One call to the agency that employs you and you're gone."

Lori shook her head. "You don't want me gone. I'm tough on you and you respect that. I care about you and you need that. You can't be mean enough or crabby enough to scare me away, and that's new for you. So here's the question. Why are you trying so hard to live your life alone?"

Gloria pointed at the door. "Get out. Get out now."

Lori was about to argue when she felt a queasiness in her stomach. She nodded and left, heading directly for the kitchen. By the time she hit the back hallway, she was shaking and feeling close to fainting.

A quick glance at her watch told her she'd gone too long without food. She knew better, but between the reporter's ambush and her morning workout with Gloria, she hadn't noticed the time.

She walked into the kitchen only to find the one person she most didn't want to see. Reid.

He looked up from the thick stack of papers he was reading and smiled at her. "I heard shouting. Should I be worried?"

She was already pretty weak, what with her blood sugar crashing, so the last thing she needed was a visceral reaction to a useless, possibly horrible, man.

But there it was—a sudden fluttering of her heart, a trembling of her thighs that had nothing to do with needing to eat and everything to do with needing a man.

But why did it have to be this one?

"We're good," she said and walked to the refrigerator, where she'd stashed a bottle of juice. But before she got there, he was on his feet, next to her.

"Lori? What's wrong? You look like crap."

"Gee, thanks."

"I'm serious." He touched her cheek. "You're sweating. And shaking."

The light brush of his fingers was nothing. Less than nothing. Yet she found herself leaning into the contact and imagining him touching her everywhere. So humiliating. She had to remember there wasn't an actual person inside. That he was nothing more than a pretty shell. A shell who liked to take pictures.

"I have low blood sugar. I'm crashing. Go away, I'll be fine."

He ignored her much as she ignored Gloria's demands that she go away. "What do you need?"

Oral sex? No, wait. That wasn't right. "Juice. Food."

"Done."

He pushed her into a chair and then got her a glass of orange juice. She gulped half of it, then let the high-sugar liquid sit on her tongue for a few seconds before swallowing.

The results were nearly instantaneous. The trembling stopped, her body relaxed and she started to feel almost normal.

"Better," she said, looking at him. "Thanks. Go away."

"That's nice," he said sarcastically. "Who crapped on your day?"

"Honestly? You. There was a reporter waiting for me outside your grandmother's front door this morning. She wanted me to confirm you were staying here, which I didn't. Just to put a little sparkle in my schedule, she showed me some pictures she'd downloaded from the Internet. Guess who was the star?"

His expression tightened as he swore. "I thought they were gone."

"You knew about them?" She couldn't decide if that was good or bad.

"They were taken about six years ago," he said grimly. "Without my knowledge. This woman I was with wanted proof to show her friends. One of them suggested she get a little more publicity, so she posted them online."

He sounded embarrassed and mad and frustrated. Lori wanted to believe he wasn't to blame, but it was difficult. "How have you been living your life?" she asked. "This sort of thing doesn't happen to normal people. The pictures, the reporter. You need to get your act together."

"I'm trying. But stuff like this makes it impossible. I even got a court order that the pictures be removed from the Web site. But they're still showing up on other sites. I don't want to talk about it anymore. You feel okay now?"

The change of topic caught her off guard. "Yes. I have to eat something."

"To maintain a higher blood sugar?"

She nodded. "Chocolate would be best. Preferably from Seattle Chocolates."

"You're kidding. That can't be good for you."

"It's not." *Like him.* "But it's my fantasy and I can have it if I want to."

He shook his head and muttered something under his breath. "Okay. Let's see what *real* food we've got."

He opened the refrigerator again and began pulling out ingredients. Shredded cheese, some cooked chicken, salsa and large flour tortillas. Food she didn't remember being in there before.

"Did you go to the grocery store?" she asked.

"I went online and they delivered. There wasn't anything in this kitchen."

At least the Internet was good for something, she thought. "Gloria's meals are delivered fully cooked. I bring in my own stuff."

He shrugged and dug around for a large frying pan. "Now we have real food."

"What are you doing?"

"Making you a quesadilla."

She wasn't sure which shocked her more—that he knew how, or that he was making one for her. "You can cook?"

"I have a few specialties. I'm very multitalented."

"I brought my lunch."

He glanced at her. "No, that's not it. Let me think. Oh, yeah. How about 'Reid, thanks so much for making me food and saving me from death.'"

She smiled reluctantly. "You have a well-developed sense of the dramatic."

"I'm used to being adored."

She was sure of that. Although some of his fans had turned against him.

She wondered what it would be like to be so much in the public eye, then decided it couldn't be a good thing. Complicating an already difficult situation was the fact that Reid had a real habit of making lousy choices when it came to women.

As he heated the pan and assembled the quesadilla, he asked, "How's it going with Gloria?"

"Great. She's making progress."

"She's a challenge," he told her. "You can say it."

"Not even under threat of torture."

He raised his eyebrows. "So I was right. Admit it."

"I won't. I still believe her family helped make her the way she is. She's alone and lonely."

"She's crabby, difficult and mean."

"She's not mean. Not to me."

"You don't know her well enough," Reid said as he slid the folded tortilla onto the hot pan.

Lori set down her empty glass and tried to find something to look at other than the man at the stove. If she didn't distract herself, she was afraid she'd start drooling.

It didn't seem to matter that his character was suspect. Her body wasn't interested in the three thousand other women he'd had sex with. It just wanted to be number three thousand and one. How sad was that?

She picked up the top sheet of paper from the stack Reid had been going through.

"What's this?" she asked as she scanned a letter from a boy wanting an autograph.

"A bunch of crap sent over by my manager," Reid grumbled. "I let his office handle all my fan mail, which might have been a mistake."

Lori remembered the slams about Reid ignoring kids in need in the newspaper article.

He flipped the tortilla. "I didn't want to bother," he said grimly. "That's my big crime. So I trusted others to take care of things and apparently they did a piss-poor job. Seth's response to everything was to send a check."

"Seth's the business manager?"

He nodded. "I was invited to a hospital opening and didn't know. They put me on the program and everything. That's not good."

"But if you didn't know, it's not your fault." Wait! Was she defending him? She resisted the need to slap herself. Didn't she consider him useless? Hello, naked pictures. That had to mean something.

"Tell that to the people waiting for me to show up." He grabbed a plate from the cupboard and slid the quesadilla onto it. "It gets worse. Some kid who was dying wanted to meet me as his last wish. But I didn't show up. Instead he got an autographed picture and a signed baseball."

Reid handed her the food, then slumped down across from her. "It all just sucks."

She was torn, both feeling sorry for him and wanting to shake him. "You're some famous baseball player, right?" she asked before taking a bite. The quesadilla was perfect—hot, with melted cheese, grilled chicken and just a hint of spice.

"Used to be."

"Then you're in a position to make a difference on a much bigger scale than most people. Things went bad. You can't change that, but you can fix things. The paper mentioned some kids who got stranded with no return ticket. Pay them back. Call the kid and go see him now. Manage your fan mail, yell at your manager or fire him. Get involved."

Reid stared out the window over the sink. "It's not that easy."

Okay, now shaking him had a definite priority over pity. "It can be. I know you were too busy with your exciting life before, but you don't have that excuse anymore. You have a responsibility. Be the person everyone expects you to be. Grow up. You might surprise yourself."

"You don't think much of me, do you?"

"No."

He gave her a slow, sexy smile. One that gave a whole new meaning to the phrase *blown away.* If he'd shown her the slightest bit of interest, she would have ripped off her clothes and done it with him right there on the kitchen table.

Of course, according to Cassie's article, Reid wasn't all that great in bed. Except she had a feeling Cassie was lying. She had to be. Everything about Reid, the way he moved, he teased, he spoke, declared that the man loved women. All women.

Well, all women except her.

Reality splashed over her like cold water. Time to end the fantasy fest. She wasn't his type. She would never be someone he could see as appealing. If he knew how he got to her, he would only pity her.

The thought of that shamed her and she spoke before she could stop herself.

"Just so we're clear, I'm not interested in you," she said coolly. "Or anyone like you. You're no one I could like or respect."

The words hung there in the silence. She desperately wanted to call them back. What had she been thinking? He was Reid Buchanan—he could emotionally eviscerate her with a couple of well chosen words.

She braced herself for the attack as he rose and stared down at her. But he didn't say what she'd expected.

"I thought you were different," he said quietly. "I didn't think you were the type to kick me when I was down. Guess I was wrong."

And then he was gone and she was alone.

Shame returned, but this time it had nothing to do with wanting a man she could never have. Instead it was about hurting someone who didn't deserve to be hurt.

She'd been trying to make herself feel better by saying he was nothing more than an empty shell— a pretty façade, not a real person. But she'd been wrong. Reid was very real.

She'd been disrespectful and dismissive. Pretty much acting the way she'd expected him to act. The way others had acted toward her.

She'd become someone she didn't like and she didn't know how to fix that.

CHAPTER FOUR

LORI STARED at the ringing phone. "Are you going to get that?" she asked.

Gloria continued to flip through the DVD magazine. "There's no one I want to talk to."

"Then I guess I'll talk to them." Lori grabbed the phone. "Hello?"

"This is Cal Buchanan. You're, ah…"

"Lori Johnston. We spoke when you called before. Hi. How are you?"

"Good. I'm phoning to check on my grandmother. I thought I might come by later and visit."

"That's great." Lori covered the phone and smiled at Gloria. "It's Cal. He wants to see you."

Gloria didn't bother looking up. "No. Tell him to go away."

Lori uncovered the phone. "She's thrilled and can't wait to see you."

Cal chuckled. "Want to let me hear her say that?"

"Not really. She doesn't always say what she means. You have to read between the lines."

Gloria glared at Lori. "Hang up this instant.

You will not answer my phone again, nor will you speak for me."

Lori took a step back so she was out of reach. "Your grandmother is doing great. She's making progress every day. Even her physical therapist is impressed and he's one tough guy to please. She's gained a little weight. Not as much as I would like, but then I'm just bitter at how good she must look in her clothes."

Gloria's scowl didn't soften. "You're annoying me. Hang up. Or tell Cal he can visit, but just him. Not that whore he married or her horrible baby."

Lori winced. She hadn't had the phone covered and based on how Cal swore, he'd heard every word.

"Why do I bother?" he asked before he hung up.

Lori put down the phone. "What is wrong with you?" she demanded. "Why would you do that? He's your grandson. This is the second time he's called, wanting to come see you. To me that shows an impressive level of commitment. If he was just being polite, he would have stopped after one call."

Instead of answering, Gloria turned her attention back to the catalog.

Lori snatched it from her and tossed it on the ground. "I'm talking to you."

"I have no interest in this conversation. You need to be careful. You're coming very close to overstepping your bounds."

"Excuse me while I tremble in fear." Lori stalked to the bookcases and turned back to face the bed.

"What's wrong with you?" she asked again. "Why are you acting like this? It doesn't make any sense. I know you're lonely. I know you're hurting and feeling a sense of your own mortality. Who wouldn't after what you've been through? So you deal with that by connecting with people. But *you* don't connect. We're talking about your family and you keep pushing them away. Why?"

"I will not discuss this with you."

"Too bad, because I'm not leaving until I understand."

Gloria folded her arms across her chest and looked out the window. Lori stared at her.

"I thought you had the most selfish grandkids in the world," she said slowly. "You'd lost your only child, you took them in, raised them, ran the family business and your reward was for them to ignore you. But it's not like that, is it? You push them away. What are you trying to prove?"

"Stay out of this," Gloria told her, her face tight with anger. "This isn't your business. You will stop right now."

"Who's gonna make me? You? You think you're so tough, but I'm not afraid of you."

One corner of Gloria's mouth twitched. "Very mature."

Lori held in a grin. Oh, my. Was that a crack in the armor? A sign of humanity? It couldn't be.

"I don't care about mature," Lori told her. "I do

what works. What's going on with Cal? Why don't you want to see him?"

Gloria turned to the window again, but this time the action seemed more about pain than defiance. "He's never respected me."

"I doubt that."

"You don't know. And that woman he married. She was pregnant with another man's baby. That child he's raising isn't his."

And people thought home care could be boring. "Did she cheat on him?"

"No. She was pregnant before they got together."

"So technically she didn't do anything wrong."

"That's not the point."

"Actually it *is* the point. Is Cal happy?"

"Any fool can be happy."

"I'll take that as a yes." She leaned against the side of the bed. "You might want to be careful about pushing people away too many times. Eventually they stop trying to get close."

"You must know this from experience," Gloria said, turning to look at her.

Lori blinked. "Excuse me? I have no idea what you're talking about."

"Of course you do. But it's not so comfortable to have someone analyzing you, is it?" Gloria looked her up and down. "How long have you done your best to ignore your appearance? One might even say you play down your looks."

Lori did her best not to react, and that included blushing. "I wear scrubs because it's appropriate for my job."

"They're shapeless and ugly. Your hair isn't horrible, but you pull it back in that ridiculous braid. No makeup, those glasses."

"They help me see," Lori said. "Blind nurses are much harder to employ."

"You use humor as a weapon. I would say I'm not the only one pushing people away. So what's your excuse? When did you stop trying?"

A long, long time ago, Lori thought grimly. When she'd realized her older sister was totally perfect and that she, Lori, would never measure up.

"So, now you don't have quite so much to say," Gloria said calmly.

"I prefer telling other people what's wrong with them, but I can handle whatever you say. I wear my hair back because it's practical. I dress like this because it's appropriate. I don't wear makeup because I have limited time in the morning and I'd rather spend it on a run than painting my face."

"Excellent excuses. Have you used them before or did you come up with them all right now?"

Lori stared at her patient. The good news was Gloria was showing a healthy, if slightly twisted interest in life. The bad news was she'd shot a few unpleasant truths right into Lori's gut while doing it.

"What do you want from me?" Lori asked. "Is there a purpose or are your comments their own kind of fun?"

"I want you to wear regular clothes. Jeans and a sweater. Looking at you in those…what did you call them?"

"Scrubs."

"Right. Looking at you in those scrubs is depressing. I'm already near death. I don't need my demise hurried along by looking at your ugly clothes."

Lori flipped up the hem of her shirt and pretended to look for a tag. "There's no warning label that being seen in scrubs can cause death."

"Insolent child."

"Crabby old biddy."

Gloria pressed her lips together, as if holding in a smile. "You will wear regular clothes starting tomorrow."

"You actually can't make me."

Gloria ignored her. "In return, there is a slight chance I might be willing to see one of my grandchildren."

That *was* a victory. And worth wearing jeans. "You have a deal."

Gloria eyed her head. "We also need to do something about your hair."

"Not likely. The price for that is you singing karaoke."

Dani waited for her large nonfat latte at the crowded Daily Grind across the street from the downtown Nordstrom.

This had always been her favorite of Seattle's Daily Grinds—probably because it was the first one her brother Cal had opened. She'd stood in line the very first day while Cal had worked the counter and waited to see if his business would take off.

It had. Now there were Daily Grinds all over the West Coast. The company was expanding and giving Starbucks a run for its money.

Of course, thinking about Cal's success made her own life look just a tad more grim, she thought with a wry smile. Decisions were going to have to be made. No, that wasn't right. She'd already made the decisions. What she lacked was action.

The barista called her name and she grabbed her coffee. It was time to give notice at The Waterfront and go look for a new job. One where she would succeed or fail based on her performance and not because of her family.

She turned, only to have someone bump into her from behind. She glanced over her shoulder and saw a pleasant-looking man backing away.

"Sorry," he said, shaking his head. "I zigged when I should have zagged."

"That's okay," Dani said.

"Did you spill?" he asked.

She liked that he visually inspected her coat instead of taking the chance to touch her.

"No. You look good." Instantly he took another step back. "Sorry. I didn't mean to say that. Not that you don't look good. You do. But I wasn't trying to compliment you. Not that I wouldn't want to, it's just…"

He stood there looking so uncomfortable, she momentarily forgot her rule of never again speaking to an unrelated man under the age of seventy-five.

"It's okay," she said with a smile. "I totally know what you were trying to say. My coat looks untouched by any form of coffee."

Relief darkened his pale gray eyes. "Exactly. I didn't spill."

"Good." Impulsively she held out her hand. "I'm Dani."

"Gary."

They shook hands and she felt nothing. Not a spark, not a hint of a spark. There was an absolute lack of sparkage. Thank God.

"It's crazy in here," she said. "I'd try to avoid the rush, but I don't know when that is."

"Me, either." A couple moved toward them and Gary took a step toward her. "I'm here several times a week for my cup of courage."

She stepped into a less crowded corner. "You get courage from coffee?"

"From the caffeine. I teach nearby and my after-

noon students are surly. This keeps me on my toes."
He raised his cup as he spoke.

He was the kind of man easily overlooked and
forgotten, Dani thought. Light brown hair, pale eyes,
pale skin. Slender. Nicely dressed, but not flashy. He
seemed sincere rather than charming, intelligent
rather than physical. All good things.

"What do you teach?" she asked.

"Theology and math at the community college.
Most of my students are taking theology to fulfill
a requirement, and everyone knows people hate
math. I should try to find a fun subject that
everyone would like."

"Is there one?"

"What did you like in college?" he asked.

"Not math," she said, then smiled. "You probably
hear that a lot."

"I can handle it."

"I took a lot of classes in restaurant management.
That's what I do now—work in a restaurant. I've
been an assistant to a chef for a while. I used to
manage a place in Renton. Burger Heaven."

He nodded. "I've been there. Great milkshakes.
Do you like being an assistant to the chef?"

"I love working for Penny, but it's time for me to
make a change. That's what I was thinking about
when we bumped into each other. That I need to
take the risk and go for it. But I'm nervous. What if
I fail? What if I succeed? I can't…"

She stopped talking and stared at him. "I can't believe I'm just blurting this all out."

"I appreciate you talking to me, Dani. I'm happy to listen."

There was something about the way he said it— as if he really meant it.

"But I don't know you."

"Sometimes we recognize a kinship in another person," he said.

If any other guy had tried a line like that on her, she would have hit him in the stomach. But the way Gary spoke the words made her think he really meant them.

"Still, I don't usually dump stuff on strangers," she muttered.

"I'm glad I was your exception." He glanced at his watch. "But I have forty-five bored students waiting to hear about comparative theology through the ages. I have to go."

He sounded as if he regretted the fact. She kind of did, too.

"Thanks for listening. I appreciate your time," she said.

"I'm glad I ran into you."

"Me, too."

They stared at each other for a second, and then he was gone. Dani walked out the other door and headed for her car.

That was good, she thought. Meeting Gary had

reminded her that all men weren't lying, cheating, smarmy weasels. There were still some nice guys around.

REID FLIPPED through the fan letters in front of him. Some were typed and sounded more like they were from forty-year-old truck drivers than actual kids, but a few really got to him.

He kept returning to the one from Frankie. A kid dying from some form of cancer Reid couldn't begin to pronounce. The kid who had asked to meet Reid as his last wish.

"Damn it all to hell," Reid muttered and picked up Gloria's phone. He punched in the number the kid had written on his letter and leaned back in his chair.

A woman answered. "Hello?"

"Hi. This is…" Reid hesitated. The letter was three months old. Maybe he should wait to say who he was. "Is Frankie there?"

"Oh, God."

The woman's voice came out in a sob. Reid stiffened as he heard what sounded like crying.

"Ah, ma'am?"

"I'm sorry. It's just…" More crying. "He's gone. It's been two weeks. Frankie died. I knew it was going to happen. It was inevitable. We all knew it. So I expected to be sad, you know? But why am I shocked? Why do I keep expecting to see him? To hear him? He was just a little boy. So little and now he's all alone."

Reid felt as if he'd taken a ninety-mile-an-hour fastball to the gut. The air rushed out of his lungs and he couldn't speak. Probably a good thing, because what was he supposed to say? That Frankie was in heaven and hanging out with the angels? Who believed that after losing a kid?

"I'm sorry," he managed at last. "I'm really sorry."

"Thank you." The woman cleared her throat. "I didn't mean to go off like that. I just can't seem to get it together." She drew in a breath. "I didn't get your name. Why are you calling?"

"It doesn't matter," Reid said. "I won't bother you again."

He hung up the phone and let the letter fall to the ground.

Two weeks. Two fucking weeks. If he'd bothered to read his fan mail even two weeks ago, he could have been there. Could have gone to see the kid.

Not that his showing up would have made any difference, but at least the kid wouldn't have thought his last wish didn't matter.

He picked up another letter from a pissed kid, basically telling him off for not bothering to show at some benefit. There were dozens more like it.

Reid closed his eyes and did his best to forget. He wasn't a bad man. Sure he had his flaws, but he worked hard at his job and he didn't deliberately hurt anyone. At least that's what he used to tell himself. Now he had no real job—the sports bar didn't count—and it turns out he'd hurt a lot of people.

His cell phone rang. He glanced at the caller ID and saw it was Seth—his so-called manager.

"What?" he said by way of greeting.

"Turn on CNN. And brace yourself."

Reid grabbed the remote and flipped to the appropriate channel. There were two former centerfold twins being interviewed.

"So this is a self-help book?" the reporter asked, barely able to keep from staring at their matching DDD boobs.

"Uh-huh," one of the blond twins said, her voice high and lispy. The sound made Reid cringe. It also made him remember a couple of nights in Cincinnati, a king-size bed and a whole lot of room service.

"We've been in a lot of relationships," the blonde continued.

"We've had a lot of men," the other one said with a giggle.

"Right." The first one smiled at the camera. "So we decided to share our experiences with other women. You know, the ones who aren't as pretty and sexy, who don't get out as much as we do."

"There are things they can do," her sister said earnestly. "Ways to be more sexy. Not just in how they dress, but in what they say and how they act."

This fabulous offer to American women everywhere came from big-haired twins wearing matching halter tops and hot pants.

"You also talk about some of the men you've been with," the reporter said.

Both sisters giggled. "Uh-huh," the one on the left said. "We know it's bad to kiss and tell, but we couldn't help ourselves."

Reid got a cold feeling deep in his gut.

"One name popped out at me," the reporter said. "Reid Buchanan's been in the news lately."

Reid groaned.

The twins looked at each other and sighed.

"We didn't want to say anything in our book," the first one said. "That would be tacky. But honestly, it wasn't that great. I mean most guys have trouble with two women, so we expect that. Sure, it's their fantasy, but when faced with the reality of us naked, it can be a little much."

"It wasn't too much," Reid yelled at the television. "It was fine. It was better than fine. I did great."

"The earth didn't move," the second one said in a low voice. "It happens."

The reporter leaned forward. "Was it a size issue?"

Reid turned off the TV and sprang to his feet. He paced the length of the room and swore. He didn't need this in his life. He didn't deserve it. He wasn't that horrible a person, was he? He should get a break.

Only no one seemed willing to give him one.

He continued to pace back and forth, but the room was too small. He had an excess of energy and no way to burn it off. He had to get out of here, but there wasn't anywhere to go.

He headed downstairs for the one person guaranteed to distract him.

Talk about idiotic, he thought as he walked into the kitchen. Lori had made it very clear what she thought of him. Did he need to be beat up more?

Except as definitive as she'd been about not wanting him, he couldn't shake the feeling that he got to her. If he did, she would hate that. Which, in a twisted way, made him happy. At least annoying her was interesting.

But she wasn't in the kitchen or the living room. He headed for Gloria's temporary bedroom.

"Where's Lori?" he asked when he saw the nurse wasn't there. "She's not avoiding me, is she?"

His grandmother slipped off her glasses, put down her book and stared at him. "Amazingly enough, the whole world doesn't revolve around you, Reid. Lori's sister is sick and Lori took her to the doctor. She'll be back in an hour or so. Can you survive on your own until then, or should I call 9-1-1 for emergency assistance?"

CHAPTER FIVE

LORI ARRIVED back at Gloria's house shortly before two in the afternoon. She walked inside only to find Reid waiting for her.

Her first thought was to turn around and hide in her car. She felt self-conscious about both their last conversation where she'd claimed she didn't want him—a big fat lie if ever there was one—and the fact that she wasn't wearing scrubs. Jeans and a sweater might be totally casual, but there was also the chance that he might interpret them as a pitiful attempt to attract him.

Or not, she thought honestly. Chances were Reid never thought of her at all. He was too busy posing for porn.

She briefly closed her eyes. No. That wasn't fair. Her stupid crush wasn't his fault. Maybe she should rethink the whole self-help book issue. It was more than obvious she needed something to get her back to her normal self. Her last trip to Seattle Chocolate, while delicious, hadn't totally cured her.

"You were gone," Reid said as she tucked her

purse on an empty shelf in the massive and mostly unused pantry.

"Yes, I was and now I'm back."

She straightened and stared at him. Why did he have to look so good? Why couldn't he be ugly or even normal-looking? Why did his eyes make her want to get lost in whatever he was saying and why did his mouth make her long for some sexual acts that might still be illegal in the more conservative red states?

She tried to push past him. When he didn't move, she said, "I have to check on Gloria."

"I just did. She's asleep. I want to talk to you."

Panic seized her. This was not a conversation she wanted to have.

"I'm busy. Let's reschedule."

He raised his eyebrows. "Busy doing what?"

"Stuff. Important stuff." She groaned silently. Talk about pathetically lame.

She couldn't handle him today. Not when she was still fighting the embarrassment of their last encounter and she was feeling emotionally vulnerable because of what was going on with Madeline.

Just thinking about her sister drained the last of the fight out of her. Her shoulders slumped and she stared at Reid.

"Fine. What do you want to talk about?"

"You can't just give in like that," he said. "It's not right."

"You're complaining because I let you win? You might want to rethink your priorities."

"Something's wrong," he said. "What is it?"

She turned away. "Nothing."

"I know enough about women to know that really means there's something but I'm going to have to work to get at it." He grabbed her arm. "Tell me."

She didn't plan to tell him anything. That was the hell of her situation. There was no one to talk to. Certainly not Madeline, who had enough to deal with herself, and not their mother who was a pretty useless kind of person.

She hated that she was tempted. Even more she hated that despite everything, she was hyper-aware of his fingers on her arm. Even through her sweater, she felt heat and need and a whole list of other desires that would go seriously unfulfilled.

"Go away," she said, able to appreciate that she was starting to sound like Gloria.

"Maybe I can help."

"Like you've helped all those kids who wrote you?" she asked, twisting free and glaring at him. "I don't think so. But, hey, if you're so big on knowing, here's the thing. My sister's dying. Okay? Are you happy now that you're well informed? She has a bad case of Hepatitis C she got from a transfusion years ago. A liver transplant could save her, but she has a rare blood type so the odds aren't good. So I'm thinking you're not going to be much help at all unless you happen to be AB negative and want to give up your liver to a really good cause."

She started out of the kitchen, but before she'd gone more than a few feet, she was swamped with feelings. Maybe Reid was a jerk, but he'd never been jerky directly to her. She had no right to lash out at him. In his own shallow way, he probably *had* been trying to help.

She glanced back at him, taking in the stunned expression darkening his eyes.

"I'm sorry," she said. "I shouldn't have said that. The doctor didn't have good news and that kind of pushed me over the edge."

Then she shocked herself and probably him by bursting into tears.

Even as the tears poured down her face, she struggled for control. She didn't cry—not ever. It wasn't allowed. She was practical and logical and take-charge. She didn't allow weakness in herself and she didn't respect it in other people.

But she couldn't seem to stop crying.

Suddenly Reid was there in front of her. He pulled her close, wrapped his arms around her.

As she couldn't seem to stop crying, she let herself lean on him for a few minutes. She let herself be comforted and held.

He was tall and strong, she thought as she held on to him. For once her thoughts where he was concerned weren't about sex. She had the oddest sense that he could be someone she could trust. Which was totally insane. He was as stable as quicksand.

Still, being held felt really nice. She gave in to weakness until the tears dried up, then she sniffed, took a step back and wiped her face on her sleeve.

"Sorry," she said, staring at the hardwood floor. It was really shiny. Maybe she should put new floors in her place.

"What happened at the doctor's appointment?" he asked quietly.

She risked looking at him and saw only sympathy in his eyes. She shrugged.

"I've known since the diagnosis that it wasn't going to be good. I mean, I'm a nurse. I can figure out the steps. But I guess it wasn't real to me before. I guess I thought nothing bad could happen to my sister. Until this, she's lived a pretty perfect life."

She sucked in a breath.

"Her doctor talked about how long she had and how we needed to think about hospice care. That really got to me. Talking about the end."

Reid reached out and took her hand in his. "What's the time frame?"

"About a year. She moved in with me a few months ago. She's starting to have bad days. She's working part-time, but that won't last long. I took this job because the hours allow me to spend more time with her and the money is great. I'm saving as much as I can so I can take off the last couple of months to be with her."

She squeezed his hand and fought tears. "She wanted to talk about that today. On the drive home, she said I shouldn't put my life on hold for her. That she was fine going into a hospice. But I don't want that for her. I can take care of her."

She had to be there for Madeline.

"Is a liver transplant the only way to save her?" he asked.

She nodded. "Unless they find a miracle cure and that's not likely to happen in time. I've been tested and I'm not a match."

He frowned. "You can't give up your liver."

Despite the pain and threat of tears, she smiled. "They use living donors now. They would take a piece of my liver. But it's a nonissue. I can't. My mom could except she drank so much for years that there isn't much of her liver left."

Lori released his hand and took a step back. "It's just like Madeline to have a weird blood type. She's totally perfect in every other way. Why can't she be O positive like the majority of the population?"

It was easier to joke than admit the real problem. There were no easy solutions for her problem or Madeline's. Lori never knew how to act or what to say. She just lived in guilt. Because as much as she loved her sister, she'd also resented her in equal measure. Which made her a pretty horrible person.

"I'm sorry," Reid told her. "I know that doesn't help, but I don't know what else to say."

He sounded sincere, she thought as she stared into his eyes. So they were both clueless. An interesting thing to have in common. "Thank you. I'm sorry I fell apart. It's not like me. Usually I can hold it together."

"It's okay. Under the circumstances anyone would."

She swallowed and forced herself to tell the truth. "You helped."

One corner of his mouth turned up. "Then that's a first for this month."

He walked out of the kitchen, leaving her staring after him. Had they just had a moment that included sensitivity? She didn't want him to be more than just a pretty face. That made him far too dangerous for her fragile peace of mind. But it seemed she didn't have a choice in the matter.

REID WALKED INTO the small den he'd turned into a temporary office. Lori's problems put his into perspective. People thinking he was lousy in bed was nothing when compared with a sister dying. Of course there were the kids who'd been disappointed, ignored and abandoned by someone who was supposed to be a hero. Telling himself it wasn't his fault wasn't cutting it anymore.

He glanced at the stack of letters. Okay, so things had gone wrong. Could he fix the problems after the fact? He grimaced as he remembered Frankie's sobbing mother. If only…

No, he couldn't fix the problems, but he could stop new ones from happening. He could do better. He could get involved and make sure the right people got what they needed.

He sat in front of the letters and saw the folder from those kids he'd tried to send to the state finals. The ones who hadn't gotten return tickets.

He read the hostile, accusing letters and felt his gut tighten. Dammit, it wasn't his fault. He hadn't had anything to do with the travel arrangements, but that didn't matter. The offer had been made in his name.

He scanned the bitter letters and found one from the coach. Not sure what he was going to say, he picked up the phone and dialed.

It took a couple of transfers, but he finally got hold of Coach Roberts. After introducing himself he said, "I'm sorry about the mess with the return tickets. I didn't know anything about the problem until a couple of days ago. The travel agency my manager hired dropped the ball. I, ah, had him send a check reimbursing everyone for their expenses. Did you get it?"

"Oh, we got it," the coach said. "It was great. It didn't cover shit, but, hey, it's the thought that counts, right?"

Reid straightened. "What are you talking about?"

"Do you really think a thousand dollars covers seventeen kids and their families?"

A thousand dollars? "No. There's been a mistake. It was supposed to cover everything."

"I don't know what the hell kind of game you think this is, Buchanan. You're the worst kind of asshole. This is a poor town in a poor part of the state. These kids come from working class families. They can't afford tickets, even on the bus. One family's car got repossessed because they had to make a choice—make the car payment or get their kids home. They picked the kids. Now you send a check for a thousand dollars like that means anything?"

"It was supposed to be more," Reid mumbled, feeling like crap. Why had Seth done it? Why such a small amount?

"Those kids looked up to you," Coach Roberts continued. "They idolized you. You made their dreams come true and then you crushed them into dust."

"I'm sorry," Reid repeated.

"You sure as hell are. A sorry kind of man. You're everything I don't want these kids to be."

He felt numb. "I want to make it up to them. Do something. Can I send them all to Disney World or something?"

"Oh, right. That would be great. Like anyone can afford a trip home from Florida. I'd tell you to stick with what you know—screwing women—but apparently you can't even do that right. Go away. No one here wants anything to do with you. We can't afford your type of charity."

And the phone went dead.

THE OUTSIDE OF THE upscale Asian restaurant was elegant. Subtle colors, a sparse but very Zen-looking garden and a patio off to the right that could be used for summer outdoor dining.

Dani parked close to the front door and walked inside. Her interview was with Jim Brace, the owner.

The décor was sparse, but beautiful. Lots of glass with accents of brightly colored fabric. The huge dining room was double the size of The Waterfront and spread out in all directions.

As it was a couple of hours before opening, there weren't many people around. She flagged a busboy who was setting tables and asked for Jim.

The man stared at her. "Does he know you're here?"

It wasn't the question that startled her as much as the worry in his eyes.

"I have an appointment with him."

"Oh, okay. I'll go get him." He started to leave, then turned back to her. "Stay here and don't touch anything."

"Promise," Dani said, wondering what it was she was supposed to not be touching.

She returned to the reception desk in the foyer and drew in a deep breath. This was her first interview and it was a big one. Jim Brace's restaurant was one of the best in Seattle. Restaurant critics argued about which was more exquisite—the food or the service. Starting here was like making a film debut in a summer blockbuster.

She reminded herself she had more than enough experience and that obviously Jim had been impressed by her résumé. If she didn't get the job, at least she would have the interview experience for the next time.

A tall, slim man walked toward her. She recognized Jim from seeing his picture in the paper and smiled at him.

"Mr. Brace, I'm Dani Buchanan."

"Call me Jim, please, and I'll call you Dani." He shook hands with her and led her toward the back of the restaurant. "Have you eaten here before?"

"A couple of times. The food is incredible."

"Secret recipes," he joked. "My mother is half Chinese and my father's brother spent years in Japan. I grew up in both places, learning the language, but more importantly, studying the food. I summered here in Seattle, so I have American sensibilities. The combination has allowed me to be incredibly successful."

He paused as a young woman in a kitchen uniform approached with a large tray.

Instead of thanking her, Jim looked over the tray, took it, then said, "You can go."

The woman bowed slightly and left.

He began putting dishes on the table. "I know you'll want to get another taste of the food. It's excellent. Our executive chef, Park, has been with us about six months. I didn't like all the changes he wanted to make, but I've let him do a few things."

"The Waterfront went through the same sort of thing when it reopened," Dani said with a smile. "Penny Jackson was determined to get her way. But who can argue with brilliance?"

"I can and do," Jim told her. "It's my place. What I say goes." Without bothering to ask what she liked, he dished up the food onto two plates.

Dani took hers and studied the eclectic offering. There were several kinds of dumplings, tempura vegetables, a casserole that smelled heavenly.

Jim poured her tea, then added a small amount of sugar. Okay, maybe it was just her, but this was a guy who enjoyed taking charge just a little too much. She would be lucky if he didn't cut up her food and put it on her fork for her.

"I've been looking for a manager for a while," he said. "I need someone who can respect my vision. This restaurant *is* me." He shrugged. "I've been called difficult."

Dani thought about all Gloria had done, letting her work her ass off and think she had a chance with the company only to finally admit Dani would never do better than Burger Heaven.

"I can handle difficult," Dani said. "As long as there are clearly defined goals and targets."

"Hey, that I can provide." Jim dug into his food and urged her to do the same. "Isn't it great?" he said when he'd chewed and swallowed.

She sampled the various dishes and had to agree. When they'd finished, Jim rose and invited her to tour the restaurant with him.

He explained about the specific arrangement of tables and how regulars who spent big had special seating areas. He preferred overbooking and didn't mind sending people away.

"Won't they be unhappy and unlikely to return?" she asked.

"Some will be, but in my experience people want what they can't have and for a lot of them, that's dinner at my place."

Dani wrinkled her nose. She was more of a "please the customer at all costs" kind of manager.

They walked through the swinging doors that separated the front of the store from the back. As they stepped into the pristine, open kitchen, she braced herself for flying insults and swearing in several languages. Instead there was an unnatural silence.

She stared at the men all working hard—chopping, blanching, prepping. The tallest of the group walked toward him. The embroidered name on his white jacket identified him as the executive chef.

"Park, this is Dani Buchanan. She's interviewing for the manager job."

Park turned to face her, then bowed slightly. But he didn't speak.

Dani had worked with enough brilliant chefs to expect attitude, opinion and a volume that would shatter the eardrums of the uninitiated.

"Hi," she said brightly. "I loved the sample menu. This is one place where making recommendations would be easy."

Nothing about Park's handsome face changed. He blinked slowly.

Before she could figure out what else to say, there was a loud clang in the back of the kitchen as two metal bowls fell into a metal sink. Jim immediately turned and spoke harshly in a language Dani didn't understand. Everyone froze in midmotion, even Park.

Jim turned back to her and shrugged. "Gotta keep the boys in line."

"Sure," she said, trying to smile and failing. There was something seriously wrong in this kitchen. It was too organized, too quiet, too perfect. Where was the controlled chaos of creativity?

Jim led her back to his large office and motioned for her to sit in one of the chairs in front of his desk.

"I believe in keeping on plenty of wait staff," he said. "I might be willing to keep my customers waiting for a table, but once they're seated, everything flows smoothly. You'll like the crew. They work hard, they're on time, they're perfect at their jobs, or they're fired."

Perfect? Who could guarantee perfection on a regular basis?

"Do you have a lot of turnover?" she asked.

"It takes a while to get the right person, but once we find a server who works, they stay a long time. The money's great."

Based on the number of reservations they had each night and the crowd that might or might not get seated, Dani could believe that.

The restaurant had everything going for it—great location, better food, cachet and five-star service. There was only one six-foot problem.

Jim talked more about the restaurant, his vision, expectations and the need to be on time, work long hours and give a hundred percent every day.

Dani listened carefully even as she tried to figure out why she had a knot in her stomach.

"I like you," Jim said unexpectedly. "I know your grandmother. Not well, but I know enough to understand if you rose to manage one of her restaurants, you've got the right stuff and you're not afraid of hard work. To be honest, I've been looking for the right manager for a long time. I think you're her. Let me write you up an offer and then we can talk again."

Dani blinked. "You're kidding?"

Jim grinned. "I know you're excited."

He kept talking, but she wasn't listening. Excited didn't exactly describe the knot in her stomach.

This was a great opportunity. Sure, Jim might be difficult, but no one could be as bad as Gloria and she'd survived her.

So why wasn't she more thrilled? Was she really getting a bad feeling or was she falling into self-sabotage? Did she secretly believe Gloria's claim that she just didn't have what it took and could never make it on her own?

Lori walked into the kitchen and found Sandy already there.

"You're early," she said.

Sandy poured herself a cup of coffee. "I know what it's like to be tired after a long day. Of course, *I'm* just waking up."

Sandy smiled at her and Lori realized she'd really started to like the other nurse. Lori considered the fact that she didn't hold Sandy's full-blown beauty against her a sign of a mature character.

Sandy waved the coffeepot at Lori who shook her head. "Not if I want to sleep tonight."

"I know. I get hyped up on coffee and then I don't fall asleep until nine or ten in the morning. My body clock is totally screwed up. Speaking of screwed, did you see those twins on CNN?"

Lori shook her head. "What twins?"

"Bimbos. Former centerfolds. It was awful.

They've written some stupid self-help book so us lesser mortals can learn to be as sexy as them. Can you imagine?"

Lori didn't know what to say. If tall, busty, gorgeous Sandy considered herself a lesser mortal, what did that make Lori? A mutant?

"They were on CNN talking about their book?"

"Uh-huh. That part was bad enough, but then the stupid reporter brought up Reid. Of course they had to dump on him and say he was lousy in bed."

Sandy pressed her lips together. "It's that damn newspaper article. Kristie and I were talking about it a couple of nights ago. The thing is, it's so unfair." She smiled, as if remembering something amazing. "I had absolutely no complaints about my close encounter with Reid and neither did Kristie. It was everything we wanted it to be."

She sighed. "Of course I was a fan and, I confess, just a little slutty at my interview. I threw myself at him. Not that he said no."

Lori couldn't think. Her mind went totally blank, which was probably for the best. Otherwise she might have exploded.

"You slept with him during your interview for this job?"

Sandy nodded. "Kristie, too. It was fun. That big desk in his office at the sports bar. Yum. I…" She stopped and stared at Lori. "Are you okay?"

No, she wasn't okay. She was furious. Not with

Reid, but with herself. For being stupid enough to
think he was a real person. He wasn't. He was just
a shallow, disgusting pretend human being.

"I'm fine," she said from between clenched teeth.

Sandy grimaced. "Oh, God. I just put my foot in
it, didn't I? I thought you'd slept with him, too."

"No," Lori said grimly. "I didn't."

Apparently she could form a club of women who
hadn't slept with Reid Buchanan. It would have a
membership of one.

CHAPTER SIX

LORI WORKED HER WAY through Gloria's morning exercises and did her best to disconnect from the usual complaints.

"That hurts," Gloria said. "Stop immediately."

"We're not working the side your broken hip is on," Lori reminded her. "We need to keep you flexible."

"As I'm unlikely to join the Seattle ballet anytime soon, this level of flexibility is not required."

"Flexibility will help with your stability. When your hip heals, you'll still be worried about falling. That will make you cautious. Knowing you're flexible and can bend in all sorts of directions will help with your confidence."

Gloria grunted and cooperated with the stretching for a few more seconds, then pushed Lori away.

"That's enough," she snapped. "I'm not paying you to torture me."

Lori hadn't slept well the night before. She had no one to blame but herself, which she hated. In truth she'd lain in bed, seething about Sandy's casual confession.

Lori had been offended on so many levels, but somewhere around four in the morning, she'd finally admitted, if only to herself, that her real pain came from the fact that Reid had never wanted her that way and he never would.

None of which was Gloria's fault, but it did mean her level of patience was lower than usual.

"You're paying me to help get you better," Lori said. "That's what I'm doing."

Gloria frowned at her. "The key is that I'm paying you. I expect professional behavior, not sadistic enjoyment of my pain."

Lori gasped at the unfairness of the accusation. "Excuse me? What sadistic enjoyment? I go out of my way every single day to make your life more comfortable. Who got you to order the movies you're enjoying? Who ran out in the rain to get you Cookies and Cream ice cream two days ago when you had a craving? Who keeps your room bright, changes the flowers, gets you books and magazines and gives a damn about you getting back on your feet?"

"I have told you not to swear around me. I won't tolerate it. If you're going to persist in that kind of behavior, I'll fire you."

"That threat is getting old."

"So is your incompetence."

Maybe it was the lack of sleep. Maybe it was the fact that Reid wanted every woman on the planet but her. Maybe it was that she'd reached her threshold. Whatever the reason, she finally snapped.

"I've had it," she told Gloria, her voice low. "I have busted my ass for you. Yes, I said ass. Live with it. When I took this job, everyone told me you were a total bitch and impossible to deal with. But I didn't believe them. The staff at the rehab facility warned me about you, said you were awful and ungrateful, but I didn't listen. I defended you over and over again. Imagine how I feel now that I find out they were telling the truth. You're all the things they said. It's no wonder your grandchildren avoid you. I sure wouldn't be here if I wasn't getting paid a whole lot of money. So here's the question. What on earth is wrong with you? Why do you act like this?"

Lori had never spoken that way to a patient before, although if anyone deserved it, Gloria did. Still, she braced herself for the scathing tirade that would end her time in this house.

But Gloria didn't say anything. Instead the old woman stared at her for several seconds, then stunned Lori by bursting into tears.

Lori stared at her for a couple of seconds, not sure if she should move closer or run for cover. But there was something broken and sad about Gloria's tears. Something that made her move next to the bed, and then gently, carefully, sit on the mattress.

She reached for the older woman and slowly put

her arms around her. Gloria clung to her, still crying, her body shaking.

"I d-didn't mean for this to happen," Gloria said between sobs. "I don't know what h-happened. I was always difficult and demanding, but now I'm horrible. I hear the things I say and I can't believe that's me talking. I never meant to become so awful. Something happened. This isn't me and it's not my fault. Nobody loves me. No one has ever loved me. I'm alone and I'm going to die alone."

Lori sucked in a breath. She felt like slime for having attacked Gloria, yet she sensed this might be an important moment in the old woman's life. She suspected that Gloria didn't allow herself much emotional vulnerability or weakness, so how best to handle the opportunity?

She considered several possibilities, then decided to go for the truth. She waited until the tears subsided, sat up, handed Gloria a box of tissues, then cleared her throat.

"You're right," she said clearly, refusing to be sucked in by the still flowing tears. "You are going to die alone."

Gloria's eyes widened. "It's not true," she whispered.

"It is true," Lori told her. "Look at how you act. Who would want to care about you? You're dismissive of people's feelings. You don't seem to ever do anything nice. You're mean and self-centered." She lowered her voice and touched the other woman's arm. "But you can change."

Gloria shook her head. "I can't. I don't know how."

"You can and you do know how. You don't want to—there's a difference. You're many things, but you're not stupid. You remember what it's like to be human."

Her patient stared at her. "No, I don't. Besides, what's the point? You're saying I should be nice to people. To care about them. But then they just take advantage of me. Besides, there are so many idiots in the world."

"There's an attitude designed to make you friends."

"I don't want friends."

"Really? Then what was the water works about? Come on, no one wants to be totally isolated. Everyone wants a sense of belonging. You're old— you'll be dead soon. Don't you want to be missed?"

Gloria opened her mouth, then closed it. "I will not be dead soon."

"You will if you don't get off your bony ass and focus on getting better."

Lori braced herself for the screaming, or at the very least another threat of firing. Instead tears filled Gloria's eyes again.

"I don't want to die alone," she whispered. "I don't want them to hate me. I want them to love me."

Lori hugged her again. "I know you do. The best way to get love is to act loving."

Gloria didn't answer. Instead she held on tight for a long time before leaning back against her pillows. She wiped her face, then said, "According to you, I shouldn't worry about being taken advantage of. I won't be around long enough to mind."

"That wasn't exactly what I meant, but if it works for you, go for it."

"Do you really think I can change?"

"If you want your life to be different. It's entirely up to you. You have the power to do whatever you want. Does this really matter? Do you want your grandchildren to love you and miss you when you're gone?"

The old woman nodded slowly. "Yes," she whispered. "I do."

AN HOUR LATER Gloria was sleeping and Lori escaped to the living room to regroup. She felt as if she'd been run over by a train.

Had she done the right thing, pushing Gloria? Would the emotional upset impact the healing process? But if Gloria did manage to change enough to reconnect with her family, wasn't that a good thing?

Lori stood in front of the massive window that overlooked the city and Puget Sound beyond. It was a rare clear day, with the sky a color of blue that God grants only after weeks of rain.

Maybe she'd been talking to herself as well as

Gloria, she thought, not sure she wanted to see the truth but unable to avoid it. Maybe she needed to be a little less bitchy with her own family. Not that she was bitchy with Madeline, but there was always that damned ambivalence lurking in the background, not to mention all the issues she had with her mother. Maybe she should—

"There you are," Reid said as he walked into the room. "I've been looking all over for you. We have to talk."

She turned slowly and looked at him. He was still one of the most handsome men she'd ever seen. Not perfect, but appealing on so many levels. She wanted to lean into his body and feel his heat. She wanted his arms around her, flesh on flesh, touching, reaching. She wanted to give herself up to him in a version of surrender that left her breathless.

On the heels of the longing came a fierce anger, both at herself for her weakness and at the man who caused it. He was easy enough to blame—especially considering what she'd so recently learned about him. In the land of Reid, the hits kept on coming.

"I don't know what to do," he said, moving close and staring into her eyes. "You have to help me. I'm totally screwed. Remember those kids, the ones I was supposed to send to their state finals? The ones who didn't have a return ticket?"

He didn't bother waiting for her to answer. "I called their coach. I wanted to make it right. Seth had sent a check and I thought things were fine. But the bastard only sent a thousand dollars. Some family got their car repossessed because of me and my manager only sent a thousand dollars?"

He ran his hand through his hair and stalked to the window. "How did this happen? How did everything get so messed up? You know what the guy said to me? The coach? I offered to send everyone to Disney World, you know, to make up for it. And he blew me off. He said they couldn't afford my brand of charity."

He turned back to her, looking genuinely confused. "It's me," he said. "Doesn't that matter?"

Something inside of her snapped. She actually felt it go and heard the popping sound.

"You are exactly like your grandmother," she began, aware of Gloria sleeping and keeping her voice low. "You are totally self-absorbed and selfish. I had thought, and let me tell you how stupid I feel about that now, that there was a person inside of you. I thought you might actually have some small crumb of decency. But you don't. You're nothing but a sex-starved, useless jerk. You're taking up space that should go to someone who actually matters."

She curled her hands into fists and fought the need to beat some sense into him. As if she could actually hit hard enough to make him notice.

"Start taking responsibility," she told him, her voice thick with anger and contempt. "You keep blaming your manager, but ultimately, you're responsible. So take the damn responsibility. Show up, do the right thing. It's really not that hard. Oh, wait, you'd have to stop being the center of the universe. That *will* be tough."

He stared at her. "What's got up your butt?"

"Oh, right. It has to be me, right? I'm a hysterical female. Oooh, maybe I have my period. There's a great excuse. But I'm going to say it anyway. Fire your damn manager. He's making you look like an ass. You do that well enough on your own—you don't need to pay someone to help with the process. You're supposed to be some hotshot baseball player. Well, with that comes responsibility. Stop letting down little kids. Be a grown-up."

"Why are you so mad at me?"

"Because you could be so much and you're not. I hate wasted potential."

He continued to watch her, looking confused, as if even he knew that couldn't possibly generate that much energy. "What's the real problem?"

"This isn't real enough for you? Look at your life. There are Internet photos of you having sex. Reporters are chasing you down to talk about how lousy you are in bed. You're being mocked on CNN. Do you sense a pattern here? You can't even hire nurses for your sick grandmother without getting laid. You slept with Sandy and Kristie. During their interviews. People don't do that. It's tacky. It's wrong. Honest to God, I'm not surprised to read that you're bad in bed. Being good in bed would mean thinking about someone other than yourself."

"HI," LORI CALLED as she walked into her house after her shift.

"Hey, you," Madeline said from the living room. "How was your day?"

"Not one I want to repeat." Lori shrugged out of her coat as she crossed to the kitchen. Once there she dropped her coat on a chair, her purse on the kitchen table and opened the refrigerator. She always kept a bottle of Chardonnay on hand for emergencies and this certainly counted as a time of need.

"That bad?" Madeline asked as Lori dug in a drawer for a corkscrew.

"In some ways good. In others, worse."

The cork popped out. Madeline collected a single glass and held it out. Lori took it and poured. Seconds later she swallowed a mouthful of the tart, fruity wine and sighed.

"Not better yet, but soon," she breathed. "So how was your day?"

"Fine. Quiet. I had lunch with Julie. Do you remember her? She was my roommate in college and one of my bridesmaids."

There had been eight and honestly, Lori hadn't bothered to learn their names.

"Uh-huh," she lied. "I'm glad you got out. You can't hang out here all the time."

Madeline tucked her auburn hair behind her ear and smiled. "I like hanging out here."

Her sister didn't fit the stereotype of the frail soon-to-be dead. She was a little pale and too thin, but that only added to her ethereal beauty. Madeline had been born beautiful and had never gone through anything resembling an awkward stage. It was one of life's sassy attempts at humor.

Madeline ignored the bottle of wine—with her liver failing, she couldn't drink. Not that she'd ever been very interested. Until recently, her sister hadn't had to deal with very many upsets or disappointments. Lori supposed that getting a death sentence put other irritations in perspective.

"What happened?" her sister asked. "Gloria making you crazy?"

"Not so much. I think we had a breakthrough today."

"Really? How did that happen?"

Lori explained about snapping and how Gloria had burst into tears and admitted to being lonely.

"She's fully capable of changing," Lori said. "The question is, will she?"

Madeline tilted her head. "I know you, Lori. That kind of moment with an elderly patient doesn't send you to the wine bottle. It was something else. Something I'm going to guess is related to a certain ex-baseball player."

Lori groaned. "Gloria lost it with me and I lost it

with him. He was going on and on about how his agent screwed up and how horrible everything is."

Her sister raised her eyebrows. "I'm going to guess you weren't as supportive as he'd been hoping."

"Not exactly." She took another drink of the wine. "I didn't mention this before because I didn't want you to think…"

Lori paused. There was no way she could fool her sister. Madeline knew her too well.

"I was talking to Sandy a couple of days ago. Somehow it came up that Reid had slept with both her and Kristie during their interviews." Her anger erupted again. "Can you believe it? Right there in his office at that stupid sports bar. It's disgusting. He was supposed to be finding appropriate health care, not screwing the staff. Does he actually have a brain, or is that a myth? Are all men like that? Is he what they aspire to? Because I think he's a nightmare on so many levels."

Madeline's green eyes were steady. "You're upset that he slept with them and not you."

"I am not. Never! I wouldn't sleep with him if…" She swallowed, then nodded slowly. "More than upset. Humiliated. I'm not like them. I'll never be like them. Guys like Reid don't even see women like me, which is fine. I don't want a man like him."

"But you do," her sister said softly. "You want exactly him."

Lori scowled. "I'm working on the problem. I'll get over him."

"Maybe you shouldn't try to."

"Oh, please. He would never be interested in me and I can't accept who he is on the inside. He's like cotton candy. Dunk him in water and he dissolves."

"But you like him."

"No. I don't like him. I despise him. I just have a powerful chemical reaction to him. It doesn't mean anything."

"Sure it does. You've never reacted to a guy this way."

"And I won't ever again." It wouldn't work. He was everything she hated in men and she was invisible to him. Oh, yeah, that was a recipe for happiness and love.

She drew in a breath. "I told him off. It didn't go well."

"He'll recover. Besides…" Madeline pushed off the counter and smiled. "Men are inherently stupid about women. You can use that to your advantage."

Lori stared at her amazingly beautiful sister and knew that dozens of men had been stupid about Madeline, but they'd managed to keep their heads around her.

"I'll figure out a way to manage this," Lori said. "A way to get over him."

"I still wish you'd try to make things work. You deserve a fling and Reid sounds like perfect fling material."

Lori supposed it was really sweet of her sister to

think that the choice was actually hers, but before she could say anything, there was a knock at the back door.

"Oh, good," Madeline said, walking toward the rear of the kitchen. "She's here."

Lori got a knot in her stomach. "What did you do?"

Just then the back door opened and their mother walked in. She smiled at both women and held up two large bags.

"I brought Chinese," Evie Johnston said. "You'll have leftovers for days."

"Great, Mom," Madeline said as she put the bags on the counter, then hugged and kissed her mother. "It smells heavenly. I'm starved."

"Good. I don't think you've been eating enough."

Evie stepped free of Madeline and smiled at Lori. "How are you?"

"Good."

Lori smiled tightly as she battled both annoyance and the sense of being the odd one out. It didn't matter that this was her house and these people were her family. Whenever she was around her mother and sister, she no longer belonged.

Evie faced Madeline. "You look good. Are you getting plenty of rest? You're doing what the doctor says?"

Madeline laughed. "I'm fine, Mom. I feel terrific. Lori keeps me in line."

"She should. She's a nurse, you listen to her as well. Lori, you need to take better care of your sister."

Lori ignored the criticism and began sorting through the boxes of takeout. She was used to her mother thinking she didn't measure up. Years ago, when she, Lori, had announced that she was going to be a nurse, her mother's semisober response had been, "You'll never pass the tests to be an R.N. and you won't enjoy emptying bedpans for a living. Try beauty school."

Madeline and her mother continued talking. Lori set the kitchen table and put the food in the center.

She would be the first one to admit Evie's life hadn't been easy. She'd married young, gotten pregnant fairly quickly and had lost her husband to another woman before Lori, her second and unwanted child, had been born.

Evie had lived her whole life in a double-wide trailer, taking whatever jobs she could hang on to between drinking binges. The only bright spot in her otherwise grim existence had been to have one perfect daughter.

Madeline had been pretty from birth, an early talker and walker. She'd been popular, friendly, charming and open to the world. Lori had been none of those things and her mother had never forgiven her for it.

Evie carried plates to the table. "Lori, you shouldn't drink wine. You know it's bad for you. Plus Madeline can't have any and it makes her feel uncomfortable to see it."

Madeline grabbed Lori's wineglass and set it by

her place. "Mom, I'm fine with it. Lori works hard. If she wants a glass of wine at the end of the day, she should have it."

"It's not right," Evie said, then pressed her lips together.

Lori wasn't sure if her mother's concern was really for Madeline or herself. Evie had been sober for nearly seven years.

"I'll put it away," Lori said as she shoved the cork in the bottle, stuck the bottle back in the refrigerator. "I wouldn't have opened it if I'd known you were coming over."

Evie looked at her. "I'm fine. Being around alcohol doesn't bother me."

"Then why do you always mention it?" Lori asked.

"Alcohol isn't good for you."

"You already said that. I hardly think an occasional glass of wine means I have a problem."

"That's how it starts."

Lori swirled her glass. "You would know."

"Yes, I would," Evie told her. "I know you think I'm critical, but I'm just trying to help."

By telling her everything she did wrong? But Lori didn't say that. Instead she dumped her wine down the sink.

"I'll get the iced tea," Madeline said. "I made a fresh pitcher earlier today. Doesn't that sound refreshing?"

It was all Lori could do to keep from running

screaming into the night. Her sister desperately wanted peace in the family and while Lori really wanted to respect her wishes, there was too much history between her and Evie.

"Lori was just telling me about her day," Madeline said as they all sat down. "She's doing home health care for a real difficult old lady and today they had a run-in."

Evie turned to Lori. "What happened?"

Lori briefly recounted some of Gloria's more outrageous behavior and the confrontation earlier that afternoon.

"I think she's really going to work on changing. I hope so. Her family keeps trying and she keeps shutting them out. What a sad way for her to live."

Her mother continued to stare at her. "You're telling her if she changes she gets a second chance?"

Lori instantly saw the dangerous direction of the conversation, but didn't know how to change the subject. "Something like that."

"I didn't think you believed in second chances," Evie said. "Or that people can change."

CHAPTER SEVEN

REID FOUND HIMSELF more restless than he would have liked. It was his damn conversation with Lori and all the things she'd said to him. While most of her ranting had been crap, a few of her choice phrases had hit home.

Admittedly it had been a poor showing of judgment to sleep with Sandy and Kristie during their interviews. But they'd both come on to him. They'd been eager, he hadn't been busy, nobody was married, so what was the problem? It wasn't as if they'd been bad choices to look after his grandmother.

But no matter how he twisted the argument around and made himself out to be the good guy, the whole situation was a little…tacky.

He was, he conceded, officially, a shitty member of the human race.

He went downstairs to the one person guaranteed to add to his guilt—his grandmother. He found Gloria admiring a modest diamond ring on Sandy's left hand.

"Hi," he said as he walked into the room. "What's up?"

"I'm engaged," Sandy said as she turned toward him and beamed. "Remember that guy I told you I was seeing? He proposed. This morning. It was so romantic."

"Congratulations," he said.

"Have you started planning the wedding?" his grandmother asked.

"Not technically," Sandy said with a grin. "But in my mind? Sure. Now I just have to convince Steve that running off to Las Vegas is romantic. There's a little chapel there that is so pretty. We could stay at the Bellagio. I've always wanted to stay at a fancy hotel like that."

"Then that's what you should do," Gloria told her as she patted Sandy's hand. "A girl only gets married once. Or twice."

Sandy laughed. "Good point."

"Obviously this happy news could change your desire to stay here. While I would really like you to continue through my convalescence, I'll understand if that doesn't work out."

Sandy shook her head. "Are you kidding? I love my job. Of course I'm staying. I love the hours and the pay is going to mean I can afford the Bellagio."

Sandy laughed and Gloria joined in. Reid stared at them, not sure what was going on. His grandmother would never approve of getting married in Las Vegas and she hated people who left before the job was done. He thought about all the science fiction movies he secretly watched and wondered if the old broad had been taken over by a pod or some kind of parasite.

Sandy chatted a little more about how wonderful Steve was, then excused herself. When Reid was alone with his grandmother, he moved close and stared at her.

"Did they change your meds?" he asked bluntly. "Are you stoned?"

A little of the woman he knew returned as she narrowed her gaze. "Nothing has changed about my routine. I'm completely fine and healing very well."

Uh-huh. "You were nice. That doesn't happen very often." Or ever.

"You're hardly around enough to know what I do." Gloria dropped her gaze to the blankets on her bed and began smoothing them. "I've decided to make some changes in my life."

He had no idea what to say to that. "Changes like…?"

"I'm going to be more pleasant. Easier to get along with. Less critical. It would be nice if you noticed."

He'd been hit by a lot of baseballs in his career, but only two had nailed him in the head. This felt a lot like that.

"Nice, as in nice?" he asked.

She returned her attention to him. "Perhaps you

could pretend the concept isn't completely foreign. Speaking of changing, it's something you need to take on, as well. Your current circumstances are inexcusable. You've brought shame to the family name and humiliated yourself. Honestly, Reid, what were you thinking, not giving your best while sleeping with a reporter? I would think, given all your experience, you would know what you were doing."

Until that moment, he'd never understood the idea of wanting the earth to open up and swallow him whole. But he did now.

His own grandmother was scolding him for not being better in bed? Did it get any worse than that?

"I'm not having this conversation with you," he said firmly.

"And yet here we are. Talking." Gloria drew in a breath. "I suspect all the accusations about disappointing children aren't your fault. You have many flaws but being cruel isn't one of them."

"Don't flatter me now," he muttered. "I won't know how to take it."

"I don't plan to flatter you. I plan to give you a few hard truths. How did the problem with the children happen?"

He pulled up a chair and sat next to her bed. "I don't know. I stay out of that sort of thing. My manager, Seth, handles all of that kind of stuff, along with booking endorsements and appearances. My accountant, Zeke, takes care of the money. He writes checks when Seth tells him to. I don't know the details of their day-to-day operation."

"That's your first mistake," his grandmother told him. "It was one thing when you were busy playing baseball, but now you don't have an excuse. What else do you have to do with your time?"

Ouch. "I work at the sports bar."

"Based on how much time you've spent around here lately, I would say that job isn't a big priority." She sighed. "Reid, you've always had it easy. You're smart, handsome and your fastball was just as powerful in the ninth inning as in the first."

Pod person, he thought as he stared at her. Definitely a pod person.

"How do you know that?" he asked.

"I would, on occasion, watch you play. And I learned about the game. It's sports, Reid. It wasn't difficult to pick up a few basics."

"You never told me."

"I didn't think it mattered."

He reached out his arm and lightly touched the back of her hand. "It would have mattered a whole lot. It still does."

They stared at each other. For the first time in his life, he realized his grandmother had cared about him. It was good to know. A little scary, but good.

She broke contact first. "This Seth fellow. He sounds like a complete idiot. It's one thing to handle your fan mail and requests for appearances, but it's another to screw it up completely. What do you know about Zeke?"

"That he's been in the business twenty years and that he's totally honest. He won't even let his clients give him Christmas presents. We're allowed to send a food basket to the office for the entire staff, but nothing else. No kickbacks, no perks. Not even tickets to the game."

"Good. Fire Seth and put Zeke in charge. You aren't going to be making any public appearances for a while. Should the need arise, I have the names of a couple of media people who know what they're doing and they're not idiots."

"You're trying to run my life," he said, not actually annoyed by her suggestions. He knew he had to fire Seth—he'd just been putting off the inevitable. But he was surprised she was taking an interest.

"You can do this," she told him. "Take responsibility. We'll change together."

"This isn't a conversation I ever thought we'd be having," he admitted.

Gloria smiled. "Surprise."

FIRST THING in the morning Reid fired Seth by phone and followed up with a fairly aggressive letter from his attorney. Seth tried protesting but quickly gave it up, which told Reid the guy knew he'd screwed up, but rather than fix it, he preferred to walk away. His next call was to Zeke.

"You heard from my attorney?" he asked by way of greeting.

"About Seth? Sure. About time."

Reid leaned back in his chair and groaned. "You knew he was a loser?"

"He's lazy. He does the least he can do and calls that a win. He's in it for the money and the perks. He likes having a successful client list."

Which explained why he'd let Reid go without a whimper. No more baseball career and since all that negative attention in the media, not much of a potential for endorsements.

"I told him to send me everything," Reid said. "I'll be forwarding a lot of it to you."

"You know we'll get the job done," Zeke told him.

"I know. How's the money situation?"

Zeke chuckled. "I assume you mean yours." There was the sound of typing on a keyboard. "Your portfolio is diversified. Stocks, real estate, a few small companies. Ballpark? One hundred and eighty-five million, give or take a few."

Reid swore silently. He'd never paid attention to things like investments. That's what he paid Zeke to take care of. He'd done what he loved for nearly ten years and he'd been paid well. He'd lived hard, but he'd never been stupid with his money.

"All that and I couldn't send those kids home from their state championships," he muttered.

"We took care of that," Zeke told him. "We sent out a check more than a month ago."

"A thousand dollars. What was that supposed to cover?"

"Two return tickets. Why? Did the family have other expenses?"

Family? "Zeke, it wasn't a family. It was the whole damn team."

Zeke swore. "I didn't know. Seth made it sound like just one family. A check for that amount had to have been seen as an insult."

"It's worse. They're families who are barely making it. The screw-up on the return ticket was financially devastating for a lot of them. One family lost their car."

"Dammit, Reid. That kind of crap isn't supposed to happen. That's why you hire people like me and Seth."

Reid was beginning to realize that Zeke and Seth were nothing alike. "I want to fix this," he told his business manager. "Can you find out how much everyone spent to get home and send them a couple thousand more than that? And the family who lost their car—let's get them a new one. And a check to cover any issue with taxes."

He heard the clicking of Zeke's computer keyboard. "Consider it done. Anything else?"

"Not right now. But soon. I'll go over the letters and requests from Seth as soon as they arrive. I have a feeling there's going to be a lot more stuff to make up for."

"We'll get it done," Zeke told him. "This is fixable."

"Right," Reid said as he hung up.

Only it couldn't all be fixed. Like the kid who had died not knowing that Reid cared about him. That couldn't be fixed or undone. How many other people had been disappointed by him? How many other disasters had his name on them?

THE NEXT MORNING Reid went looking for Lori. Sometime in the night when he once again couldn't sleep, he'd had an uncomfortable realization.

Lori had been upset because he hadn't slept with her. He'd slept with the other two nurses but not her.

He wanted to tell her not to take it personally, but she was female and of course that's how she would see things. How could he explain that he hadn't slept with her because he hadn't seen her that way? Oh, yeah, there was a conversation he was dying to have.

He told himself to forget about her and the other nurses and her possible hurt feelings, except he couldn't. Bad enough the world thought he was a jerk—he didn't want Lori thinking that, too. Even though it was probably too late to change her mind.

He found her in the kitchen. She was rinsing off Gloria's breakfast dishes and putting them into the dishwasher. She narrowed her gaze when he walked into the room but didn't say anything.

She'd changed her clothes, he thought, noticing she'd replaced her normal scrubs with jeans and a sweater. The more fitted style suited her, drawing his attention to curves he previously hadn't noticed. Interesting.

She straightened and pushed up her glasses. "What do you want?" she demanded.

"To meet your sister."

The words weren't the ones he'd planned and he had no idea where they'd come from.

"No," Lori said flatly.

"Why not? She's dying. You said she's dying. Maybe she'd like some company. I'm good company."

"You're not and the answer is still no. Madeline isn't some freak show you can visit to fill your day. Go annoy someone else."

Her attitude was really starting to piss him off. What had he ever done to her? "I'm trying to help," he told her. "I bring comfort to the dying."

"Obviously not sexually."

The unexpected snipe cut right through his who-gives-a-shit veneer. He crossed the two steps separating them, grabbed her arm and fought the need to shake some sense into her.

"It wasn't my fault," he yelled. "It was my first year away from the game. My team was in the playoffs. They'd just lost. I was drunk. So what if I was more interested in drowning my pain than showing that woman a good time? I had an off night.

Everybody else gets an off night, but not me, right? I'm good in bed, dammit. Better than good. I've been clawed and made women scream on a regular basis."

Her steady gaze never wavered. "I'm yawning," she said in a low voice. "That's how interested I am in this conversation."

He swore, jerked her close and kissed her.

He hadn't planned to. He was just so pissed off and there weren't that many acceptable ways for a guy to let off a little steam.

So he pressed his mouth to hers and let all his frustration and anger and okay, maybe hurt, pour into the kiss.

He buried his free hand in her hair and was surprised to find the curly waves were kind of nice to touch. He moved a little closer and tilted his head slightly, getting a better angle on kissing Lori because it was starting to feel good. Damn good. Who knew?

Lori found herself just standing there, not sure what to do with her arms, her hands or even her body. She felt awkward and stupid, but the one thing she knew for sure was that she never ever wanted the kiss to end.

His mouth demanded things from her and she found herself wanting to give them. But even as he took and insisted, his lips weren't too hard. There was just the right amount of pressure and heat and promise to make her want to lean into him and beg.

She liked the way he smelled and how he was exactly the right height. She liked the feel of his hand in her hair and the first teasing, erotic brush of the tip of his tongue against her lower lip.

Had she had access to her brain and any voluntary functions, she would have pulled back. It was the sensible thing to do. It was the only thing that made sense. But she didn't, so it wasn't her fault when she put one hand on his shoulder and parted her mouth.

He nipped her lower lip. The gentle bite shocked her. She gasped, he chuckled, then swept inside, claiming her with a passionate dance that took her breath away.

He kissed like a man who loved women. He kissed like a man who understood that sometimes kissing wasn't just a stepping stone on the path to something better. That it could be—if done correctly—a destination.

He kissed like he meant it and made her feel she'd been waiting her whole life for this moment.

Heat flared inside of her, burning through her body, making her weak. She felt uncomfortable in her clothes and in her skin. She wanted him touching her everywhere and she wanted to touch him back. She wanted to know what his perfect body would feel like, naked and straining. She wanted him inside of her.

The image of them together in that way was so

vivid, her body clenched in anticipation. He deepened the kiss and she met him stroke for stroke, following him back to his mouth to tease and explore and excite.

Then, as suddenly as the kiss had begun, it was over.

He stepped back. "You're trembling."

Was she? She felt the tremors race through her body. Okay, so maybe she was.

"Low blood sugar," she told him in a foolish attempt to protect herself. "I didn't have enough protein at breakfast."

Reid stared at her for a long moment, then he began to smile. It was a slow, self-satisfied, *male* smile. One that spoke of his superior ability to bring a woman to her knees with just a kiss.

He was still smiling when he walked out of the kitchen. Lori stared after him, not sure who she was mad at more. Him for turning her on and then leaving, or herself for responding in the first place.

TWO DAYS LATER Reid let Walker and Elissa into Gloria's house. Walker's expression was as unreadable as usual, but Elissa looked ready to jump out of her skin.

"Command performance," Walker explained by way of greeting. "Gloria called and asked us both to come by."

Elissa bit her lower lip. "You're sure about the

both of us part? I'm sure she just meant you. She doesn't like me and I find her really, really scary."

Walker smiled down at the woman standing next to him. "You can wait here with Reid, if you want. I'm not going to force you."

She sighed. "Of course you're not, because that's the kind of guy you are. But because you're being so nice, I'll feel guilty for being afraid, so I'm just going to come in with you and be polite. I can do that. I was raised by very nice people."

Reid thought about reassuring Elissa, telling her that Gloria had been through something of a change. But as he wasn't completely sure the change was going to last, he decided to keep quiet.

"I can come in with you, if you want," he offered. "If it gets ugly, I'll take Elissa out so you're not forced to kill your grandmother."

"Sounds like a plan," Walker said. "How's your life going?"

Reid led the way down the hall. "I'm still doing damage control. Every day some other woman comes forward and says the earth didn't move for her. It's grim and humiliating, but at least it's a distraction. I fired my manager and I'm going through all the boxes he sent over. There are so many requests and letters that went unanswered. I hate knowing there are kids out there assuming I'm an ass."

"What are you going to do to fix it?" Walker asked.

"I'm still trying to figure that out."

Reid wasn't so sure what to do. The job was daunting.

LORI SMOOTHED the sheet on Gloria's bed, then tucked in the end, all the while wishing she weren't so on edge.

She'd spent the last couple of days trying to ignore Reid. After that kiss they'd shared, she didn't know what to say to him. Just as annoying, she hadn't run into him, which made her miss him, which really bugged her. She hated that with a simple brush of mouths she'd gone from a completely capable in-charge woman to a sighing, mooning giggler desperate to see the man of her dreams.

Yesterday she'd taken both a morning and evening run, in an effort to tire herself out enough to let her sleep. It hadn't worked. The second she'd closed her eyes, she'd seen his face and felt the damp heat of his kiss. Reliving the sensations over and over had kept her up half the night.

"Ladies," Reid said as he entered the room. "We have company," he told his grandmother, who sat reading in a chair, then gave her, Lori, a wink. "My brother. Two for the price of one. Of course, *he's* taken."

Lori straightened and tried to speak, but it wasn't possible. With less than a couple dozen words, he'd reduced her to brainless silence. It was so humiliating.

A second man walked into the room. He looked

enough like Reid for her to be able to guess their relationship. With him was an attractive woman with long brown hair and blue eyes.

"So you came," Gloria announced. "Good. Walker, Elissa, nice to see you. This is Lori, one of my nurses. Lori, my grandson and his girlfriend. Oh, did you bring your adorable daughter, Elissa? I'm sorry, I can't remember her name."

"Ah, Zoe," Elissa said, a puzzled look on her face. "She's in school."

"Too bad. Maybe she could come along next time. Children add such positive energy to a room."

Lori glanced at everyone's stunned expressions and took that as her cue to leave. Gloria was working the program. Sure, it would take time to convince her family that the change was genuine, but Lori was confident that would happen.

"You didn't hit her over the head, did you?" Reid asked as he walked out beside her. "I checked her medication so I know you're not drugging her."

She tried to ignore his nearness and how she was so aware of his breathing. "Why can't you simply accept that she wanted to make a change, so she did?"

"You should have come along sooner," he muttered. "Life would have been much better. The last time Gloria met Elissa, she threatened to have her fired, evicted and maybe arrested. All because Elissa dared to date Walker."

"She's not like that anymore."

They'd reached the kitchen. Lori moved to put the island between them—she had a feeling a physical barrier would help her maintain control—but Reid grabbed her hand and held her in place.

"It's because of you," he told her. "You're the reason for the change."

It was difficult to think with his fingers touching hers. "She's the one who made the decision. I simply pointed out that being nicer might be in her best interest."

"Why don't you want to take credit?" he asked.

"It's not necessary."

She tugged free and took a step back. She didn't want to stand there anymore, having him look at her as if she mattered. As if she were someone special in his life. How could she ever believe that?

Why him? Why couldn't she have had a strong physical reaction to someone else? Someone not so far out of reach. She didn't mind that she could never have Reid. What she hated was being pathetic and knowing that if he ever figured out how much of a crush she had on him he would pity her. That would be the worst.

A few minutes later Walker came out for coffee.

"I wouldn't have believed it," he told Reid.

Lori busied herself setting out a tray.

"She's a totally different person," Walker continued. "Warm, friendly. She told me I was doing a good job and I think she made a joke."

Reid grinned. "Hang in there, big guy. You'll get used to it."

"I hope it lasts."

"Me, too," Reid said. "But if you want a for-sure answer, talk to the master."

Lori looked up to find them both staring at her. She shrugged. "I'm not the master of anything. Gloria was feeling lonely and sorry for herself. I just pointed out that the reason people avoided her is that she's incredibly difficult to be around. I suggested she try being nicer."

"That's it?" Walker asked. "No water torture?"

Lori smiled. "She's been through a lot. The heart attack, the recovery from her hip. She's in pain and feeling vulnerable. I think both of those events pushed her to want to do something different. I'm hoping the changes are permanent, but I can't promise."

"Either way, it's a miracle," Walker said. "We owe you big time."

Reid walked over and before she knew what he was going to do, he put an arm around her. "I'm the one who found her. Don't forget that."

Walker shook his head. "You're never going to grow up, are you?"

"Not if I can help it."

He gave Lori's shoulders a squeeze, then he released her. He and his brother returned to Gloria's room with coffee and a plate of cookies. She was left alone in the kitchen.

His touch hadn't meant anything. She knew that. It had been a quick, casual embrace and if he knew it had left her shaken, he would feel bad for her.

"An impossible situation," she murmured into the silence.

She knew better and yet here she was. Trapped.

She was going to have to get over Reid and fast. And she knew exactly how to make that happen.

CHAPTER EIGHT

DANI PLACED HER ORDER for her latte and then moved to the right to wait for her name to be called. She glanced around the crowded café and stiffened slightly when she saw Gary.

He was bent over what looked like a pile of term papers, a red pen in his hand.

Dani turned back to the counter and waved when her name was called. After collecting her latte, she hesitated. While she'd enjoyed speaking with Gary a couple of weeks ago, she didn't know if she wanted to go up and say hello. She wasn't interested in any man romantically and from her limited personal experience, men weren't interested in being friends.

Before she could duck out, she heard him call her name. She turned and smiled.

"Hi, Gary."

"Hi." He waved her over, then motioned to the empty seat on the other side of the tiny table. "Do you have a moment?"

She barely hesitated before nodding. There was

just something about him, she thought as she took a seat. He defined…nice.

"Looks like a lot of work," she said, motioning to the papers. "Are they good?"

"Some. The assignment was to compare three religions, past or present, finding similarities and differences. There are a few Web sites that provide very tidy lists. Some of my students went there and copied the lists. They won't be happy with their grades."

"I can imagine. Going online is easier than going to the library."

He nodded. "I don't object to using the Internet for research, but I do expect them to assimilate what they've learned and write it up using their own words."

"Sounds reasonable."

He smiled. "They won't see it that way. So, how's the job search going?"

She shrugged. "Not as well as I would like. I think…" She hesitated, then leaned forward. "I turned down a great job. It was at a very popular and upscale restaurant. The food was good, the money excellent. In theory, it was everything I wanted."

"But?"

"But I had a funny feeling. I just didn't like the owner. I can't even explain what it was specifically. He was a little over the top, but that's fairly typical in the business. There was just something about him. Something…"

"Dark? Dangerous? Threatening?"

She smiled. "Thanks for helping. Actually he was…cold. The staff seemed afraid of him and not in a respectful way. More like they were worried he was going to have them shot at dawn. And the kitchen was too quiet."

Gary frowned. "How can a kitchen be too quiet?"

"Have you ever worked in a restaurant?"

"No."

"They're crazy places—especially in the kitchen. It's hard work with a lot of pressure. The kitchen staff is loud, insulting, especially if they're gifted. But it wasn't like that. I just wasn't comfortable." She sighed. "I turned down the job. I still can't believe it."

"Sounds to me like you listened to your gut. Finding the right job is important. It helps define who you are as a person. Why would you want to spend the majority of your time in a place that didn't feel right?"

She stared at him. "When you say it like that, I feel positively in tune with the universe."

"You are. Dani, this has to be right for you. You're not desperate—don't settle."

His gaze was steady, his expression kind. She nodded slowly.

"You're right. I'll keep looking until I find the right job. Maybe then I won't regret all the years I've already wasted."

He raised his eyebrows. "You're too young for regrets."

"You'd be surprised." She sipped her latte. "My family owns restaurants. I've wanted to go into the business my whole life. My parents died when I was young and my grandmother raised me and my three brothers. There was always something tortured about my relationship with Gloria—that's my grandmother. It was as if she didn't really like me." She paused. "I should probably stop talking now."

"Not on my account," he told her. "I'm a good listener."

She frowned slightly. "Yes, you are. Why is that?"

For a second, she would swear he looked uncomfortable, then he smiled. "It's a gift. Go on. Gloria was acting weird."

She smiled. "More than weird. I got my master's and came home to go to work in the family business. There are four restaurants in all. Two fine dining places, a sports bar and a place called Burger Heaven. She put me to work there, which was fine. I was more than willing to prove myself. But years went by and I couldn't get her to talk to me about moving up the food chain. Nothing I did made her happy."

She shook her head. "I finally quit."

Gary studied her. "There's more to it than that, Dani. But if you're not comfortable talking about it, I understand."

She believed him. He would be okay with her

moving on. Yet there was a part of her that wanted to tell the whole story, to share it with someone outside of the family.

"Gloria and I had a huge fight. I demanded to know why she'd been holding me back. She said it was because I wasn't a real Buchanan. My mother had had an affair and I was the result. She was never going to let me work anywhere but Burger Heaven. She said I wasn't worthy. So I quit."

Gary nodded slowly. "She sounds like a very unhappy woman."

Dani blinked. "You're taking her side?"

"Not at all. I'm saying that if she raised you and then later refused to see your potential because of who your father is, there are a lot of rules in her life. That doesn't usually make people happy."

"I hadn't thought of it that way. Honestly, and I know this makes me sound like a horrible person, but I don't care if she's unhappy. She's been so mean to me for so long."

"So you quit and now you're going to find something you like."

"I am. No matter how long it takes."

"What about your father? Are you also looking for him?"

"No." Dani sipped her latte, then set it back on the table. "I'm afraid," she admitted. "I'm guessing he didn't know about me, but what if he did? What if he just didn't care?"

She wasn't looking for any more rejection in her life right now.

"Is that enough of a reason not to go looking for him?" Gary asked.

"So far it's working just fine."

"He's your family. What is more important than that?"

Good question, she thought. "So what about your family?" she asked.

"Two sisters, both married. Between them they have seven kids." He grinned. "I love being an uncle."

"No kids of your own?"

His expression tightened slightly, then he relaxed. "I've never been married."

He had to be in his mid to late thirties, she thought. While not everyone got married, it was strange that Gary hadn't. He was a great guy. Kind and sensitive and easy to talk to. The kind of man who...

Duh, she thought, wanting to smack herself on the side of the head. Of course. He was gay.

She looked him over. All the signs were there. His low-key occupation, the perfect grooming, his interest in actual conversation, the lack of any sexual spark.

Relief spilled into pleasure. If Gary was gay then maybe they could be friends. She could use a few more friends in her life.

"I WOULD HAVE COOKED," Madeline said as Lori stirred the simmering beef and filled a pot of water for the noodles.

"I've got it," she said. "You cooked all week."

Madeline leaned against the counter. "I cooked twice, we had takeout twice and leftovers once. I'm not overwhelmed with work."

"You should be resting."

"You should try to catch your breath," her sister told her.

Lori set the pasta pot on the stove and turned on the heat. "I'm fine. The whole breathing thing is fine."

"You looked panicked—like we're going to be firebombed any second."

Lori did her best to smile. "I have no idea what you're talking about."

Which was a big, fat lie, she thought grimly. Madeline was many things, but stupid wasn't one of them. Of course Madeline wasn't anything bad or negative. She was perfect. Physically, mentally, spiritually. She was what the rest of the world aspired to be.

Lori had given up being bitter about that years ago. It was a matter of accepting her sister's amazingness or live her life chronically cranky. She'd decided to move on. These days all she allowed herself was a little ambivalence.

The fact was Madeline couldn't help being beautiful and smart and charming. So when Lori had realized she didn't know how to get her feelings for

Reid under control, she'd decided to manage them the only way she knew how. Introduce him to her sister.

He'd been bugging her about it for a while, so she'd decided to give in to him. She'd invited him over to dinner and he'd accepted. She knew exactly what would happen when he walked in the door. It was the same thing that had happened with every other guy she'd ever brought home—not that there had been that many.

He would take one look at Madeline and fall for her instantly. After the third time it had happened, Lori had stopped bringing guys around. Until now.

It would be like ripping off a bandage, she told herself. Sharp momentary pain, but then it would be over. She would watch Reid succumb to her sister's charms and she would finally be able to squash her own feelings for him.

"It's not going to happen," Madeline said quietly.

Lori looked at her. "I have no idea what you're talking about."

"Interesting, because I know exactly what you're thinking. You can't stand that you have a thing for Reid so you've brought him here, thinking he's going to fall for me."

Lori shrugged. "It's a good plan."

"It's a stupid plan. He's not going to be interested."

"You don't know that." Lori smiled. "I'll even put money on it."

"Did it occur to you that the other guys weren't

as interested in me as you think they were? That by expecting the worst, you pushed them away?"

The unfairness of the accusation really bugged her. "Excuse me? Once they met you, you were all they talked about. Face it, Madeline, you never went through an awkward stage. You grew up beautiful. I had to work my ass off to pass for average. I've made peace with that. I have a life I'm proud of. I'm doing the best I can."

"No, you're not. You're hiding. You don't try because it's easier not to have expectations."

Madeline's words hurt. "Thanks, Ms. Perfect. It's always exciting to get your professional take on things. Whether you want to accept it or not, the bottom line is, guys adore you."

"Vance didn't."

Two words spoken so quietly that someone in the next room couldn't have heard them. Lori swallowed, her anger fading to dust.

"Vance is a total loser who is possibly the stupidest man on the planet," she said.

"Don't say that," Madeline told her, her large brown eyes filling with tears. "He was my husband."

Lori hated that her sister had any feelings left for Vance. The bastard had taken off the second Madeline had been diagnosed. Apparently the marriage vows hadn't meant anything to him.

Before Lori could figure out what to say, the doorbell rang.

"Your young man," Madeline teased.

Lori glared at her. "Don't make me kill you. I'm more than capable."

"Cheap talk."

Lori huffed out a breath, then stalked to the front door and pulled it open.

Any ideas she had for a clever greeting flew out of her head when she saw Reid standing on her tiny porch, smiling at her.

The overhead light illuminated his handsome face. His leather jacket emphasized his broad shoulders and narrow hips. He looked sexy, masculine and as out of reach as the moons of Saturn.

"Hi," he said and thrust a paper-wrapped spray of flowers at her. "I was going to bring wine, but I went on the Internet and it said someone with your sister's disease shouldn't drink."

She stared from him to the beautiful flowers. "So these are for Madeline?"

"What? No. They're for you. These are, too." He handed her a box from Oh! Chocolates.

Okay, now she was confused. He'd brought her flowers and chocolates? Her?

"Come in," she said, stepping back.

"Thanks."

He stepped into the house, turned and kissed her. Just like that. A quick brush of mouth on mouth, then he was shrugging out of his jacket and looking around.

"Nice place," he said.

Lori couldn't move. She also couldn't think or breathe or very possibly stay alive much longer.

He'd kissed her. Kissed her. As if… As if… Damn, she didn't know as if what, but it was weird. They didn't kiss. Well, there had been that one time, but since then, nothing. They weren't dating. This wasn't a date. Did he think this was a date?

Before she could begin to function again, Madeline walked in the room.

"You must be Reid," she said, crossing the room looking tall and beautiful and oh so delicate. "I'm Madeline."

"Hi. Nice to meet you."

They shook hands.

Lori braced herself for the lightning strike. Oddly, Reid looked away from her sister.

"I was telling Lori this place is really nice," he said.

"Isn't it?" Madeline smiled. "Lori and I grew up pretty poor. We lived in a double-wide until we moved out. We both vowed to have a real home of our own. I wanted a trendy high-rise condo, but Lori always said she wanted a house where she could own the ground it stood on."

Lori cringed in embarrassment, but Reid nodded. "Makes sense." Then he actually turned his back on Madeline and looked at her. "You'd hate my place. I live on a houseboat. No land at all."

She didn't know what to say or how to respond.

He was talking to her. Her and not Madeline. How was that possible?

"I, ah…" She began and then pressed her lips together. "The, ah, houseboat sounds very nice. Everyone loves being on the water, right?"

He grinned. "Liar."

She blinked. Was he teasing her?

Life was suddenly very confusing. She glanced down at the flowers.

"I should get these in water," she said and ducked into the kitchen. Maybe if she left Reid and Madeline alone the sparks would fly. Only he followed her and watched as she tried to reach a vase on a high shelf and then gently pushed her aside to grab it himself when she couldn't stretch that far.

"Zeke and I have been talking," he said as he handed over the glass. "About ways to salvage my reputation."

"Who's Zeke?" she asked.

"My accountant. I fired Seth—he handled things like bookings and endorsements, and there aren't going to be any of those anymore. So we talked about what I could do to improve my image. He mentioned a big benefit. What do you think?"

She filled the vase with flowers and set them into the container. As she had no knack for arranging, she was officially out of ways to occupy herself. She turned to him.

"It's a gesture," she said. "Don't you think people

are going to see it as such? You need to do something more. Something with a little staying power."

As soon as the words were out, she wanted to call them back. Or disappear into the floor.

Staying power? Why those particular words? They were too close to what that reporter had said about Reid in that awful article.

"What I meant…" she began, only to have him grin at her.

"I know what you meant. Something more significant."

"Right."

"You weren't talking about my ability to—"

"Not at all," she said quickly. "I'm sure that's…"

He waited, his eyebrows raised.

"Fine," she mumbled.

"Better than fine."

"Right. Spectacular."

He grinned. "Exactly."

"I LOVE EVERYTHING about this house except the lack of a dishwasher," Madeline said when they'd finished dinner and cleared the table. She'd sent Lori off to rest and Reid had offered to help with the cleanup.

"It's original," Madeline continued. "Very forties. She bought that old stove from a place that restores them. She'll let me keep a microwave on the counter, but heaven forbid one of the precious cabinets be taken out to make room for a dishwasher."

He looked around at the brightly colored kitchen. The walls were yellow, the cabinets white, the tiles red and white with splashes of yellow.

"This suits her," he said.

"I agree."

He reached for a dish cloth and grabbed the first plate she put in the rack. "I thought you'd look different."

"Sick, you mean?" she asked.

"Something like that."

"That will come. Right now most of the symptoms aren't visible. I have some bruising on my torso—a sign that my liver isn't working well. I'll look worse as the disease progresses."

"Should I not be asking about this?"

"I don't mind talking about it," she told him. "It's a part of my life now."

And her death. He'd never known anyone who was dying before. Gloria was old and had come close to death, but this was different. Madeline was still in her early thirties.

"You seem calm," he said.

"Some days."

"I don't think I'd be calm."

She smiled. "You never know what you're capable of until it happens. I was in shock and didn't know what to do. Lori handled pretty much everything. She came to the doctor with me, asked all the right questions. My husband left and she's the one who bullied the attorney to make sure I didn't get screwed."

"He left because of you getting sick?"

"Oh, yeah. It was charming."

"I'm sorry," Reid said, feeling awkward.

"Me, too. At least we didn't have kids. Leaving me when things got tough was bad enough, but leaving them…" She rinsed a glass. "Okay, this is officially time to change the subject. Let's talk about something happy."

Just then Lori stepped into the kitchen. "I can help," she said.

Madeline sighed. "No, you can't. You cooked dinner. We're cleaning up. Go rest."

"I'm not tired."

"Then watch TV. Read a book. Contemplate the ever expanding universe."

"I'm going," Lori muttered and left.

Reid stared after her. "She's acting weird, even for her."

Madeline smiled as if she knew a secret. "It will pass." She rinsed another plate and handed it to him. "Lori is really special."

"I agree."

"I wouldn't want to see her get hurt."

Okay, so he wasn't as quick on the uptake as he could have been. Madeline wasn't making conversation. She was probing and warning.

Normally that sort of thing made him want to run into the night, but now he found himself willing to have the conversation. Why was that?

He supposed some of it was that he liked Lori. He liked talking with her, annoying her, even kissing her. The kissing had been really good. Better than good. Under other circumstances he would have taken things further.

Need filled him. It had been a hell of a long time since he'd gotten laid. Under the circumstances, it was going to be a while longer. After that damn article, he wasn't exactly eager to be with anyone. Not when he knew what the woman in question would be thinking. But Lori was different. She was…

He became aware of Madeline staring at him.

"Sorry," he said. "What was the question?"

"I didn't ask one."

"Right. You were going to warn me to stay away from Lori."

"Now why would I do a thing like that?" She began rinsing flatware. "I'm the oldest. It wasn't easy for Lori when we were kids. I was smarter, prettier, more popular." She paused and wrinkled her nose. "Gee, that makes me sound like an egotistical bitch. But it's true. Mom was drunk all the time, Dad was gone. He ran off while she was pregnant with Lori. We didn't have any money and it was hard. Add to that the fact that Lori grew up in my shadow. It's no surprise that she can't decide if she loves me or hates me."

Reid stared at her. "Lori doesn't hate you."

"I know. That's what's so great about her. She could and no one would blame her. Least of all me. But she doesn't. She invited me to come live with her as soon as she found out about my disease. When I hesitated, she physically packed all my stuff herself and hired the movers. She's my rock."

She reached for a pot. "This has got to be so hard on her. I'm the reason her childhood sucked, she loves me more than anyone in the world and I'm dying. How on earth is she supposed to reconcile that?"

Reid didn't know what to do with all the information Madeline had dumped on him, but he didn't doubt it was true. He could feel it in his gut.

"How did you figure all this out?" he asked. "Lori didn't tell you."

"Of course not. She wouldn't want to burden me with what she wrestles with. But I watch and listen. She's so much more than she believes she can be."

"I know."

She looked at him. "I thought you might. So what are you going to do about her?"

"I have no idea."

Lori wasn't his type. She wasn't the kind of woman to enjoy a hot night and move on. He wasn't good for anything else. Which meant avoiding her was the best solution for both of them.

Yet he found himself wanting to be with her. Not just in bed, but out of it as well.

"You'll figure it out," Madeline told him. "Just try not to hurt her. She's more fragile than she looks."

He thought Lori was a rock, but maybe there was more to her than just sarcasm and being everyone's source of strength. Maybe there were sides of her no one saw.

"I don't know what's going to happen," he admitted. "This isn't the sort of thing I'm any good at."

"Then maybe it's time you learned."

REID SAT IN HIS OFFICE at the sports bar and went through invoices. He generally passed any paperwork to the three assistant managers who really ran the place, but today, for some reason, he wanted to feel useful.

He sorted the paperwork by vendor, then went onto his computer and compared this month's bills with those from the previous three months. He wasn't sure what he was looking for but it seemed a logical way to figure out if anyone was trying to hide kickbacks or stealing.

He heard footsteps in the hallway.

"I swear, I saw him," a woman said as she and her friend walked past his office on the way to the restrooms. "He's so good-looking. And I don't care what that bitch reporter said. He was great in bed."

"I thought so, too. It could have been a little longer, but then it always could have been a little longer."

They laughed. The sound was cut off when the bathroom door swung shut behind them.

Reid turned his attention back to the computer, but his concentration was shot.

He had no idea who those women were or when he might have slept with them. For all he knew, they'd had a threesome. At least they hadn't been complaining about his technique.

But that wasn't much comfort. He turned off his computer and left the paperwork on the desk. Nothing felt right anymore, he thought as he grabbed his jacket and headed out. He needed something to do with his day—something that mattered. Pretending to run the sports bar and hiding out at Gloria's didn't cut it.

He drove east, crossing Lake Washington, then turned aimlessly through Bellevue. He stopped in front of a large sporting goods store and stared at the display. God, he missed baseball. Sports had always been a way for him to escape. They had given him purpose and a goal.

He grabbed his cell phone and dialed a familiar number.

"What's up?" he said when Cal answered.

"Not much. Where are you?"

"Not at the sports bar," Reid told him. "Is there a place in Seattle where kids need sports equipment? Like a school in a poor part of town or a club or something?"

"Sure. Hold on." Reid heard typing, then Cal continued, "There are a couple of after-school places where poor kids go. They probably need supplies and equipment. Why?"

"I gotta do something. You got an address?"

Cal read it off, along with a phone number. After Reid hung up with Cal, he called and asked to speak to the director. A woman got on the phone.

"Do you have a yard there where kids play?" he asked.

"Yes." She sounded cautious.

"How's the equipment situation? I'd like to send over some balls and bats and other stuff. You could use it?"

"Of course. Always. Who is this?"

He hung up.

Two hours later he was parked across the street from a beat-up old building. About thirty kids gathered around the large delivery truck. They cheered when the equipment was unloaded.

"I don't understand," an older woman was saying. "This man just called and asked if we needed it. Are you sure it's free?"

"Everything's been paid for," the delivery guy said. "Just sign that you received it and we're good."

The woman smiled, then signed.

Reid shifted into first and drove away.

CHAPTER NINE

REID ARRIVED back at Gloria's house to find Lori waiting for him. It was after four and her shift had officially ended. Sandy's car was parked in the large circular drive, which meant Lori had no reason to stay.

Except to see him.

Watching those kids with their new sports equipment had gone a long way to making him feel less like a loser. Having Lori hanging around to see him cemented his good feelings.

"You stayed," he said as he smiled at her.

"I have to talk to you. Privately."

He liked the sound of that. For reasons he couldn't explain he kept remembering that kiss. He'd wanted to repeat it, but had never found the right opportunity.

He followed Lori to the back of the house. There was a small den, with a television and stereo equipment on one wall.

Lori shut the door behind him. He moved toward her expectantly. She stopped him with a single sentence.

"Some TV producer called here, looking for you," she said.

His desire froze and disappeared.

"What did you tell him?"

She pressed her lips together. "Her. I lied. I said I didn't know who you were and that I had no idea what she was talking about."

"Thanks."

"Not thanks. I don't want to have to do that sort of thing. The reporter looking to ambush someone was bad enough. Now this."

"I can't stop them. What do you want me to do?"

"Not be this way. I don't get it. I can't begin to understand who or what you are. On the one hand, you have moments of kindness and intelligence. On the other hand, you seem willing to have sex with most women in this country. Or any country, I'm guessing. None of this makes sense."

Her energy went beyond annoyance. She seemed as much confused as frustrated.

She put her hands on her hips as she faced him. "How can you be so interested in volume? How can you not care about the person inside?"

"Because for you it's all about the person inside," he said.

"Of course. I want to have a relationship to go with my sexual encounter. That probably sounds really backwards to you."

"It doesn't," he said as he wondered about the men

in her life. Who were they and why wasn't she married? Had she been the one to resist or hadn't anyone asked?

"Are you seeing anyone?" he asked.

"What? No, but that isn't the point."

"I get the point. I was just curious."

She folded her arms over her chest. "We're not talking about me. Explain the thought process, Reid," she said. "Why on earth do you act this way?"

There were a hundred different answers he could give. Slick lines he'd used before. But he didn't want to share any of them with Lori, so he settled for the truth.

"I'm not the kind of guy women marry," he said. "I'm not the kind of guy women get serious with."

Lori waited a few seconds, opened her mouth, then closed it. "That's it? You're a dog when it comes to women because it's not your fault?"

"I'm not a dog. I'm very clear on what's going to happen and what isn't. I tell the truth."

"You're right. I'm sorry." She crossed to the leather sofa and sat down. "You're saying you act this way because the world has low expectations and you've chosen to live down to them?"

Not exactly how he would have phrased it, he thought, feeling uncomfortable. How had they gotten onto this topic to begin with?

He crossed the room and sat at the other end of the sofa.

"You don't think very much of me," he said.

"You don't give me reason to think better."

She was right. Most of the time he didn't care what women thought of him. Enough worshiped him that he didn't give a damn about the rest. But for some reason Lori was different.

He drew in a breath. "There was a girl," he said slowly. "Jenny. I met her when I was drafted into a farm team."

He looked at Lori. "That's a minor league baseball team. All the major league teams have farm teams to groom players."

She smiled and even with her glasses, he could see the corner of her eyes crinkle. "I know what a farm team is," she told him. "I'm not a huge fan, but I'm not totally ignorant."

"Good. So I met Jenny and it was amazing from the beginning. She was pretty and smart and funny and I was crazy about her."

Lori shifted on the sofa. Her mouth twisted slightly, then she said. "So you were normal once."

"More than that. I was in love."

He didn't like remembering how it had been back then. The good times with Jenny had been the best, but the crash…he'd wondered if he would ever recover.

Lori's hazel eyes darkened slightly. "I can't imagine you in love. You mean like being faithful and wanting a future in love?"

Her voice sounded tight. He wanted to believe

that was about envy or something, but he had a feeling it was just a whole load of disbelief.

"I asked her to marry me."

Lori's breath caught. "I didn't know."

"No one does." He leaned forward, resting his forearms on his thighs and stared at the ground. Without wanting to, he remembered everything about that night. It had been warm, but raining. The rain was the reason he hadn't been playing. A three-day soaker had trashed the field. He could smell the dampness in the air and someone's cooking a couple of apartments over. He and Jenny had been sitting on the steps leading up to her place.

He remembered the feel of her body so close to his, the way her long straight blond hair had gleamed in the moonlight. He'd looked at her and known she was the most beautiful woman he'd ever seen. She was all he'd ever wanted—someone he could love forever. So he'd asked her to marry him.

"She said no." He spoke the words flatly, as if they had no meaning. As if he couldn't remember what it had been like to hear her faint giggle of surprise.

"I'm sorry," Lori said.

"Don't be sorry yet, because that's only part of it. She said she wasn't interested in marrying me. She thought I was a lot of fun and great in bed, but marriage was out of the question. I wasn't the kind of guy women married. She was actually seeing someone. He was going to propose and she was going to say yes. I was the kind of guy women had a last fling with, but not the kind anyone wanted to be with for the long haul."

LORI HAD A RESTLESS NIGHT and a difficult morning. She couldn't seem to concentrate on what she was doing, mostly because she kept reliving her conversation with Reid.

While she knew he was telling the truth, she still had trouble believing any woman could reject him so easily. Sure, he was too good-looking to be real but he was charming and fun and just thinking about having him kiss her again was enough to make her weak at the knees, which made her want to pound her head against the wall out of sheer humiliation, but there it was. The reality that Reid was the kind of guy women loved. Even smart women who knew better. Apparently self-awareness was very different from immunity.

She couldn't get her mind around the fact that someone he'd been in love with had walked away from him. Had, in fact, rejected him cruelly. There had to be more to the story.

Lori knew many of her questions would never be answered—especially the one about why this was so fascinating to her. She didn't want to know the answer to that.

She finished clearing the dishes from lunch and loading the dishwasher. Then she went to check on Gloria.

Her patient was reading in bed. Gloria set down her book when Lori entered the room.

"My oldest grandson's wife is coming to visit," Gloria said, her voice sounding more resigned than pleased. "She had a baby recently. The biological father came from a sperm bank, if you can believe it. I'll never understand why Cal wanted to get back together with a woman who would do that sort of thing. He could have done so much better than some breeding cow who…"

Lori raised her eyebrows.

Gloria drew in a breath, then let it go slowly. After a second, she spoke again. "My grandson's new wife is coming by to visit. She's bringing her new baby. Won't that be lovely?"

Lori grinned. "I think you'll enjoy the company."

"I like babies," Gloria said slowly. "Regardless of where they…" She paused again. "Penny is very pretty. I'm sure her baby will be especially attractive."

"You're making progress," Lori told her. "How does that feel?"

"Awkward and foolish most of the time," Gloria admitted. "But you're right. It makes a difference. I want my family in my life and if this is what it takes, then I'm willing to do it."

"The things we do for love."

Gloria stared at her. "Or don't do. Why aren't you married?"

"No one asked."

"I find that hard to believe. You're perfectly capable."

Lori knew that there was a genuine compliment buried in the less than elegant words. "I should have that stitched on a pillow. 'Perfectly capable.'"

"You know what I mean. You're the sort of woman who would make someone a good wife."

"You'd think that, wouldn't you? But apparently men everywhere decided they could live without me." She spoke lightly, not wanting to admit there might be any pain inherent in her situation. She was nearly thirty years old and no man had ever fallen in love with her.

Her sister's theory was that she deliberately picked men she could never care about so it was easier for her to keep her distance. Lori wasn't sure. She'd never been in love, so maybe Madeline had been right. And she did tend toward men who were safe.

Except for Reid. Not that she could ever really care about him, but he was someone she could dream about.

She'd gone her entire life without having a crush on someone. Why did she have to have one now? And on him?

"You're not sexy enough," Gloria said.

Lori stared at her. "Excuse me?"

"Men are stupid about sex. Always have been. You don't try to make yourself attractive."

"I dress appropriately for my job."

Gloria shook her head. "Don't pretend that this is how you are during the day and it's totally different the rest of the time. You've made a career of blending into the background. I'm not fooled. Hand me my purse."

Lori reached for the leather handbag by the bookcase and passed it across to her patient.

"Maybe I like my life," she said, more than a little annoyed. "Maybe I don't appreciate your criticism."

Gloria slipped on her reading glasses and pulled out a Palm Pilot. "I'm the queen bitch, girly. What makes you think I care?"

Lori tried to hide her smile, but couldn't. "You're not all that."

Gloria looked at her over her glasses. "I'm all that and more. Write this down." She read off a phone number. "You want Ramon and only Ramon. Tell him I sent you. That should put the fear of God into him."

"Who, exactly, is Ramon?"

"My hairdresser. And don't panic. I'm an old woman and he does what I say. But with your hair, he could do something amazing."

Lori resisted the need to finger her long, wavy hair. It had always been a disaster she didn't know how to control. Deep down inside, she'd always wondered if a great cut could make a difference. But she'd been afraid to try before, so she'd left her hair long and kept it back in a braid.

Still, she was tempted. Would changing her hair

make Reid see her differently? And how much did she hate that he was the first place her mind zipped?

"Thanks," she said. "I'll think about it."

"You'll call," Gloria said. "That's an order."

"Yes, ma'am."

"Good." She glanced at the clock. "Now put my purse away and help me to the bathroom. Penny will be here any minute."

TWENTY MINUTES LATER Lori opened the door to find an attractive woman holding a baby on the wide porch. The woman seemed tense and apprehensive.

"Penny Jackson," the woman said with a tight smile. "Not Buchanan. Which I'm sure Gloria hates. For a woman who was a pioneer in her day, she has some very particular ideas about the rest of the world. Not that I care. I don't care. Except she's Cal's grandmother and my grandmother-in-law, so even though I don't want to care, I actually do."

She paused, sucked in a breath and seemed to relax. "You're probably thinking you don't want to let the insane inside. I totally get that."

Lori grinned. "I'm a professional. The insane don't scare me."

"Good to know. What about mean old ladies?"

"I'm fearless."

"I wish I was."

"You will be. I'm Lori Johnston, Gloria's day nurse," she said as she stepped back. "Come on in."

"Do I have to?" Penny asked, but she stepped inside. "I'm married to Cal, Gloria's oldest grandson, which you might have figured out from my senseless rant. This is Allison."

Lori stepped close to smile at the baby, ignoring the audible ticking of her biological clock. All she had to do was see a small child and her body sent up hard to ignore get-pregnant-now messages.

"She's beautiful," she said honestly, gazing down at the sleeping baby.

Allison was all pink skin and pale wisps of hair. She smelled like powder and vanilla and her mouth was that perfect rosebud shape women spent the rest of their lives trying to duplicate.

"I think so," Penny told her. "You should see Cal. He's crazy about her. I know some men are freaked out about babies, but he's not. He wants to be a part of everything. He's even crabby that I'm breast-feeding because it means he can't help." She sighed. "He's a great guy."

Lori felt a flicker of envy. Not because she was the least bit interested in Penny's husband but because she was stupid enough to want a great guy for herself. Which wasn't likely to happen. She had never been in love. Not even once. Obviously there was something wrong with her.

Her lack of love wasn't all one-sided—after all, no one had ever been in love with her, either. Although she wasn't sure if that made the situation better or worse.

Lori grabbed the large diaper bag hanging from Penny's shoulder.

"I'll put this in the kitchen for you," she said. "Would you like anything while you're visiting Gloria? Tea? Decaf? A sandwich?"

Penny sighed heavily. "I want to say a speedy escape, but I have a reputation for being tough. Difficult even. I once stabbed a man. It was an accident, but still. I refuse to be afraid of one small old woman."

Lori felt her eyes widen. "You stabbed someone?"

Penny shrugged. "Assuming I survive this, I'll give you the details." She raised her head and thrust out her chin. "Okay. I'm braced."

"You don't need to be braced," Lori told her. "You'll do fine. Gloria has changed."

"So I've heard, but as I've yet to see any flying pigs, I'm reserving judgment."

Lori resisted the need to say, "You'll see." Instead she led the way into Gloria's temporary quarters.

"Penny's here," she said as she stepped aside to let in Cal's wife and the baby.

Gloria raised her bed and smiled welcomingly. "Penny! How delightful to see you. Thank you so much for coming. I know you must be busy, between taking care of Allison and cooking those delicious meals at the restaurant."

Penny came to a stop and stared at Lori, then looked back at Gloria.

"Come here," Gloria said, coaxingly. "Oh, what a beautiful little girl. So precious. She's perfect and she looks just like you."

Lori did her best not to look smug as she stepped out of the room and shut the door behind her.

AN HOUR LATER Cal arrived with Reid on his heels. Both men carried large takeout bags from the Downtown Sports Bar. Lori knew that was where Reid supposedly worked, although he hadn't been going in much. Not that she blamed him. The whole world wanted to talk about how lousy he was in bed or find out if he wasn't. Under those circumstances, she supposed that laying low made sense.

"Your wife and daughter are already here," Lori said as she took the bags from Cal. "I'll get this ready to serve. Do you want to eat in Gloria's room or the dining room?"

Cal glanced back at Reid who tilted his head toward the study, where Penny and Allison were still entertaining Gloria.

Cal looked doubtful. "I want to be in the mood to eat."

"You will be," Reid told him. "Trust me. Go on. Say hello. Give it five minutes. If she bugs you, we'll eat out here."

"You're setting me up. I can feel it."

"Would I do that to you?" Reid asked, looking innocent.

"In a heartbeat." Cal disappeared down the hall.
Reid followed Lori into the kitchen.

"How's it going with Penny?" he asked.

"I haven't heard any screaming, so that's a good
thing."

"It is."

He began unpacking the bags. She did the same,
trying not to say anything as she opened containers
of chicken wings and various sauces, spinach-and-
artichoke dip with chips, fried shrimp, potato skins
and taquitos.

Behind her, she heard a low chuckle. She turned
to find Reid grinning at her.

"Say it," he told her. "You're dying to yell at me
about the food, aren't you?"

"I have no idea what you're talking about."

"Liar."

He was standing close enough for her to see the
various shades of brown and gold that made up his
irises. His lips curved into a smile that made her insides
get all squishy. Suddenly nothing about the food
bothered her. Instead she wanted to press up against
him and have a second go-round of that kissing action.

Several things prevented her from acting on any
impulses. For one thing, except for the brief greeting
at her house, he'd never tried to kiss her again, which
wasn't a good sign. For another, they weren't alone
in the house. But the real reason was she was terrified of being rejected.

Reid was the kind of man who took what he wanted. She was right there, practically begging. His lack of response was answer enough.

"You hate the food," he said.

It took her a second to figure out what he was talking about. "I'm sure it's fine."

"It's not healthy."

"I'm not going to be eating it."

The right side of his smile curved up a little more. "Come on, Lori. Give in. You want to yell and I'm willing to listen. You might even get through to me. Look at all that fat, those empty calories. Not a vegetable in sight. Well, except the spinach and artichokes. So that's something, right?"

Thoughts of kissing faded as indignation flared inside of her. She knew that he was baiting her and didn't mind in the least. A loud argument about his disgusting eating habits might make her forget how much it hurt to want someone who didn't want her back.

"You're a grown man, not some teenager," she said. "You know better. Worse, you've been a professional athlete. I know you've been educated on what is best for your body. If you expect any kind of peak performance, you have to give your body something to work with. This garbage will kill you. That's the bad news. The good news is you'll go slowly, so you'll have plenty of time to enjoy your fade to black."

"That's my girl," he said.

She narrowed her gaze. "I'm serious. Eat a real vegetable. Some fruit. A lean protein. With this kind of food, you might as well drink drain cleaner and be done with it."

"He's not going to listen."

She turned and saw Cal standing in the doorway to the kitchen. "I know. I'm ranting because I need to, not in an effort to change him."

"That makes sense." Cal walked toward her. "Although if anyone could get through to him, I'm guessing it would be you. You seem capable of working miracles."

For a second her heart froze in her chest. She felt the absence of beating and a distinct coldness.

She could change Reid? How? Because he'd said something to his brother? He'd hinted that he cared about her, or that he…

"I don't know what you did to Gloria," Cal continued, "but it's damned incredible."

Oh. Right. Gloria.

Her heart resumed a disappointed beat.

"I only pointed out the possibilities," she said, going for cheerful and hoping she didn't fail. "She made the decision to change. It's a work in progress and she's doing great."

"More than great," Cal said. "I don't know how to thank you."

"No thanks are required."

Reid put his arm around her shoulders and hugged her close. "Can I pick 'em or what?"

"You don't get credit for me," Lori told him, ignoring the heat his touch generated. "The nursing agency sent you a list of names and you picked me at random."

Reid looked wounded. "You don't know that."

"I'm willing to put money on my guess."

"She doesn't take your crap," Cal said. "I like that."

"She keeps me honest," Reid said. "No one's done that before."

Lori tried to take pleasure in the compliment but she didn't want to keep Reid honest. She wanted to keep him up nights with unquenchable desire. Like that was ever going to happen.

"Honest, huh?" Cal raised his eyebrows. "Interesting."

"Yeah, yeah. Fascinating," Reid grumbled. "Let's eat. Gloria must be hungry."

Lori wrinkled her nose. "There's no way your grandmother will eat this horrible, greasy food."

"You think you know everything," he said, stepping away from her. "But you don't."

Then he handed her the plate of wings with the bowl of dipping sauce in the middle.

"Cal, grab the rest of this," he said. "I'll bring in plates and napkins. Tell Penny I don't want any complaints about the food. Now that she's a hot chef, she complains too much."

Lori felt awkward as she carried the food into Gloria's room. There was a little too much family for her comfort and she didn't want anyone to think she assumed she was one of them.

But when she entered the study, the number of chairs pulled up to Gloria's hospital bed indicated a party of four joining the elder Buchanan.

Lori hovered and fussed with the food and the plates until Reid pushed her into a chair and took the one next to her.

"I should—" she began, only to be cut off when he handed her a plate covered in fried food.

"Eat," he said.

"But…"

He picked up a taquito and placed it between her lips. "Eat."

She ate.

Conversation flowed easily. She listened, rather than participated, as they talked business and family. She'd already met Walker and could place him, but Reid and Cal's sister, Dani, was still a mystery to her.

"Walker has a handle on the business," Cal was saying. "Sales are up at The Waterfront."

"I'm a little annoyed by that," Penny admitted. She'd placed the baby on the bed next to Gloria and pulled up the side bars to keep everyone safe. "I was gone for nearly two months. How could sales be up without me there to supervise the meals? I hate the thought of being replaceable."

"You're never that," Cal told her.

Gloria chewed, then swallowed. "Obviously you left a well-trained staff in place. Plus, Walker mentioned something about an increase in advertising. That wouldn't have helped if not for your excellent menus."

Cal and Penny exchanged a look of surprise, then Penny murmured, "Thank you."

Lori felt like a proud parent watching a child in her first play. She wanted to remind them all that Gloria wasn't really evil. She'd just lost her way. But Lori didn't want to break the mood by saying that. Instead she enjoyed the death food and the way Reid sat close to her. Was it totally stupid of her to pretend that this was real? That she was one of them and that Reid…what? Cared about her?

The longing was as intense as it was foolish. If she were friends with someone in her situation, she would tell her friend to get over the guy who was out of reach and move on with her life. That time spent dreaming was just a waste.

Reid passed her a couple of chicken wings. "Secret recipe," he whispered in her ear. "You'll love them."

As he spoke, he winked. Talk about charming. Now that she knew a little more about his past, she couldn't keep telling herself he had the emotional depth of a cookie sheet. There was more to the man than just good looks and a way with women.

The information hardly helped her situation. He

was still as out of reach as the moon and she was nothing more than a coyote howling for what she would never have.

CHAPTER TEN

CAL, PENNY AND the baby left just as Sandy arrived for her evening shift. She helped Lori pack up the leftovers.

"Take any of this," Lori said. "I doubt Gloria will have seconds and Reid doesn't need them."

Sandy grinned. "I don't know. I think he looks pretty great."

"I was thinking more of his heart than how he fits in jeans," Lori said dryly. "And aren't you engaged?"

"I'm in love, but I'm not dead. He's still a fine-looking man. Any reason you're not going for some? I know he's interested."

Lori felt a shift in the space-time continuum. She glanced at the clock on the microwave and half expected to see it moving backward.

"Excuse me?" she said, her voice low and breathless. "I don't think so."

Sandy shrugged. "I could be wrong, but I don't think so. He looks at you like…" She paused, then said, "Like you matter. You're important to him."

"Reid? Me?"

Lori hated how desperately she wanted the other woman's words to be true. Once again she was the poster girl for pathetic.

"I have a brain," she said. And fairly small breasts—an obvious fact she didn't share.

"Reid takes what's easy because he can," Sandy told her. "But none of us mean anything to him. There's something about him. Something that makes me think he's been through something bad. I don't know. Maybe not."

Sandy was surprisingly perceptive, Lori thought. The other woman had guessed what Lori had never imagined. Remembering Reid's sad tale about love and rejection made her want to find him and tell him she was sorry for assuming he was too shallow to have actual feelings. It also made her want to ask for the rest of the story. There had to be more than he was telling her.

"You do what you want," Sandy said. "You're going to anyway. But don't count Reid out just yet. I think he's hot for you."

Lori didn't know what to say. Worse, she could feel herself blushing, which she hated.

Sandy was a great person with a generous personality. She wasn't the type to be cruel on purpose. No doubt she actually thought Reid could be interested in Lori—a fact that made Lori question her intelligence.

But what was worse was the awkward combination of hope and resignation Sandy's faith inspired. Lori *wanted* Reid to have feelings for her. But as much as she wished that, it was so unlikely as to be impossible to imagine. It was like being sixteen again—but with a level of self-awareness that made her ache.

"I should be going," Lori said. "See you tomorrow."

"Have a great night."

Lori collected her purse and jacket, then walked toward the front of the large house. But as she passed the staircase, she found herself turning and climbing up.

Her first couple of days in Gloria's employ, she'd explored the old mansion. But after getting a basic layout of the place, she'd never gone looking around again. Once Reid had moved in, she'd decided to make the upstairs off limits.

Even so, she had a good idea of which suite he'd claimed for his own. In the back of the house was a bedroom, living room, bathroom combination with a balcony and a great view of the city.

She walked to the half-open door and knocked.

From the hallway, she couldn't see anything, but seconds later, Reid appeared.

She'd just spent most of the afternoon with him, so seeing him shouldn't have been any big deal. But it was. Her blood raced through her body and she had the amazingly stupid urge to flip her hair over her shoulder. Fortunately, it was safely secured in a tight braid and therefore unavailable for flipping.

"Hey," he said with a slow, easy grin that made

her insides shimmy and shake. "I thought you'd gone home."

"I'm going now," she murmured, barely able to form words.

What was it about this man that got to her? Why him? Why now? Sure he was good-looking, but she'd never been into appearance before. So what else? What combination of chemistry and need made her unable to dismiss him?

He stepped back and she followed him into the living room of his suite. The furniture was elegant but comfortable, the colors dark. Like everything else in Gloria's house, it was perfect.

Reid wore jeans and a sweatshirt. Sometime after coming upstairs, he'd kicked off his boots and wore only socks on his feet. He was still substantially taller than her, which made her feel feminine and incapable of rational conversation.

There was an open bottle of beer on the coffee table. She recognized the label as one from a local microbrewery.

"Want one?" he asked.

She shook her head, then changed her mind and said, "Sure. Thanks."

He collected her a beer from a built-in refrigerator disguised as an end table, opened it and handed it to her.

She took the icy bottle, then put down her purse and perched gingerly on the edge of the sofa. He joined her at the opposite end, looking interested and expectant. Right. Because she didn't usually spend her free time up here.

"I'm sorry about before," she said slowly. "About what I said and what we talked about."

He frowned slightly. "Can you be a little more specific? I don't exactly remember what moment you're thinking of."

"Oh. Sure. Before. I was ragging on you about the women you're with and you told me about Jenny. I didn't know there was something like that in your past. I shouldn't have judged you."

He picked up his beer and took a sip, then turned his attention back to her. "You like judging me. It makes you feel superior."

Guilt and embarrassment made her flush. "That is so untrue," she said, lying and proud of it.

"Come on, Lori. You think I'm totally useless."

"Not useless. Just lazy."

"Ouch."

"You don't try because you don't have to. Like with Jenny. Did you really just give up on love because she rejected you or was it a convenient excuse to never fall in love again?"

"Double ouch. You really don't like me, do you?"

She saw a flicker of emotion in his eyes. Had her questions hurt him? She knew he was capable of being wounded, she just didn't think she could do it herself.

"I do like you," she said impulsively. "A lot."

"Really?"

Oh, God. She could feel herself blushing. "What I mean is I think you're a great guy. You just like to hide your assets."

He raised one eyebrow and she blushed again.

"My assets," he said slowly. "Interesting. And they would be…?"

He was baiting her. She wanted to think he was flirting with her, but she wasn't totally sure.

"You're smart, you care about people. You have a heart, you're perceptive. But you conceal all that under a façade of being superficial and useless."

"Playing baseball isn't useless."

"I wasn't talking about your job, I was talking about your attitude. You act as if none of this is your fault. Like sleeping with the nurses. You want me to believe it just happened. But it didn't. You made it happen."

She felt a little more comfortable and relaxed slightly. "You don't take responsibility in your relationships. Now I kind of know why."

"I see you're still very comfortable judging me."

"I don't mean what I said in a bad way."

"Of course not." He studied her. "You're angry I didn't try to sleep with you."

It was her worst nightmare come true. For possibly the third time in as many minutes, she felt hot with humiliation, only this experience was about a thousand times worse than the others. She couldn't speak, couldn't breathe, could only try to brace herself for the fact that he was going to tell her exactly how unappealing he found her. He would be kind about it, of course. He would say something polite but the message would be the same. Not her, not ever.

"You didn't ask," he said, staring directly into her eyes. "You went out of your way to make sure I knew you thought I was a bug, which I could have handled. But the not asking?" He shrugged. "That's why."

She felt as if her brain was caught up in a feedback loop. Information swirled around, repeating itself over and over again.

"You slept with Sandy and Kristie because they asked?"

He nodded.

She opened her mouth, then closed it. There had to be more to this, she told herself. "You're saying you only sleep with women who offer?"

"Pretty much. If they come on to me, or show up naked in my room, I'm game."

She couldn't believe it. "So you want a relationship where all you have to do is show up?"

"It's not a relationship," he told her. "It's sex, and yes."

"And women do this? They show up and offer themselves?"

"On a regular basis."

"You have no other standard?"

"No husbands or serious boyfriends." He grinned. "I don't want my ass kicked."

"But if you could take the guy, then married would be okay?"

He shook his head. "That was a joke, Lori."

"I'm not sure it was. I can't believe that's your only benchmark. So any age? Any appearance?"

"I like women. All women. Always have."

But there had to be something else driving this. "You aren't that much of a dog," she said. "You have feelings. You have to want more."

"Why? Because you do?"

They were *so* not going to talk about her.

"Because you're a real person, not a sexual machine."

He grinned. "I like the idea of being a sexual machine."

Sometimes he was such a guy. "Reid, I'm serious."

"Why? What's the big deal? You want to figure this out and you already know the answer. Don't make it more complicated than it is. Women offer and I say yes. That's it."

She wanted to accuse him of lying, but she had a bad feeling he was telling the truth. "I'm offended by the stupidity of women who walk around offering."

"Why? They're getting what they want."

She had a bad feeling he was right. "And you are, too?" she asked. "Your standard of answering the call of 'come and get it' is met? I can't believe you don't require more of yourself. Based on what you're saying, if I'd walked in here and said 'hey, big guy, want to get some?' we'd be having sex right now?"

She hadn't thought her question through. She'd just been talking. But now the words were out there and she couldn't remember ever being more horrified.

Because the tension in the room had cranked up considerably and Reid was looking at her in a way he never had. She was hyper-aware of him, of his maleness, of how much she wanted him. She'd voiced her greatest desire and by doing so, had opened herself up to her greatest fear.

He was going to reject her.

Oh, sure, he liked her enough to do it nicely, but the result would be the same. He was going to be kind and she was going to be devastated.

"I need to get going," she said as she stood and started to back out of the room. "You're busy and I should get home. This has been great but…"

He stood and grabbed her hand. She tried to tug free of his hold, but he didn't let her. Darkness invaded his eyes, but not in a scary, slasher-movie kind of way. Instead it was as if there was something smoldering in his gaze.

She groaned silently. Smoldering? Was she so far gone she was thinking words like that? What was wrong with her?

Stupid questions, she thought grimly. What was wrong with her was about six foot three, all muscle, charm and with some kind of body chemistry that reduced her to quivering without trying.

"I'm not your type," he said, staring at her, as if trying to figure out what she was thinking.

She opened her mouth, then closed it. What was she supposed to say to that?

He took a step closer. Or maybe she'd just stopped pulling back. The humiliation was inevitable. Why not get it over with so she could hit bottom and start the healing process?

"You would never in a million years want a guy like me," he continued. "You think I'm shallow and useless."

What? "That's not true," she told him. "I think that you're…"

She'd always read that people tended to use less than ten percent of their brains, which left a vast untapped wilderness of who knows what swirling around in there. Her eleventh percent suddenly jolted to life.

"You think I don't like you," she said, barely able to believe it was true. "You're afraid I think you're a total waste of space."

"Not afraid. You've told me exactly that, more than once. In many ways."

She had, she realized. When they'd first met. But why would her opinion matter? He couldn't possibly…there was no way he actually, maybe, *liked* her, was there?

On the heels of that unexpected revelation came the thought that maybe she'd hurt him. It didn't seem likely, let alone possible, but once the thought formed, she couldn't let it go.

"Reid, I don't think badly of you," she whispered. "I can't. You're not what I thought." She smiled. "Sometimes you're worse, but mostly you're better."

He continued to hold her hand as he stared into her eyes. There was something compelling about his gaze, something that made her lean forward and wish.

"You confuse the hell out of me," he admitted. "I prefer my women simple."

Inadequacy swamped her. She jerked her hand free and stepped back. "I won't keep you anymore."

She started to turn, then he was there, in front of her, pulling her close, swearing softly, which was crazy enough, but then his mouth was on hers and crazy morphed into unbelievable.

She didn't pull back because she couldn't and she didn't want to. She gave herself up to the slow brush of his mouth on hers. The kiss was slow. Sexy and enticing, but at a speed that implied they had all the time in the world.

He reached up and rubbed his thumb against her bottom lip. Her instinct was to bite down on his thumb, but that seemed too aggressive and sexual and it wasn't anything she'd ever done before, so she stood there, feeling awkward and stupid.

"Relax," he murmured, stepping closer until they were touching everywhere. He took off her glasses and put them on the coffee table. "Unless you don't want to be doing this."

She wasn't sure what "this" was, but if it involved feeling the hard planes of his chest against her breasts and their thighs rubbing, she was all for it.

"I'm fine," she murmured.

"Fine?" His voice was teasing. "Wow. I'm excited now. I've made you feel fine. Maybe I *do* deserve what they said about me in the newspaper."

She wanted to tease back, but she was too scared. She stared into his dark eyes and wished for inspiration.

"Reid, I…" There weren't any words. She had no idea where this was going, but she didn't want him to stop. More would be better. But how to say that?

In the end she gave up on saying it right and simply leaned forward a few inches and kissed him back. Lightly, almost chastely, lips on lips, her hand pressing against his chest.

He was warm all over. Heat seemed to radiate from him. She was aware of that, along with the faint scent of his body. He smelled clean and tempting at the same time. All man and sin and sex.

Need flickered to life. Maybe she was like all those other women, offering herself to him in the hopes that he would take her on. If so, there was nothing she could do about it. She was afraid of being rejected, but for once in her life when it came to a man, she was more afraid of not trying.

She raised herself up onto her toes, wrapped both arms around his neck and kissed him again. This time she put her body into it, leaning into him, trying to convey her desire with something as simple as a kiss.

For a second nothing happened. But just as she felt the waves of humiliation rising up inside of her, he wrapped his arms around her body and kissed her back.

He tilted his head and swept his tongue across her bottom lip. She opened for him instantly, wanting everything he could give her. When he eased inside, she met him eagerly, kissing him back.

Their tongues circled and stroked, rubbing, reaching, playing. He moved his hands up and down her back, each time dipping lower until he cupped her rear. When he grabbed her curves, she felt a surge of wanting rush through her. At the same time, she instinctively arched forward, bringing her belly into contact with his erection.

He was hard! The happy thought filled her brain like a confetti explosion. He was really, really hard. Guys couldn't fake that.

She was so happy, she started to laugh, which made him pull back and study her.

"You're going to make this difficult, aren't you?" he asked.

She couldn't stop grinning. "No, I'm not. I'm enjoying myself."

"You're not supposed to laugh."

"There are rules?" she teased, then rested her hands on his shoulders, pressed against him and rubbed her belly against his erection. "Come on, Reid. We can play, too."

"I didn't think you'd be the play type."

She wasn't, usually. But these were not normal circumstances.

"I'm not excited about playing escaped prisoner and the warden's wife, but I don't need every moment to be solemn."

He raised one eyebrow. "Have you ever *tried* escaped prisoner and the warden's wife?"

"No."

"Then you can't know if you'll like it or not." He stepped back and grabbed her hand. "Come on."

CHAPTER ELEVEN

LORI LET Reid lead her through the living room and into the massive bedroom. She had an impression of dark furniture and a bed the size of her kitchen. He released her, turned on a small lamp on the nightstand, then pulled back the comforter.

Oh, God. They were going to have sex.

It was what she wanted, she reminded herself. It had been what she'd wanted practically from the first moment she'd seen him. But this all felt strange. It was too conscious. She liked to feel a little swept away with her intimacy.

He turned back to her and she had no idea what to do. Was she supposed to take her own clothes off? He was a man used to being adored by women. All women. So how, exactly, did he expect things to go?

"Shoes off," he said as he approached.

"Okay."

She toed off her thick nurses' shoes and kind of kicked them away. Instructions made things easier.

He moved behind her.

"Relax," he said, his voice low and close to her ear.

"Not likely."

"Want to bet?"

"Sure. I keep alternating between excitement and terror, which I probably shouldn't tell you. I'm just not sure how things are going to—"

He kissed her neck.

He stood behind her, his hands on her shoulders. There had been a little breath of air as a warning, but even so the kiss had caught her off guard.

She had no real thoughts about her neck. It was fine, it supported her head, sometimes she remembered to put sunscreen on it. But she'd never considered anything about it erotic.

She did now. He pressed an openmouthed kiss against her suddenly sensitive skin and made her break out in goose bumps. He squeezed her shoulders, holding her in place as he slowly, so slowly, kissed his way down to the top of her crew-style sweater. Then he shifted to the other side and did it again.

That was it—a simple kiss. Lips on skin with a slight flick of his tongue. But it was one of the most sensual moments of her life.

Her breasts felt heavy and swollen. She wanted his hands on them, his mouth on her nipples. Between her legs, flesh heated.

She started to turn toward him, but he wouldn't

let her. "Not so fast. We've got a lot of work to do first."

Work? What work?

He dropped his hands to the hem of her sweater and tugged. She helped him pull off the garment and happily toss it onto a chair by the armoire. Once again she tried to turn toward him and once again he stopped her. Then his mouth returned to her neck.

He kissed her slowly, thoroughly. He moved down her shoulder and took a gentle bite. Shivers rippled through her. He rested his hands on her hips, just holding her in place. She couldn't help thinking that his hands could be doing other, more interesting things. Then she got lost in the way he nibbled across her back and licked down her spine.

Nothing was rushed. Over and over he kissed her, teased her, until she felt that time had actually stopped. They were alone on a different plane. Need pulsed in time with her heartbeat, but she understood the appeal of making it last.

He returned to her neck and licked the sensitive skin behind her ear. The action both aroused and tickled. She giggled softly, then caught her breath as her bra fell off. She hadn't even felt him unfasten it.

He moved his hands to her waist, then slid them up her ribs. At the same time he bit down on her left shoulder, then licked away any hint of pain.

She didn't know what to think about first—the feel of his mouth or the movement of his hands. But when he reached her breasts, she allowed herself to get lost in those feelings.

Still standing behind her, he cupped her curves. With his thumbs and forefingers, he captured her nipples. Pleasure shot through her and her breath caught. Her legs began to tremble.

He teased her tight flesh over and over, brushing the tips and sending ribbons of need all through her.

"Open your eyes," he murmured in her ear.

The words startled her so much, she did as he asked. She looked down and saw his tanned hands caressing her pale skin.

A blush heated her cheeks, but she couldn't seem to look away. Not when he again rubbed her nipples and she could both see and feel what he was doing. Then he moved close, pressing his erection against her rear, making her wish they were naked so he could be inside of her.

She knew she was wet. She could feel the dampness of her panties. She wanted him touching her there. She *needed* to feel him touching her everywhere.

Without thinking, she reached for the button on her jeans. She unfastened it, then had the zipper halfway down before she realized what she was doing.

"Don't stop," he whispered, as he continued to stroke her breasts. "Don't stop."

So she lowered the zipper all the way, but she couldn't seem to find the courage to push down her jeans. Fortunately, that wasn't required. He dropped his right hand to her belly then went down, down, down, slipping under her bikini panties. His warm fingers found their way through her curls and between her legs. He went right to the core of her and found it on the first try.

She was swollen and ready. The first touch made her gasp. The second made her want to scream.

He used his first two fingers to pleasure her, finding a circling rhythm that sent her spiraling into madness in a matter of seconds. It was as if he could read her mind, or maybe just her body. Not too fast, not too slow and most important, the perfect amount of pressure.

She sagged against him, letting him support most of her weight. Her legs threatened to give way at any moment, but she didn't want to move. What if he stopped and never started again? She would die from the need.

Round and round, moving faster and faster, pushing her closer to the edge of her release. Need filled her, making it difficult to breathe or think. She wanted to beg or scream. She wanted more.

Even as he touched her between her legs, he also caressed her breasts, moving back and forth, squeezing her sensitive nipples and pushing her closer and closer to coming. Her muscles tensed in anticipation, yet she didn't want to come. Not yet. Everything felt too good.

Without thinking, she shoved down her jeans and kicked them free. Then she widened her stance, giving him more access. In response, he slipped both fingers inside of her, filling her. She felt her hot, wet, swollen flesh part for him and it wasn't enough.

"I want you inside me," she said, stunning herself by speaking the thought aloud. She could feel his hard-on pressing against her from behind and she wanted more.

"Soon," he told her. "Just relax."

Relax? Relax? He moved out of her and was once again circling that sensitive part of her. She was seconds from coming, not sure how she was going to keep standing long enough, but she didn't dare suggest a shift in positions because then she might miss the whole thing and that would kill—

He stopped and stepped back.

Lori felt the breath leave her body as she struggled to understand what was happening. She was naked, except for socks and how embarrassing was that, seconds away from possibly the greatest climax of her life, begging Reid to be inside of her and he was *stopping?*

He moved in front of her, pulled her close and kissed the hell out of her. There were lips and tongues and reaching and then his hands were between her legs and rubbing and she was so damn close.

Her climax exploded without warning, making her cling to him in an effort to stay standing. Muscles convulsed and throbbed as pleasure poured through her. She might have screamed, she wasn't sure—but as they were kissing, it didn't much matter.

The man knew what he was doing, she thought hazily as he continued to touch her, drawing out every ounce of amazing without pressing too hard on her suddenly sensitive flesh. Then, when the shuddering had stopped and she could breathe again, he eased her back onto the bed, lay down next to her and stroked her face.

Without her glasses, the room was blurry, but Reid was close enough to be exactly in focus.

"Still fine?" he asked, the corners of his mouth twitching with an almost-smile.

She sighed. "Better than fine. Much, much better."

"Good."

He sat up and pulled off his University of Washington sweatshirt. Despite her weakened condition and general sense of well-being, she couldn't help notice the perfectly toned abs and his smooth, muscled back. The man was a walking, breathing advertisement for great genes, a challenging workout and the sense to take advantage of both.

Maybe it was tacky, but she couldn't help wanting to see the rest of the package.

She reached for the button of his jeans.

"Impatient?" he asked.

"A little."

"I like that in a woman."

While she took care of business on her end, he stretched out an arm behind her and tugged on the coated rubber band holding her braid in place.

She abandoned his jeans. "What are you doing?"

"Unfastening your hair. I've been wanting to see it loose for weeks now."

"My hair?"

"Uh-huh."

After what had just happened, she was more than willing to give him anything he wanted. So she sat up and reached for her braid.

"Get naked," she told him.

"Yes, ma'am."

He pushed off jeans and briefs a lot faster than she was able to deal with the braid. Apparently not sure what else to do with his time, he leaned in and licked her right nipple.

Despite her recent orgasm, fire shot through her, all the way down to her crotch. She fell back on the bed and resisted the need to grab his head and hold him captive over her breasts.

"You're distracting me."

"Ignore me."

He knelt over her and drew her nipple into his mouth. First he flicked his tongue against the sensitive peak, then he sucked. Hard.

Forget the hair, she thought as she closed her eyes and gave herself up to the experience of being seduced by Reid Buchanan.

He moved back and forth between her breasts. He used his mouth, his tongue and his fingers to explore every inch of them several times over.

She writhed beneath him, feeling her body ready itself for a second round. Her insides hungered to be taken by this man. He was hard again or still or always and she subtly tried to shift so that he could slide inside of her. But he resisted.

"Soon," he said against her breast.

"You told me that before."

"I'm not lying."

Before she could complain, he began moving down her body. First he kissed her breastbone, then her belly. He teased her belly button with his tongue and continued his journey south, finally reaching his destination between her legs.

Lori closed her eyes and decided to accept her fate at the hands of a man determined to make her boneless. She thought about mentioning the fact that she'd already come once and that it was unlikely it would happen again. Except there wasn't anything ordinary about making love with Reid, so who knew what would happen.

He parted her with his fingers. She felt anticipation, the coolness of his breath followed by the warm, erotic touch of his tongue.

Oh, yeah, she thought as she relaxed into the slow, steady movements. Just like that.

He circled her with the tip of his tongue, then used

the flat part to stroke her senseless. He was a man on a mission and she found that she liked that. He was patient, he read her body and she found her muscles tensing in anticipation about forty-five seconds after his first touch.

She'd always needed a slow build, but not today. She went from intrigued to panting in far too short a time. Even as the pressure inside her increased, she tried to figure out what it was he was doing that was so great. Then she decided she didn't care and lost herself in the ride.

He caressed her, moving back and forth against her center. Need made her part her legs more, as if trying to offer all she was to him. She was torn between going for it and making it last longer. Everything felt too good, she thought as she felt herself getting closer and closer.

Her legs began to tremble. She clutched the bottom sheet and dug her heels into the mattress. He moved a little faster, then gently inserted a single finger inside of her.

She hung suspended for a heartbeat, then two. Tension built until she knew she was going to be ripped apart. It was her last conscious thought as her release crashed through her, causing every muscle to contract and her whole body to get lost in perfection.

She cried out, caught her breath and cried out again. She pushed against him, needing more, wanting everything and then getting that and more.

She rode his finger, gasping with thanks as he pushed in two. She felt herself contract around him. It was too much.

She couldn't wait to do it again.

A few minutes later her heartbeat had slowed from hummingbird speed. She lay on the bed, exhausted and exhilarated. She wondered if she would ever be the same again.

"Mission accomplished," she told him. "I'm officially boneless."

Reid lay next to her, his head propped on his hand. He smiled slowly. "I'm glad."

"No, seriously. This was amazing. You could get your own cult."

Her words made him smile. He liked that he'd pleased her. No, more than liked it. He felt as if he could take on the world.

Everything about her screamed satisfaction. Her skin was flushed, her eyes dilated. She looked like a very happy woman.

"I don't need a cult."

"Are you sure?" she asked. "I could be president."

Her eyes were hazel. He'd never noticed that before. They were large and sexy and he found himself wanting to get lost in them.

He'd wanted to please her for a couple of reasons. First because he always liked his partner to enjoy the experience, but also because he had something to prove. That damn article still haunted him.

But somewhere along the way, that hadn't mattered anymore. He'd wanted to make the experience great because of who Lori was. Because he wanted to please her. Specifically her.

She sat up and unfastened the rest of her braid, then flopped back down on the bed. He reached out and fingered a wavy curl.

She turned toward him. "At the risk of being greedy, I'm ready for more."

So was he. He'd been hard and ready since she'd showed up. It had been a hell of a long time.

He opened a drawer in the nightstand and grabbed a condom and quickly put it on. Then he pulled Lori close and began to kiss her.

Her body felt good against his. She was soft and yielding in all the right places. He liked how she smelled and tasted and responded. He liked pretty much everything.

She reached between them and touched him.

"Oh."

Oh? He was about to ask what was wrong when he realized he wasn't hard. Until maybe three seconds ago, he'd been a rock. Now…nothing.

"Give me a second," he said and reached for her breast.

He was fine, he told himself. Everything worked. Everything *always* worked. He was a fucking machine.

He tried to find humor in the play on words, but couldn't. Then he focused on how great her breast felt in his hand. Then he did his best to remember a porn movie he'd seen. Any porn movie. Crowds and crowds of people doing it. A whole stadium humping.

It didn't work. He wanted her. He wanted her bad. He wanted to be in her and coming and feeling great. But his body refused to respond. If anything his dick shrank down to the size of a grape.

He rolled onto his back and swore. Humiliation made him rest his forearm over his eyes and wish to hell he was anywhere but here.

"Reid?" Lori's voice was soft and tentative.

He raised his other hand. "Don't," he told her. "Whatever you're going to say, just don't. I want to totally be in the moment, so later, when I'm asked, I can point to this as the official low point of my life. I know it's the newspaper article. I know it's pressure. But knowing doesn't help."

"There's a bright side."

He lowered his arm and looked at her. She was bent over him, her long hair teasing his arm.

"There's no damn bright side," he said, trying not to sound angry at her. "This doesn't happen to me. I know guys say that, but for me, it's true. It sure isn't you. I enjoyed what we were doing. It was all I could do to let you come first and not just take you in the first five seconds. I'm better than this."

She smiled. "Better doesn't come close. Right this minute, you're the best sex I ever had. Seriously.

So what does that say about my life? Talk about putting things in perspective."

Against his will, he started to smile. She grinned, then began to chuckle.

"I'm pathetic," she said, still laughing.

"No. Never. You're beautiful."

And she was. Naked and flushed and smiling at him. Without thinking, he kissed her. She parted and then he was in her mouth.

God, she felt good. He touched her body, stroking her everywhere. He reached between her legs and she parted for him. She was so wet and hot. He wanted to be there.

Without thinking, he shifted so that he could push inside of her. He had a moment of panic, knowing he couldn't possibly, but then he was filling her. He was hard, he thought with relief. Then being hard didn't matter. Not when he could thrust into her and take them both the long way home.

CHAPTER TWELVE

LORI DID HER BEST to slow her breathing. It was kind of embarrassing to still be panting ten minutes after the fact. But considering all her body had been through in the past half hour, maybe it was to be expected.

She still felt boneless and incapable of actual movement. Every part of her groaned with satisfaction.

Reid shifted so that she lay next to him. He wrapped an arm around her and ran his hand down her side.

"Amazing," she breathed. "Seriously, that cult thing? I'm totally there."

Instead of answering, he kissed her. There was tenderness in the gesture and without warning, she felt tears in her eyes.

Tears? After sex?

That got her attention. She sat up and glanced at the clock on the nightstand. It was nearly five—a full hour after her shift ended.

"I should be going," she said, mostly because of the unexpected emotion, but also because she rarely arrived home much later than this. "Madeline will wonder what happened to me."

"Let her get her own guy," Reid said, pulling her back into his arms. "Call and let her know you're not going to be home for dinner, then stay with me."

Several thoughts filled her brain at once. In no particular order they were the fact that Reid seemed to *want* her to stay. Didn't guys want to do the deed, then cut and run? She would have bet a lot of money on the fact that he was one of them. A guy who was only in it for the sex shouldn't want company after. So was he just an anomaly or was this a different situation?

She knew which she wanted it to be but it wasn't like she was going to be asking the question.

Second was the "let her get her own guy" comment. As in he was her, Lori's, guy? On what planet?

Finally the fact that she wanted to stay but was afraid. Afraid of caring, afraid of feeling, afraid of him crushing her like a delicate girl bug over-whelmed by feelings.

A strong, self-actualized woman would face her fears. A smart woman interested in survival would disappear into the night.

He handed her his cell phone and then he smiled.

The smile got her. They were naked, in his bed and she'd just had the most incredible sexual experience of this or any other life. Why would she want to walk away from that?

"Hi, it's me," Lori said when her sister picked up.

"How interesting," Madeline said, a smile in her

voice. "According to the caller ID, I should be talking to Reid Buchanan."

"I'm, ah, using his cell phone."

"Are you going to tell me why?"

Lori knew she would confess everything later, but right now she didn't want to get into the details. "I wanted to let you know that I'll be a little late tonight."

Reid pushed her onto her back and began licking her breasts. Despite the liquid fire pouring through her, Lori did her best to keep her breathing totally normal.

Madeline laughed. "Who would have thought my totally straightlaced sister would fall for a bad boy baseball player? Have a good time."

Reid grabbed the phone, said, "Don't wait up," into it, then disconnected the call and slipped his hands between her legs. "Where were we?"

Thirty minutes and two orgasms later, Lori resurfaced. She lay on her side, facing Reid and lightly traced his features.

"You're very good-looking," she said.

He frowned. "Don't say that."

"Because it's a bad thing?"

"Because it's one of the things you don't like about me."

"That's not true. I like that you're pretty."

He winced. "No guy wants to be called pretty. I'm not pretty."

"You're close."

He grabbed her hand and pressed a kiss to her palm. "You think I'm shallow and that I've skated by on my talent and good looks."

"A little. Do you want to tell me that you've done any differently?"

"I want to, but I'd be lying." He ran his fingers through her hair. "Now this is pretty."

"Gloria wants me to cut it."

"What do you want?"

"I don't know. I've always hated my hair. When I was younger, it was a hideous color of red. I was teased all through school. It's gotten better in the past few years, but with the waves and everything, I don't know what to do with it. So I ignore it."

"Ignoring something doesn't make it go away," he told her.

"If you're going to get all deep and sensitive, a lot of women are going to be disappointed."

"What about you?"

This was the second time he implied that she mattered in some way. Lori hated how much she wanted that to be true.

"I'm open to change."

"Except when it comes to your hair."

He had her there. "Maybe I should get it cut."

"You should do what makes you happy."

Being with him made her happy, she thought as she pressed her hand against his bare chest. She liked the feel of warm skin and the way the hair there tickled. She still couldn't believe that she was here, naked, able to touch him however she wanted.

He stroked her cheek, then rubbed his thumb over her lower lip. "Why nursing?"

"I wanted to help people and I wanted to be needed." She drew back slightly, startled by her own honesty.

"Good reasons," he said.

"Partially altruistic, partially selfish," she admitted. "I also wanted a career that I could count on. I knew that I would have to take care of myself financially and nursing has made that happen."

He smiled. "No plans to marry a rich guy?"

"No plans to marry anyone."

"Why not?"

She had a fairly clear understanding of why not. The bottom line was she didn't trust any man enough to believe he could love her.

"I'm not the marrying kind. I'm okay with that."

"You don't believe that humans have a biological need to pair bond?" he asked.

She blinked at him. "What did you say?"

His smile turned smug. "I went to college."

"Where you majored in cheerleaders and being charming."

"I got a degree in cultural anthropology."

The surprises kept on coming. "Why?"

"I thought it sounded cool and would get me women."

She laughed. "At least you're honest."

"I try to be."

"Okay. Back to your original and slightly startling question. Yes, I suppose most people need to pair bond. But the need is stronger in some than in others. It's not a big deal for me. I just want to be able to take care of myself. Buying my house put me on that road."

"Your whole face changes when you talk about your house."

"Does it? I guess because I really love the place. I love that I can decorate it however I want. I love the size and the location. I love that I have an emergency fund in case I need a new water heater or there's a plumbing problem. I love that every month I add a little extra onto the mortgage payment so I can pay the place off in fifteen years instead of thirty. I feel safe there."

His dark gaze never left her face. "Feeling safe is important to you."

He wasn't asking a question, which was fine. He was plenty smart enough to figure out her issues.

"I grew up in a double-wide in Tacoma. It was no one's idea of a great life," she said.

"Madeline mentioned your mom was difficult."

"Oh, really?" She flopped onto her back. "What else did my sister tell you?"

"That you were the one your mother took things out on."

That was true, Lori thought sadly. "My mother used to drink. A lot. She was a pretty mean drunk."

"And now?" he asked.

"She's been sober seven years."

"So that's good, right?"

"I guess. She's trying to put the pieces back together."

Reid leaned over and lightly kissed her. "Are you going to let her be successful?"

She looked up at him. "Don't get too insightful. It will change my opinion of you."

"I can handle it. Are you going to answer the question?"

"I don't know," she admitted slowly. "Sometimes I really want her to make this work. I want her to be successful."

"But?"

"But I'm still mad as hell at her." She wrinkled her nose. "I know that's awful. She's my mother. She's putting her life back together and I'm still pissed because of how she treated me when I was twelve. I should get over it and move on."

"That's your head talking. Not your heart."

She narrowed her gaze. "Excuse me, but a degree in cultural anthropology doesn't mean you get to play pretend psychologist with me."

He grinned. "What if we play it naked?"

"We are naked and the answer is no."

He kissed her again. "You're not easy."

"Thank you. It's been my life's ambition to not be easy."

"So really. Why aren't you married?"

He had a streak of tenacity she hadn't expected. There was no way she was going to admit the real reason, so she settled for truthful but slightly off the mark.

"No one ever asked," she told him, not bothering to mention she didn't let anyone get close enough to think about asking.

Nothing about Reid's expression changed. "Any near misses?"

"Not one."

"So did you not meet the right guy or were you scared?"

Okay, now they were getting a little too personal. "Hey, what about you?" she asked. "All these questions apply."

"I don't date many guys. Sure, I tried for a while but it was just a fad."

She laughed. "You know what I mean."

"I fell in love once, remember? I was willing to do the marriage thing."

With a woman who didn't want him, Lori thought sadly. Life was nothing if not perverse.

DANI WALKED INTO the Daily Grind and glanced around for Gary. Sometime in the past couple of weeks they'd established a standing coffee date. She waved when she saw him already seated at a table in the corner. What did it say about her life that the best guy she'd met in years turned out to be gay?

"How's the job search going?" he asked as she took the seat opposite his.

"Okay. I've had a couple more interviews, but nothing I've really clicked with. The problem is I love working with Penny at The Waterfront. Sure it's hard work, but we're all part of a team." She grimaced. "Could I sound more like a cliché?"

"Probably not, but is that bad? Would you rather work in a place where you're not part of a team?"

"No and no. That's why I turned down the last job offer. I know you said to be patient and you're right. It's just…" She took a breath. "I hate to admit this, but with Walker running the company, I kind of don't want to move on. Dealing with him makes me feel connected to my family."

"They'll still be your family, no matter where you work," Gary told her. "Are you still thinking about looking outside of Seattle?"

"I should, but I haven't yet. I don't want to move away."

"Then you don't have to. There's no law."

He smiled at her—a sweet, gentle smile that made her happy they'd become friends. He was a good man and knowing there could never be anything sexual between them helped a lot. She didn't need to make another mistake in the man department.

"I can't blame you for wanting to stay here," he told her. "I would never leave Seattle. All my family is here, as well. I love them all, even my sister who has spent the past six months setting me up with every single woman she knows. It's getting so I'm afraid to take her calls. The last woman was very nice, but she had this grating voice…"

He kept on talking, but Dani wasn't listening. She was too stunned to do anything but stare at him.

If his sister was setting him up with women then that meant… "You're not gay?" she blurted without thinking.

Gary paused in the act of raising up his container of coffee. Confusion drew his eyebrows together. "You thought I was gay?"

Oh, God.

She wanted to bolt from the room and disappear into the crowd outside. How could she have been wrong about that? What would he think of her? Worse, he was such a sweet guy and she really liked him and now she'd practically shouted that there was something about him that made her think he wasn't into women. No straight guy was going to take that as a compliment.

"I'm sorry," she whispered, forcing herself to look at him. "I shouldn't have said that. I didn't mean…"

So what hadn't she meant? There weren't a lot of interpretations to "You're not gay?" It wasn't as if she could pass off the line as him not understanding what she meant.

She opened her mouth, then closed it again.

Gary sipped his coffee. "Gay," he said slowly. "Interesting."

She drew in a breath. Interesting wasn't bad. "You don't hate me?"

"No. Why would I?"

"Some men wouldn't consider the comment flattering."

"I can see that. It makes me want to dress better."

She risked a smile. "You dress fine."

"A little too conservative," he said with a shrug. He glanced down at the ivory shirt and dark slacks he wore. "My sister keeps getting after me to try a little color. Maybe a pink shirt," he teased. "Of course that would make me look more gay."

She felt herself blush. "You're taking this really well."

"It's kind of exciting. I've never thought of myself as having a secret life before." He leaned toward her, his pale gray eyes bright with excitement. "So what made you think I was gay?"

"I'm not sure. You're nice and quiet and you've never tried to pick me up. Not that every man does. I'm not all that."

"You kind of are," he said.

Dani didn't know how to take that. Was Gary flirting with her? And if he was, how did she feel about it?

"You're not married," she said.

"You're not, either."

"I used to be. My divorce is barely final."

"Hard time?" he asked sympathetically.

"No worse than anyone else's, I'm sure," she said. "Hugh wasn't a bad guy." She paused. "Wait a minute. You know what? He was. He was totally awful."

She explained how she and Hugh had met in college and how in his senior year, he'd been injured playing football.

"I stood by him all through his surgery, his therapy," she said. "I'm not asking for a reward, but I stayed. I loved him and even though I knew he'd be paralyzed from the waist down forever and that we could never have a normal physical relationship again, I wanted to marry him."

"What happened?"

"We got married. I bullied him into finishing his degree and then continuing his education. Eventually he got a job as a professor. I worked at Burger Heaven. I thought we were happy."

They hadn't been, of course, but she'd thought their problems were just like everyone else's. A little boredom, a few too many weekends spent on separate activities.

"It wasn't perfect," she continued. "But I thought…" She shook her head. "I was wrong."

"He asked for a divorce?"

"Not just that. He told me I hadn't grown enough as a person. That I hadn't kept up with him. It was totally humiliating."

She remembered wanting to scream at the unfairness of the accusation. She'd wanted to point out that all her free time had gone into looking after him and supporting the two of them. If she hadn't grown it had been because she'd been busting her ass for him.

"Worse," she continued, "It turned out to be total crap. He'd been having an affair with one of his students. Or maybe more. I'm not sure. I caught him cheating."

"I'm sorry," Gary said and reached out to take her hand in his.

She let him and then studied their joined fingers. His touch felt nice. Safe. There wasn't even one tingle, but after all she'd been through, she'd decided that sexual attraction was highly overrated.

"So you'll get over him," he told her. "You'll recover."

"I'm over Hugh," she said wryly. "If only my sad story ended there."

"It doesn't?"

"Oh, please. Why make a fool of myself once when I can easily do it again?"

He winced. "What happened?"

"Rebound guy. Ryan. He was perfect. Charming, handsome, caring and everything I needed to help me get over Hugh. He knew exactly what to say, how to say it."

"So what was the problem?" Gary asked.

"He was married. Yup, a lying, cheating weasel

dog. I thought about having him shot. One of my brothers used to be a Marine. But in the end I let him live."

"Probably for the best. You wouldn't like prison."

"At least I wouldn't have to deal with my very tragic love life."

"It is a unique story," he said.

She smiled. "I agree. I doubt you can top it."

"I can't. So now what?"

"Now I find a new job and look for my father. Which is mostly your fault. You keep talking about the importance of family and now I have to go for it. I just don't know how to start."

"Have you tried a private detective?"

She shook her head. "I never thought of it before. Maybe one could help. I don't have very much to go on." In truth she had nothing, but miracles happened.

"I can give you a couple of names. Both really good at what they do."

She pulled her hand free. "Excuse me? How does a guy who teaches theology and math know about private detectives?"

"I'm a man of many talents."

"Apparently. Okay, sure. Names would be great."

He pulled a pen out of his jacket pocket and then passed over a napkin. "Why don't you give me your number and I'll call you with the information."

Fifteen minutes ago she wouldn't have hesitated to give him the information. Gay Gary was safe. But if he wasn't, and why would he lie about that, things were different. What if he called her for other reasons? Like to ask her out?

Dani wasn't sure how she felt about that. Getting involved should be illegal in her case. Yet this was Gary. She liked him and nothing about him even hinted that he could ever be a threat. Of course the neighbors of serial killers always went on about how nice they were.

Still she wrote down her cell number and passed it back to him. Sometimes you just had to take a chance on people.

LORI ARRIVED FOR WORK a few minutes early. She locked her car, then stared up at the imposing house. For the first time since being hired to help Gloria, she didn't want to go inside.

She could come up with a thousand reasons why, but they all covered up a single truth. She was scared. Truly, down to her bones, terrified.

Yesterday and last night had been incredible. Being with Reid had made her feel in the best way possible. They'd made love one more time before she'd finally gone home. It had been well after midnight and Madeline had waited up.

The teasing had been worth it, Lori thought as she walked toward the front door and let herself in with her key. She'd endured the teasing happily because she was still glowing from all that Reid had done to her body.

And it wasn't even all about the sex. It had been great—but not really the best part. The best part had been being with him. Spending time with the man and finding out she liked him even more than she'd thought possible.

Which made the morning after even more awkward. What had their time together meant to him? What was he thinking? Was he sorry? Did he want to pretend it had never happened? What were his expectations? She supposed she should be asking the same of herself and assuming she got a say in how things went, but that was a level of maturity she wasn't going to reach in this lifetime. She would have to settle for being terrified he had regrets.

Because she didn't. She wanted more of last night. She wanted to talk and laugh and touch. She wanted to be with him in every way possible.

She was realistic enough to accept that a good part of his interest in her was due to the fact that he was basically trapped in the house. There weren't the regular hordes of admirers all around. When that changed, so would his opinion of her. But until then…

She knew that as a strong, self-sufficient woman she should demand answers. Instead she decided that not acting scared out of her mind would be enough of a win for today.

She hung up her coat in the hall closet and set her purse on the shelf, then walked into the kitchen.

Reid was already there. He stood with his back to her, which meant she could look all she wanted, so she did.

Her gaze dropped to his butt, which deserved its own billboard campaign. A hot, needy quivering began low in her belly. She must have made a sound because he turned.

For a second he just looked at her. She couldn't seem to bring herself to move. Fear tightened her chest until her heart hurt. Then he smiled.

It was a slow, sweet, sexy smile. The kind designed to reduce a sensible woman to a puddle. It about did her in. Then he walked over, put his arm around her waist, pulled her to him and kissed her so thoroughly she practically floated.

"Morning," he murmured.

"Hi." Was that low, sexy voice hers?

"Did you sleep well?"

"Not really." She'd been too busy thinking about what they'd done to want to sleep.

"Me, either. You get inside my head. I can't decide if that's good or bad."

She couldn't, either.

He stared into her eyes. "I went out and got you scones. I know you like them. I didn't know what kind, so I got one of each."

Scones? He'd noticed she had a thing for scones?

"You didn't have to do that," she murmured.

"I know I didn't *have* to. I wanted to."

And just like that, the walls that had protected her so well, for so long, tumbled into dust.

REID MET PENNY in her office at The Waterfront. He and Penny had been friends through her first marriage to his brother, during the divorce and the years she and Cal had been apart. They were still friends now that she and Cal had remarried.

"You didn't bring Allison into work today?" he asked as he took a seat. "I like holding her."

"Because like every other female on the planet, she adores you." Penny tossed down her pen. "I don't get it. She's only a few months old and the second you hold her, she gets spacey. It must be chemical."

He grinned. "I've got it. Not my fault, but there it is."

"Oh, please. Did you want to talk about yourself or did you want to visit with me?"

He loved riling Penny. "I get a choice?"

"I'm ignoring you," she said. "Did you know Walker and Elissa are ready to start looking for a wedding venue? I was hoping they'd have it here, but Walker wants a non-Buchanan location. Which makes no sense to me. If it's not here, I won't be cooking."

"Maybe he doesn't want you to cater his wedding."

The wrong thing to say, he realized as Penny glared at him.

"Why not? Are you saying my food isn't fabulous enough? Is there even one chef in the entire state who is better than me?"

Reid held up both hands. "Truce," he said. "Deep breath. This isn't about your cooking. Did it occur to you that your brother-in-law might want to have the wedding somewhere else so that you could come and enjoy yourself as a member of the family rather than have to sweat cooking for a couple of hundred people?"

"No," she admitted. "But my food would be way better."

"It would. Think of how much Walker loves you. He's willing to make the sacrifice and give up your talent."

"You're playing me," she grumbled.

"Maybe, but I'm doing a hell of a job at it."

"You don't stink," she said and leaned back in her chair. "Okay. Maybe I'll allow them to go somewhere else. But I'm going to insist on catering the rehearsal dinner. What do you think about something with crab? And maybe—"

He groaned and dropped his chin to his chest.

"What?" she demanded.

"Not menus. Please. Anything but that. We can even talk about shopping. Just not menus or food choices or anything food-related."

"All right. Another topic. My choice." She studied him. "Are you dating Lori yet?"

Trust Penny to find a new way to torture him. She was good and he could respect that.

"We're not dating," he said calmly. They'd had a hell of a good time in bed the other night, but that wasn't dating.

"Why don't you ask her out? You like her. And don't bother denying it. I can tell when I see you together."

"I'm not going to deny it. I do like Lori. She's great."

She was a whole lot more than that. Pretty and sexy and smart. She didn't let him get away with crap, which he respected.

Penny's eyebrows rose. "Oh, my. So it's possible I phrased the question incorrectly. Let me try again. Are you and Lori involved?"

He couldn't seem to stop the grin he felt pulling at the corners of his mouth. He had a feeling Penny could see just about everything she wanted from the look on his face.

"We're involved," he admitted.

She shook her head. "I don't know what to say. You like a woman you're involved with. It's not convenience or something to do to fill the time. This means something to you. Have you figured out that makes you practically normal?"

"I'll never be normal, but don't sweat it. Lori can handle me. No problem."

CHAPTER THIRTEEN

"SHE WAS JUST SO imperious," Lori complained. "Ask for Ramon. Tell him I sent you. Who does she think she is? European royalty? She's some old woman with a broken hip. I don't take orders from her."

Madeline smiled serenely from the other side of the leather couch in the quietly elegant, upscale salon.

"Poor Gloria," she said. "All this angst because she gave you the name of her hair person, as a favor, in case you forgot. As for taking orders from her, you kind of do. It's part of the job description."

Lori cupped her impossibly large latte and scowled. "If you're going to be logical, we're not having this conversation. I just can't believe I'm here. What was I thinking? Nothing can be done with my hair. It's impossible. Reid won't even notice, and if he does he'll think it's hideous."

Madeline sipped her own coffee. "Reid?" she asked innocently. "Why would he matter?"

Lori stared at her sister. "I'll kill you, I swear. Don't test me."

"Oooh, violence. So it must be about him.

Besides, you've never been willing to do anything for a man. Why is this one different?"

"He just is," Lori muttered, not wanting to get into something she hadn't totally figured out for herself.

Madeline smiled kindly. "Reid already thinks you're great. He's falling for you."

As much as Lori wanted that to be true, she knew better. "One night of sex does not a relationship make."

"Sometimes it helps. Why would he risk being intimate with someone he has to see every day if he didn't care?"

"I don't know. It had been a long time and I was accessible? Gloria warned me about him. I should have listened."

"Honey, you were gone from the moment you saw him."

It was true, although she'd rather be tortured than admit it. "I'm not like them," she said instead. "Those other women he sleeps with. I'm not all fluff and beauty."

"So he's changing. Now he wants a little substance with his pretty. Why is that a bad thing?"

Because those words would never describe her, Lori thought, more resigned than hurt.

"I can't do it," she mumbled. "I won't."

"So you're going to give up?" her sister asked. "That's terrific. You meet a great guy you can't stop thinking about and for reasons that make absolutely no sense, you walk away without even trying. Does it ever occur to you that the best things in life require a risk? They don't just show up and shower you with everything you want."

Lori set down her coffee a little harder than necessary. "Easy for you to say. If I remember correctly, that pretty much describes your life. When did you ever work for anything?"

"I showed up and got the job done," Madeline said quietly. "Yes, I had some advantages. I know that, and they helped. Maybe being pretty got me on the cheerleading team, but it didn't keep me there. I had to bust my ass to learn the routines. College wasn't easy for me, either."

"Did studying get in the way of your social life?"

Lori hated how she sounded even as she spoke. When she least expected it, she got lost in the bitterness of her past.

"I'm sorry," she said quickly. "This isn't about you, and I know it. I'm overreacting."

"I know." Her sister smiled at her. "You're afraid. You've never really tried before when it came to a guy."

"Ouch. I'm trying to bond here. Stop pissing me off."

"I'm telling you the truth and you know it. I've loved you from the second you were born, Lori. You're my best friend. I want so much for you, yet over and over again I've watched you walk away from what you want because you're not willing to take a chance. I would hate to see you lose Reid for that reason."

"I don't know that I have him," Lori told her. "I don't think I do."

"Then go after him."

"Easy for you to say. When have you been hurt by a guy?"

As soon as the words were out, Lori desperately wanted them back.

"I'm sorry," she whispered. "I'm so sorry."

Madeline shook her head. "It's okay. I'm the perfect one, remember?"

It was an old joke between them, but this time it was hard for Lori to smile.

"I know it's hard for you," Madeline said. "You want him and he's amazing and that terrifies you. But you have to try. He's too good to let go."

"I don't know how to compete with those other women. We have nothing in common."

"Has it occurred to you that that might be a good thing? You've told me that Reid isn't into relationships. He's more a one-night-stand kind of guy. But that's not happening with you."

"Technically it was just the one night," she muttered, then shrugged. "But yeah, he's not hiding from me or anything."

"So maybe you're exactly what he's looking for."

"Maybe I'm not."

Madeline frowned. "I've had it with you. I'm dying, dammit, so you have to listen to me. You care about this guy. You're going to be fully engaged during this relationship. You're going to give it your all and if it ends badly, then you'll have the satisfaction of knowing you have nothing to regret."

Except possibly a heart that could never be whole again.

But instead Lori said, "I hate it when you play the death card."

"Go with your strengths, baby. Besides, the hair can be just the beginning. We can do a whole makeover thing. Clothes, makeup. You'll make Reid crazy."

While Lori liked the sound of that, there was still reality to face. "I'm not…you know…pretty."

"Of course you are. Or you can be. You hide in those hideous scrubs, or *that*." She pointed at Lori's sweater.

Lori glanced down at the plain brown sweater she wore over jeans. "What?"

"It's the definition of ugly. It's too big and the color sucks the life from your face. You're a blob in that. You have a great body—show it off. Flash a little boob at the guy. Men are basically as emotionally developed as the average dog. Show them the goodies and they'll do almost anything."

"That's hideously sexist."

"But true."

Lori was tempted. She'd always stayed out of the

game because it was easier than competing. But nothing had ever mattered to her as much as Reid. Madeline was right. Some things were worth the risk. And if she got crushed like a bug, then she would figure out a way to go on despite the pain. Plus, she could hold the whole thing over her sister's head, and that was always fun.

"Okay," she said as a tall, painfully thin man walked toward them.

"I am Ramon," he said. "Who is Lori?"

"I am," she said as she rose.

"Ah, yes. Gloria mentioned you had wild hair." He smiled. "I like wild hair on a woman. It reflects her spirit, yes?"

Lori didn't have the heart to tell him that her spirit was less "wild" and more "aging domestic tabby."

"So, what are you looking for?" he asked.

She drew in a breath, then went with the truth. "A miracle."

LORI WAS STARING at herself in the department store mirror so intently that she nearly ran into a pole. Madeline stopped and laughed.

"It's you," she said, sounding pleased. "Honest-to-God you."

"I can't believe it," Lori admitted.

Ramon had performed the requested miracle and it had been worth every penny of the hundred-and-twenty-dollar bill.

He'd started by chopping off about six inches of her hair, which had nearly given her a heart attack. Then he'd snipped and sliced and used a razor, thinning her hair and giving her layers. The whole time he'd raved about the various colors in her hair, how she would never need highlights and how beautiful the curls were.

Lori had protested, saying she had weird waves, not curls, but she'd been wrong. Apparently wearing her hair long her whole life had pulled the shape out of her curls. But now, with her hair just below her shoulders, there were curls. Lots of them.

Ramon had shown her how to use a couple of different products that both defined and separated the curls. He'd explained how she could blow dry her hair straight if she had the time and was interested in an upper body workout. Then he'd turned her to face her reflection and she'd nearly fainted.

Her hair was fabulous. Light and sexy and moving, and the color was incredible. Mostly auburn, but with hints of gold and blond.

Before Lori could bask in her newfound wonderfulness, Madeline had dragged her to the back of the salon where an evil woman had waxed her eyebrows. The pain had been intense, but brief. A total makeover had followed.

Desiree had promised a five-minute routine that would change everything. Lori had timed her. The makeup had taken seven minutes, but when she'd seen the results she decided not to complain about the extra time.

Her skin was luminous, her eyes huge. Lip gloss drew attention to her mouth that suddenly appeared full and really sexy.

Now, in the department store, Lori shook her head. "I can't believe that's me."

"It is. Although, honestly, the glasses have to go."

"I can't wear contacts," Lori said, tearing her gaze away from her reflection and following her sister into a department filled with really cute casual clothes.

"There are other solutions," Madeline said. "Like Lasik surgery."

"I'm not having a laser burn off my cornea just so I don't have to wear glasses."

"Beauty is pain. Besides, wouldn't you like to see the digital clock in the morning?"

"I can see it just fine."

"If you lean forward and drag it right to your face. Come on, Lori, it's perfectly safe. Millions of people have had it done and they love the results."

"You're just flapping your lips. It's easy for you to talk—no one is discussing burning off your cornea."

"Fine. I'll let the glasses thing go. Let's find you some great jeans."

Thirty minutes later Lori had three pairs of jeans that fit perfectly. She buttoned up the first of the blouses Madeline had brought her.

"It's more fitted," her sister said. "See how it follows the curves of your body. That's a good thing. I brought in some sweaters, too. And look—no brown."

"Very funny."

But Lori wasn't about to complain. She liked the dark green shirt her sister had picked out. It brought out the green in her hazel eyes.

Madeline forced her into colors she would never have tried on her own. Teals and dark purples, a fun sweater in a range of colors from dark orange to pale peach. The pile kept growing until Lori was sure she could feel her credit card trembling in fear.

"I don't need all this," she said, although she wasn't sure how she would pick her favorites. Funny, but when she shopped on her own she hated the process. Nothing seemed right.

Her sister walked into the crowded dressing room with a simple black dress.

"I know what you're going to say," Madeline began. "'Where would I wear it? It's too expensive. It's not my thing.' Yada, yada. So you're going to try it on and then we'll talk."

Lori took the dress, put it on a hook, then pulled her sister close.

"I love you," she said as they hugged. "I want to make sure you know that."

"I love you, too," Madeline told her.

They smiled at each other, then Lori reached for

the dress. "I really don't have anywhere to wear this."

"No one cares."

They had to make a trip to the car to dump all the packages. Lori thought they were finished, but Madeline dragged her back into the mall and steered her toward a familiar store. Well, familiar from seeing it on the outside. Technically, Lori had never been inside.

"No way," she said, balking at the entrance. "I'm fine."

"You're not fine. You wear ordinary panties and your bras are too plain. You're with a great guy. He deserves a little lace and silk."

With that, Madeline pushed her into Victoria's Secret. "Trust me, he'll love it."

If he wanted to see her in her underwear again, Lori thought, both intrigued by the prospect of something sexy and nervous about Reid's reaction to the new her.

Madeline began collecting scraps of silk and lace, beautiful bras with matching bikini panties. When she paused by a display of thongs, Lori shook her head.

"There is absolutely no way in hell you're getting me into one of those."

Madeline's grin broadened. "Want to bet?"

REID WALKED INTO Cal's office at the corporate head-quarters of The Daily Grind and slumped into the leather chair opposite his brother's desk.

"What's up?" Cal asked. "You look beat."

"I'm good. Still reading all the mail that was sent over. I've sorted it into piles by date."

"Sounds organized."

"It's hell. So many kids write to me. Some of them want something but most of them are just trying to connect with me. They think that if they can see me or talk to me that it's a big deal."

"You're a famous guy."

"Famous for what?" Right now Reid felt about as important as last season's program. "I've wasted the past year of my life. I got injured and it was my own damn fault."

Cal leaned forward. "When you blew out your shoulder? That wasn't your fault. You swerved to avoid some kids on the mountain. It just happened."

"That's what I told you," Reid said, finally ready to admit the truth. "There weren't any kids. I was drunk. That's why I lost control and snowboarded into a tree. That's why I lost my career. I was drunk and stupid. Then I read about these sick kids and I realized I don't have the right to complain about anything. I should spend every day making their lives better."

"That's not your job," Cal told him. "Life doesn't work that way."

"Then how does it work? I can't be useless anymore. I've gotta make some of this right. I just don't know how." He slumped lower in his seat. "The press is still all over me. I get chased a lot when I go out."

"It was a story designed to capture the world's attention."

"You know what? That doesn't even bother me so much anymore." What did he care about some woman he couldn't remember? He knew how good things had been with Lori. Funny how that mattered a whole lot more now.

"I want to leave the sports bar," Reid said. "I'm going to talk to Walker later."

"You just said the press thing didn't bother you anymore."

"It's not about that. I need to do something different. I'm not the right guy for the job. I don't want to sit around and tell stories all day. I want to…" That was the hell of it. He didn't know what he wanted to do.

"You're rich, right?" Cal asked.

"Need a loan?"

"I'm good. I was thinking about you. You've got more money than you can ever spend."

"True."

"So start a foundation. A real one. Endow it with enough money that it functions off the interest, then set it loose on the world."

Reid straightened. He didn't know anything about foundations except that they did good stuff. He remembered how much he'd enjoyed watching those kids get that sports equipment. "I could focus on what I wanted," he said more to himself than to Cal. "Kids and sports."

"More than that," his brother said. "You're the guy everyone is interested in. You can get in places the rest of us can't. You can get people to notice just by showing up."

Reid knew that was true. When he made a call, he got through. "I could give without anyone knowing it's me."

"Is that what you want?"

Reid thought about all those letters and requests and how coldly they'd been answered.

"I don't need credit for doing the right thing," he said quietly. "Not anymore."

LORI WALKED INTO Gloria's room and braced herself for any number of comments. She was wearing new jeans and a fitted sweater. Despite her inexperience, she'd managed to reproduce Ramon's riot of curls and she'd done the makeup thing without poking herself in the eye with the mascara wand.

But now that she was here, she felt awkward and foolish. Like a goat trying to pass as a gazelle.

"Good morning," Gloria said, looking up from her paper. "Did you enjoy your day off?"

"Yes. How are you feeling?"

"Like an old woman with a broken hip. It aches a little this morning, but I'll survive."

"I was hoping for life on a higher plane. Just surviving isn't fun."

Gloria smiled. "You think you can perky your way out of me noticing the changes, but you're wrong. Now stand in the middle of the room and turn slowly."

"You don't pay me to model."

"I pay you to cater to my whims. Now go on."

Feeling foolish and a little self-conscious, Lori did as instructed. She stood in the center of the room and turned in a slow circle.

Gloria studied her, then nodded slowly. "Better," she said. "Much better. You saw Ramon?"

"Yes. He did the cut and showed me how to use some fairly sticky products on my hair."

"The clothes are nice, as well. You finally look like a woman instead of a blob."

Lori chuckled. "Blob, huh?"

"If I had to see that brown sweater one more time, I was going back to the skilled nursing facility."

"I doubt that."

"Your sister help you with your clothes?"

Lori thought about saying she was more than capable on her own, but they both knew it wasn't true. "Yes. She picked everything out. It's kind of embarrassing that I don't know what looks good on me."

"You do now." Gloria leaned forward. "But we have to do something about those glasses."

"I can't wear contacts and don't start on me about

the Lasik surgery. I'm not interested in getting my corneas burned off, okay?"

"It's not like they burn off the whole thing, but fine. You look lovely. Reid will be very impressed."

Lori froze. Technically she'd had sex with Reid under Gloria's roof, but it had never occurred to her that her patient knew about it. She couldn't. That would be too humiliating for words. They had to be talking about something else. Reid in general. Or the fact that Lori had a crush on him, which no one was supposed to know either.

"I didn't do this for Reid," Lori mumbled.

"Of course not, dear. I just want you to be careful. I care about you and I don't want to see you get hurt."

Lori appreciated the gesture. She knew Gloria spoke from a place of caring and concern. But what really got her was the assumption that Reid would do the hurting. That there was no way she could ever be the one to leave or wound him.

Yes, it was realistic, but just once she would like to be the one with the power instead of the one left begging.

"I'll get your coffee," Lori said, and walked out of the room.

She entered the kitchen and was startled to find Reid already there. He looked up, started to speak, then stopped and stared at her.

"What?" she demanded. "Is there a problem?"

"No. Hi. I'm glad to see you. I missed you yesterday."

"I get a day off."

She knew she was being a bitch and the real reason had nothing to do with him.

"No one's saying you don't." He moved close and kissed her. "I like your hair."

"I got it cut." She felt stupid and self-conscious.

"You weren't sure you wanted to before. It looks good." He smiled. "In fact, you're gorgeous."

"Now," she said, unable to keep the hurt out of her voice. "You forgot to say now. But, hey, it's great to be out of the ugly camp and in with you beautiful people."

"What's wrong? Why are you mad at me?"

She wasn't. She was mad at herself, but he was easier to yell at.

"I'm pathetic," she announced. "Horribly pathetic and I hate it. Why can't you have a crush on me? Why can't you be worried I won't be interested anymore?"

"What makes you think I'm not?"

She grabbed the coffee pot and poured, then glared at him. "Oh, please. Get real. I had a makeover. I'm actually wearing makeup and a thong. And I've done it all for you. To what end? What's my point? This is crazy and it's all your fault."

"My fault? What? How?"

She heard him sputtering as she left, but didn't turn around. Talk about a mistake, she thought grimly. Who was she fooling? She didn't fit in. She never would. Trying was a mistake. Better to be safe and not risk the pain.

CHAPTER FOURTEEN

VALERIE'S GARDEN WAS a restored old Victorian on an acre lot. To the right was the parking lot, but the rest of the house was surrounded by a wild and beautiful garden. Even in winter there were lush plants and hedges, trees and pathways that called to Dani. She wanted to wander the stone walkways and discover all the secrets of the beautiful space.

Instead she walked through the front door and into the open dining area.

She was greeted by a young woman in khaki pants and a white long-sleeved shirt covered by an apron edged in embroidered flowers.

"We're closed for lunch," she said with a smile, "but I can probably persuade the chef to whip up something to go. How does that sound?"

Dani appreciated the effort and made a note of the server's name. "Thanks, Bethany. I'm Dani Buchanan. I have a two-thirty appointment with Valerie."

"Oh, right. She's waiting for you. Her office is right this way."

Bethany took her to the back of the house, then

up a narrow flight of stairs. Valerie's office had once been a bedroom. The wallpaper was floral and mostly purple. Valerie herself was a fifty-something woman who had long graying blond hair pulled up on top of her head and wore flowing, romantic clothes.

"Dani Buchanan, Val," Bethany said.

"Wonderful." Valerie stood and stepped around her painted desk. "Dani, I'm so happy to meet you. I've been looking for a manager forever. It's so difficult to find the right blend of philosophy and talent, but based on everything Penny told me about you, I have a wonderful feeling about this interview."

"Me, too," Dani said, shaking the other woman's hand and making a mental note to call her sister-in-law and thank her for the plug.

"Good, good. All right. Let's start with talking, then I'll show you around and we'll finish up with a minitasting. I told Martina, our head chef, to dazzle you."

"I look forward to it." Dani sat in a white wicker chair that was surprisingly comfortable.

"She's brilliant. Beyond brilliant. Are you a vegan?"

Dani hesitated, then shook her head. "I'm sorry, I'm not. The job description said that wasn't a problem."

"It isn't," Valerie assured her. "The only issue we'll have is a familiarity with the various dishes. While you'd have that anywhere, it's more important here. Our serious vegans want to know exactly what they're getting, while those who are experimenting often want ideas for home cooking."

"Learning the menu isn't a problem."

"Good. We're fanatical about fresh here. I have seasonal vendors who provide most of our produce. They're amazing."

Dani thought about Penny's insistence that everything be as fresh as possible.

"The right ingredients make all the difference," she said.

Valerie smiled. "I like you already. Come on. I'll show you around."

They toured the supply areas upstairs, then moved downstairs and met the few members of the serving staff who were still hanging around, having a late lunch together and talking. She saw the wine cellar, the two main dining rooms along with three small rooms that could be used for private parties.

The kitchen took up the rear of the house. It was light, bright and filled with delicious smells. Martina was a tiny woman with a big smile.

"I know Penny," she said by way of greeting. "She says good things about you."

She and Dani shook hands, then Martina introduced her staff.

"Most kitchens are difficult, stressful places," Martina said. "I try to be different. We all want to please our guests. I prefer harmony. Of course I'm more than willing to knock a few heads together if necessary."

Dani really liked the restaurant. She liked the staff and Valerie and Martina. She liked the location, the ambience and how no one seemed terrorized.

"Go on and sit," Martina said. "I'll have Gerald bring out the first course. I did up a little tasting menu for the two of you."

"Wonderful," Valerie said. "Thanks, hon."

Valerie led the way to a small table by the window. In winter the view of the garden was impressive. Dani could only imagine what it would be like in summer.

"I hope things work out with you," Valerie said as they took a seat. "But even if they do, I'm tempted to pretend to interview a couple more people just to have Martina keep making her tasting menu. It's delicious. The best of what she does. We're starting with a vegetable quesadilla with a few spicy surprises and a leek soup you'll die for."

Gerald, a good-looking guy in his early twenties, appeared with a tray and a pitcher of iced tea.

"House blend," Valerie said as he poured.

He then served small cups of soup and set a plate of steaming tortilla wedges between them.

Dani sipped the tea, then stared at her glass. She wasn't a huge tea drinker, but she certainly enjoyed a glass of it from time to time. But this one tasted odd. Like it had been steeped in celery juice or cucumber water. It wasn't a great combination.

She then tasted a spoonful of the soup. Leeks were fairly innocuous, so she wasn't expecting much. Certainly not the sharp tang of licorice.

"Anise?" she asked after she'd forced herself to swallow the unpleasant liquid.

"Fennel mostly. A few other herbs that bring out the distinctive flavor. The stock is a cauliflower base we make up fresh every day. Guests beg us for the recipe or to at least sell the stock to them, but Martina keeps it all a secret."

Dani nodded and smiled, but on the inside, she felt the first hint of worry. She loved Valerie and her restaurant. It had never occurred to her that she could find the exact place she wanted to work and be unable to eat the food.

Things would get better, she told herself. They had to.

But they didn't. The vegetable quesadilla was more awful than the soup, which turned out to be the highlight of the meal.

Part of working in a restaurant at the manager level was the need to be enthused about everything served. Not only would Dani be eating it herself every day she worked, she would also have to talk about it with guests and make recommendations. How could she do that if she couldn't even choke down one meal?

"Isn't this incredible?" Valerie asked as she scooped up a forkful of a lentil casserole with an unfortunate spice combination that tasted and smelled like bad tuna.

"Martina is innovative," Dani said.

This was so unfair, she thought bitterly. The restaurant was her dream job. Why couldn't Valerie have a passion for steaks or Thai food or anything else? Something she, Dani, could enjoy, or at least tolerate. And how could she tell Valerie the truth?

She was saved from having to come up with a polite version of "yuck" when Valerie got an urgent call from her root vegetable vendor. She promised to be in touch with Dani shortly.

As Dani walked to her car, she glanced back at the beautiful old house. If Valerie called with an offer, she would have to figure out a polite way to tell her no. Then she would have to keep looking.

Her dream job was out there…it had to be. She would keep looking until she found it, no matter how long that took.

LORI HOVERED by the stairs for most of the afternoon, wanting to see Reid, but in a casual way. The most sensible plan was to simply go up to his rooms, knock on the door and talk to him. It was the mature thing to do. The problem was, she wasn't feeling especially mature these days.

She'd been lurking for so long that she was startled when he finally appeared and she didn't know what to say.

She stood at the foot of the stairs for his whole journey down and still couldn't come up with a way to say what she needed to.

"I was scared," she said at last, which without an explanation probably didn't make much sense.

Reid stood in front of her and waited.

"I don't want to do this," she continued. "I don't want to try. I don't want to risk the pain."

"Are you breaking up with me?"

She tried to read his expression and couldn't. What was he thinking? Did they have enough of a relationship for there to be a breakup?"

"It's too hard," she admitted. "I'd done all this stuff and sure, some of it was me, but it was mostly for you and what if you didn't notice or didn't care? What if I'm yet another in a long line of one-night stands? Does any of this matter to you? Am I getting involved with someone who has no plans to be involved with me? I've never gone out with a guy like you. I don't know the rules. I've been warned to protect myself from you and while I appreciate the information I want to know why no one is warning you. Maybe I'll break your heart."

"Maybe you will," he said.

"I'm not saying I want to," she clarified.

"Yes, you do."

Did he really think that? "No. I just want to be equals in this. I want to be more than a supplicant at the altar of Reid."

"I have an altar?"

"You know what I mean." She shrugged. "That was all." She turned to leave.

He grabbed her arm and held her in place. Then he moved close, put his hands on her waist and drew her against him.

"Why do you doubt yourself?" he asked. "You look great. You looked great before. If you're happy with what you did, then I'm happy. You don't have to change to get me interested." He smiled, but continued to stare into her eyes. "I think I've already proved that. Several times over."

She appreciated the reassurance and refused to let herself point out that there hadn't been a repeat performance of that single, amazing night. She stepped back.

"I'm not looking for a one-night stand," he continued. "As for you hurting me, of course it could happen, Lori. I have as much on the line as you do. You're right—we're not equals. You have the advantage."

"Oh, please." Who was he kidding?

"You don't trust me," he said. "Why?"

"Because… Because you're Reid Buchanan and I don't know how to be in a relationship. Because I'm afraid. Because this is hard."

"So you run?"

"It seems a good plan."

"Maybe you could find another one."

She stared at him, not sure what to say. Did she

want to stay? Not because he asked or because Madeline said it was a good idea, but for herself?

"I'm not running," he said. "You think that doesn't terrify me?"

"You're trapped here."

He touched her face. "You're wrong. There are a thousand places I could be. I'm here. With you."

She liked how that sounded. In the past, she'd always avoided making the effort. Maybe it *was* time to change that.

"I'll stay," she whispered.

"I'm glad."

DR. GRAYSON WAS a friendly woman who listened as Lori told her sad tale of being unable to wear contacts.

"How long has it been since you tried?" the doctor asked. "The new soft lenses are mostly water and many of my patients don't feel them at all."

"It's been about five years," Lori said. "Maybe longer."

"Do you want to try a pair now?"

Lori really didn't but somehow her makeover seemed incomplete. Besides, as spineless as it made her, her recent encounter with Reid had inspired her to go to the next level, or at least talk about it.

Dr. Grayson pulled out a plastic container of contacts. "You're a perfect candidate for Lasik," she said. "If that interests you."

Lori was too caught up in watching the doctor put liquid onto a seemingly innocent piece of flexible plastic to do more than murmur, "I'm not wild about the idea."

She swallowed hard, then tried to relax as the contact got closer and closer to her eye. When it was nearly touching, she flinched.

Dr. Grayson chuckled. "This goes better if you leave your eye open. Do you want to try putting it in yourself?"

"Not even for money."

"Okay. Deep breath. Here we go."

The contact slipped onto her eye. Lori could instantly see better out of that one eye, which was kind of nice. Maybe this wasn't so bad. Maybe she'd overreacted to the whole contact lenses issue. Then she blinked.

It was like having a boulder in her eye. Pain shot through to the back of head and tears poured down her cheek.

"Get it out, get it out," she said quickly.

"Okay. Look up. Keep your eye open."

Then it was gone. Dr. Grayson handed her a tissue. "So maybe contacts aren't for you."

"Maybe not."

"There are a lot of great styles in glasses."

Lori blinked several times to clear the tears, then looked down at her glasses. Maybe it was time to admit defeat.

Five minutes later she walked out into the waiting room. Madeline stood up.

"You're not wearing contacts."

"I'm not a good candidate."

"Oh. Okay. Now what?"

Lori pulled the appointment card out of her back pocket and tried not to hyperventilate.

"Now I get my corneas burned off by a stupid laser."

A TRUTH OF BASEBALL IS that the pitcher is going to get hit by a few balls. Either throws that go wild or an unexpected low hit that flies right down the middle. Reid had taken his share of knocks and he remembered how each one hurt like hell. The ones that hit him in the gut had pushed the air out of his lungs.

He felt like that now—as if he'd been sucker punched. He wondered if he would ever catch his breath again. Sure he'd done the right thing, but damn.

He walked into the kitchen and saw Lori making Gloria's lunch. She turned, smiled, then put down the knife she'd been using and hurried over to him.

"What's wrong? Do you feel okay? Are you sick?"

"I'm good."

"You look awful." She touched his forehead. "You don't have a temperature, but you're a little pale."

"I'm fine. Just getting used to the fact that I gave away one hundred and twenty-five million dollars."

Her eyes widened. "You did what?"

"Gave it away. I'm starting a foundation. Its mission is to help get kids involved with sports. We'll give away equipment, build play fields, send kids to camp, that sort of thing. At least that's what we're working out right now. The details."

Lori touched his arm. "Impressive. That's a lot of money."

"I'm just getting that."

She smiled. "So are you poor now? Do you have to get a job?"

"I'm trying to do the right thing, but I'm not crazy. I have money left. Besides, I have a job. I've quit the sports bar and now I'll be working at the foundation."

"Running it?"

"No. I'm hiring experts for that. I'm going to be the front man. I was talking to Cal about it. I want to do something. Those letters..." He shook his head. "They haunt me."

She squeezed his arm. "It wasn't your fault."

"It was my picture and fake signature that got sent to those kids. When I think of how disappointed they must have been..." He didn't want to think about it, but he couldn't seem to stop.

"I don't want it to happen again," he said firmly. "I'm going to make sure I get it right. I'm a celebrity of sorts. I can use that. I'll go out there and meet people. I'll get other donations, bring focus to important causes. Who knows—maybe I can even make a difference."

Even saying the words felt uncomfortable. While he'd tried to be a decent guy, he'd really only ever cared about himself and his family. Taking on the world's troubles seemed daunting. So he would start small. One problem at a time.

"You'll be great," she said. "Maybe this was your destiny all along. Maybe you were supposed to end up here, doing this kind of work."

He wasn't a big believer in destiny, but maybe she was right. But if all this was his destiny, what did that make her?

He stared into Lori's eyes, liking the way the colors swirled together. She was so beautiful, he thought. Beautiful and bossy and sexy as hell.

He dropped his gaze to her mouth and thought about kissing her. Kissing Lori was a great way to spend a day. Of course there was the issue of Gloria, and Lori being in the middle of preparing lunch, but…

He stared more intently. Something was different. Something was…

"You're not wearing your glasses," he said.

She nodded, her mouth pulling into a slight smile. "I know."

"Contacts?"

"We're not compatible."

"Then?"

"Lasik surgery."

He winced. "I thought you were never going to do that."

"I changed my mind. It wasn't bad at all. They gave me a tranquilizer and I let them burn away. The whole thing took about fifteen minutes. There isn't any downtime at all. Madeline even watched."

He grimaced. "Eye surgery? No, thanks. When did you have this done?"

"Yesterday."

"And you're okay?"

"I'm great. I can see perfectly." Her smile broadened. "It's kind of a miracle. And no more glasses."

He sensed he was on dangerous territory. If he said or did the wrong thing, he could really piss her off.

"I'm glad you're happy," he said carefully. "You looked great before and you look great now."

"You're so politically correct."

"I don't want you to beat me."

She laughed. "When have I ever beaten you?"

"You were very disapproving when we first met."

"I thought you were useless."

"Plus you were wildly attracted to me and you hated that."

He'd been teasing and expected her to deny his statement. Instead she looked away. "I need to finish Gloria's lunch."

"Lori?"

She shrugged. "It was stupid, but, yes, I did kind of have a crush on you. I hated that I did. Men like you never notice women like me."

"All evidence to the contrary," he said. He wanted to jump up and down and yell that Lori liked him, but he had a reputation for being cool, so he didn't.

"If you hadn't had to hang out here, nothing would have happened," she said.

"My loss."

She looked at him, her eyes wide. So many emotions raced across her face, he couldn't read any one of them.

"I don't know how to deal with you," she admitted.

"Why do I have to be dealt with?"

She sighed. "I don't know what's going on. We're not dating. We're friends, I guess. It's confusing. I'm confused."

"Me, too." He kissed her.

He liked her. He liked being with her. He wanted to keep being with her. But if she was asking him to define what they had, he was the wrong guy.

"I have something to ask you," he said. "Something important."

"Okay."

"I want you to think it through before you answer."

"You're making me nervous."

"No reason to be. Will you be on the board of directors for my foundation?"

She looked as stunned as if he'd just transformed into a cartoon character.

"What? I don't know anything about being on a board. I don't know anything about sports or charity work. Reid, you don't have to do this. Seriously."

"It's not about experience," he said. "You don't have to worry about that. The other members of the board are pros at this sort of thing. But I want you on the board as well. You won't let me get away with any crap. I trust you to kick my ass when I need it. You're the most down-to-earth person I know. You'll keep me and the foundation grounded. It's only a few hours a month. You'll get paid for your time, but it's not big bucks."

Lori couldn't believe what he was saying. Reid actually wanted her to serve on an advisory board for a new foundation funded by a hundred and twenty-five million dollars? Her?

"That's kind of a long-term commitment," she said. "If things don't go well between us, you'd be stuck with me."

"I'm good with that. No matter how much I pissed you off personally, you'd never mess with the foundation."

She wouldn't, of course, but she appreciated that he knew it, too.

Making a difference had a lot of appeal. Who wouldn't enjoy being in that position? It was a once-in-a-lifetime opportunity, compliments of a man she'd once thought of as having the emotional depth of a cookie sheet.

She walked into his embrace and hung on tight.

"I was wrong about you," she murmured, burying her face in his shoulder. "You're much more than a pretty face."

"I'm overwhelmed by your flattery."

She chuckled, then raised her head and looked at him. "You didn't have to do any of this. You could have lived off your millions and not given a damn about anyone."

"I'm still going to live off my millions."

"You're a good guy. Don't hide that. We need good guys in the world."

In truth, she hadn't expected him to be one of them. But now that he was, it made him even more irresistible.

She felt her heart give a little zip. As if it had just opened up to Reid. As if she could now let him inside. The thought of caring more was terrifying, but how was she supposed to stop herself? He was better than she could ever have imagined.

He kissed her lightly. "You'd better feed my grandmother. She's skinny and needs to eat."

"You're right." But he didn't let her go. Instead he kept his arms around her.

"What are you doing later?" he asked. "After work?"

Anticipation exploded inside of her. "I don't know. What did you have in mind?"

"My place." He jerked his head toward the ceiling. "Say four o'clock. I'll be the good-looking guy waiting for you."

She would be the quivering female, but there was no reason to actually say that.

"Sounds like fun," she whispered instead and stepped back.

Reid looked at the clock. "That's a long time from now."

"Four whole hours."

"You still wearing a thong?"

There was something in his voice. Something low and throaty that made her thighs twitch.

"Uh-huh."

He groaned. "Ask my grandmother if you can leave work early."

CHAPTER FIFTEEN

LORI WAS BOTH excited and nervous as she climbed the stairs. She was pretty sure she knew what Reid had in mind—the concept if not the details. While she was thrilled at the thought of being with him again, she wondered how this time would be different from the last. Before she'd been totally swept away by the moment. Now she was not only aware of what they were going to do, but she had her own growing feelings to contend with.

Making love now would probably send her into a female frenzy of bonding. Did she want to take the chance of connecting more? Did she have a choice?

She reached Reid's room before she'd decided. The door stood partially open and she stepped inside.

She was met by soft, seductive music, lit candles everywhere and the man of her dreams walking toward her. As he took her in his arms and kissed her, she knew the answer to the question was no, she didn't have the strength or the will to walk away from him. She was going to play this to the end. If she got hurt, she would deal with the pain.

"I didn't think you'd ever get here," he said as he kissed his way down the side of her neck.

She wore a long-sleeved shirt. He unfastened the first couple of buttons, then pushed the fabric off her shoulder so he could kiss her there.

"I have chocolate wine and chocolate-dipped strawberries," he murmured against her skin. "Prepare to be seduced."

"Chocolate wine?"

"You'll love it," he said. "Trust me."

Her mind and her body fought for her attention. On the one hand, it was impressive that the original Mr. "I take a woman who is willing and does the asking" had put himself out there. On the other, the warm brush of his lips made her not really care about anything else.

He straightened and pulled her into his arms. They began to sway to the music, a sexy, sultry Norah Jones song that had a beat built in desire.

Reid kept one hand on the small of her back and slipped the other through her hair, then he kissed her.

His mouth was warm and demanding. She parted for him. He slipped inside, his tongue brushing hers in a way designed to excite her. His body was hard and unyielding, already aroused. The feel of his erection against her belly sent heat and need spiraling through her.

He wanted her. He wanted *her*. Impossibility battled with reality and reality won. She threw both arms around him and abandoned herself to the moment.

She kissed him with all she had, meeting him stroke for stroke, then closing her lips around his tongue and sucking. He stiffened, his arousal pulsed, then he nipped her bottom lip and pulled back.

"How about the chocolate wine?" he asked.

She opened her eyes. "Not necessary."

"But I have the whole seduction planned. Especially the chocolate part."

Which was sweet. He'd obviously gone to a lot of trouble. She appreciated the gesture. "Seriously, later, I'll be all over that chocolate wine. But not right now."

She stepped back and toed off her shoes. After pulling off her socks, she dropped her jeans, then tossed them onto the sofa. She moved up against him, took his hands in hers and put them on her butt…the very butt left bare by the thong she was wearing.

His breath caught. He squeezed her curves, then eased one hand around to her hip. He pushed the scrap of silk down her legs and she stepped out of it. Then he slipped his fingers between her thighs and began to touch her with an expertise that took her breath away.

He found her center and began to tease it, moving slowly around the heart of her desire, but not quite touching it. He did that again and again, until she was close to begging. She stood, her legs parted, her hands on his shoulders, needing him to keep her balanced and at the same time wanting him to rock her world. Just when she was about to give in and shove his hand into place, he slipped a single finger inside of her and pressed his thumb exactly where she needed him most.

Sensations rippled through her. Tension rose as muscles tensed and her breathing increased. He knew exactly how to do that, how to circle and rub and excite. It was as if he had been hard-wired into her brain and could feel what she was feeling.

With each second he touched her, she moved closer to her orgasm. There was no ebb and flow, no reaching and hoping. It was just a steep, slick, wet, downhill slide to paradise. She dug her fingers into his shoulders and prayed her trembling legs continued to support her. She supposed she could have suggested they move things to the sofa, but she didn't want to break the mood of the moment. Not when she was already so close.

"Look at me," he whispered.

Startled, she did as he requested, opening her eyes and staring into his.

Fire lurked there. Bright, hot need that excited her more.

"I like doing this," he said, his voice low and heavy with his own need. "I like touching you, arousing you. I like how wet you are and how I can feel you shaking. I like everything about your body.

The softness of your skin, the way you start to contract even before you're totally over the edge. I want you, Lori. I want you bad."

His erotic words quickened her breathing. She started to close her eyes, but then forced them to stay open.

"Come for me."

It was more of a request than a command, but it was enough. She crashed over the edge, her body convulsing in perfect pleasure. He kept his thumb on her even as he mimicked the act of love and thrust two fingers inside of her, in and out. Contractions shuddered through her and she groaned out her surrender.

She had barely come back to reality when he leaned in and kissed her. She kissed him back and savored the feel of his body against hers. This was only the beginning, she thought happily as he unfastened the last few buttons on her shirt, unhooked her bra and tossed both on the floor. Then his hands were on her breasts.

He cupped her curves before touching the very tip of her tight nipples. After a couple of seconds, he broke the kiss and bent his head so he could take her right breast in his mouth.

He sucked deeply, pulling at her skin while his fingers caressed her other breast. The connection between her sensitive breasts and her still throbbing center strengthened. She felt each stroke, each lick, each circle of his tongue deep inside. Despite the extraordinary orgasm of a minute or two ago, she found herself getting aroused.

Suddenly she wanted him naked. She wanted their bodies pressed together, joining and staying that way until they were both exhausted. She tugged at his sweater.

"Get your clothes off," she insisted. "Now."

"I like it when you're bossy," he said with a grin, then obliged her request. His feet were already bare so all that was required was for him to pull off his sweater, jeans and briefs. Then she could see all of him.

He had a perfect body, she thought as she walked around him, touching whatever interested her most. His shoulder, his back, the curve of his butt.

She did what he had done that first time they'd made love. She snuggled up behind him, pressing her body against his and began to touch him everywhere.

He was too tall for her to see over him, so she closed her eyes and imagined what he looked like. She explored his chest, paying particular attention to his nipples. She stroked them, then squeezed them. He groaned softly. At the same time she trailed kisses across his back, punctuating them with little, soft nips.

She moved her fingers lower, down his flat belly, then out to his narrow hips. She brushed across his muscled thighs, before taking him in both hands.

He was hard—that always unexpected male combination of impossibly rigid flesh encased in the softest of skin. She explored his length, then circled the head, running her fingers along the sensitive underside before returning to the base and dipping her fingers to explore his testicles.

She wanted him as much as she'd ever wanted anyone. Okay, if she was going to be honest, she wanted him more. She wanted him inside of her, taking her, claiming her.

There it was—her secret truth. She wanted to be claimed by this man. Nothing between them but naked flesh and desire. And hearts, she thought, emotions welling up inside of her. She wanted him to care with a desperation that took his breath away.

The longing, deeper and more powerful than any she'd ever known, threatened her arousal. So she pushed it away to be dealt with another time. She dropped her hands, moved around to stand in front of him and kissed him.

He responded like a starving man. He kissed her hard and hot, touching her everywhere. He also began nudging her backward, toward the bedroom.

His hands were on her breasts, between her legs. Frantic, urging and she soon found herself just as eager. Then she was on the bed. There was a second's delay as he slipped on a condom, then he was inside of her, filling her, taking her with an intensity that gave her no choice except to give herself to him and enjoy the ride.

"DISASTER," Dani said as she sank into the chair opposite Gary's at The Daily Grind. "It was a total disaster. I loved everything about the place. Valerie was great, her staff was charming and happy. Martina, the chef, is someone I would love to work with."

"So how was it a disaster?"

Dani glanced around, wanting to make sure no one from Valerie's Garden happened to be lurking in the area, then spoke in a low voice.

"The food was hideous. Seriously awful. I hated everything. Even the iced tea. Apparently I don't have an upscale vegan palate. If only they'd given me a regular cheese quesadilla, I would have signed up in a heartbeat. Or if it had been nearly any other kind of food. Even if I'd only sort of liked it, I probably would have tried to make the job work, but I'm telling you. What they served bordered on nasty."

Gary chuckled. "They probably won't want you in their ads."

"Probably not. I'm seriously bummed. Why did it have to be like this? I feel like Goldilocks. So far, nothing is exactly right."

Gary reached across the tiny table and patted the back of her hand. "You'll find something. I know you will."

"I hope so," she grumbled, even as she tried to figure out what she felt about him touching her.

"I'll keep looking," she said. "I'm determined to

further my career. I'm getting calls, so that's good. I just have to be patient."

"That's the attitude," he said. "Did you talk to the private investigator?"

"Yes. Thanks for giving me her name. She's great and we got along, but she said without some more information, she can't help me."

Dani wasn't surprised. She knew absolutely nothing about her father except for the fact that at one time he'd existed.

"I haven't got a clue about him," Dani said. "No name, no address, not even a description. I've asked my oldest brother Cal if he remembers anything but he doesn't. He was pretty young and I'm sure my mother was careful to keep him away from the man she was having an affair with."

Gary pulled back his hand and took a sip of his coffee. "What about papers from your mother? Letters? Notes? A date book?"

All good ideas, she thought. "I don't know of anything like that. I'll ask my brothers, but I don't hold out too much hope. There's only one person who might know something and getting her to talk would take a miracle."

"They happen."

"Not in my world."

Gloria? Help her? Her brothers swore the old woman had changed, but was it enough? Gloria had made it clear she loathed Dani.

"I don't want to give her the pleasure of going to her and asking," Dani said flatly. "She doesn't deserve it."

"What do you deserve?" he asked. "If there's a chance of getting what you want, isn't that worth an awkward conversation?"

She smiled. "Oh, sure. Be rational."

"I'm a math teacher. What did you expect?"

She sighed. "I know you're right. I just can't stand the thought of going begging, which means you're going to say then I obviously don't care enough about finding my father."

She drank more of her coffee. "Maybe I'll talk to Reid. He's living in Gloria's house and spending the most time with her. If he says she's really willing to help, then I'll ask."

"Now you have a plan."

She looked at him. "You think I should go face the dragon."

"Our fears get bigger than they should be if we don't see them in the light of day."

"That would be the theology teacher speaking," she said.

"Maybe, and a little of the man."

"We never talk about your life very much," she said, realizing she didn't know that much about him. "You're very good at asking questions."

"I'm very interested in your life," he told her. "My days are often similar."

"And I'm living in the middle of a soap opera. I'm thrilled to know I can at least entertain my friends."

"We appreciate it," he said lightly, then leaned toward her. "Dani, would you like to go to dinner with me sometime?"

He was asking her out. She'd wondered if he would and how she would feel about the invitation. But now that it was here, there was no sense of panic or the need to avoid taking things to the next level. Gary was a great guy. She really liked him. He was kind and honest. The total lack of physical chemistry might be a good thing. She'd been burned by passion enough lately.

"I would love to go to dinner with you," she said.

REID WAS FEELING LIKE pretty hot shit. It was sunny and relatively warm, he'd decided what to do with his life and last night he'd seduced the hell out of Lori. He hadn't taken what was offered, he hadn't gone along with what was easy. He'd planned the evening, reduced her to a puddle and then he'd made her scream.

He liked knowing he could do that to her. He also liked that there was no pretending. He could read her body nearly as easily as he read his own and he knew exactly how to please her. Being with her made him feel good. He found himself wanting things he hadn't thought about in a long time.

The realization should have scared the crap out

of him. Instead he found himself thinking about the future. Playing a serious round or two of "what if."

What if he didn't walk away from Lori? What if things developed between them? What if she fell in love with him?

He knew she liked him. Not just the crush she'd admitted to, but real liking. She wouldn't have slept with him otherwise. He wanted to take credit for her physical transformation, but he knew it had very little to do with him. She'd used him as the excuse, but in truth she'd wanted to make a change for a long time. Lori wasn't comfortable hiding anymore. It had just taken a while for her outsides to figure that out.

But could she fall in love with him? Was she willing to take that ultimate risk? He knew that on the surface he was a great catch. Healthy, good-looking and rich. But what about on the inside? He'd never committed to a woman in his life. He'd only offered once. As Lori had pointed out, he'd then used that moment as an excuse to stop trying.

That wouldn't be enough for Lori. She had high standards and he wondered if he could measure up.

He poured more coffee from the pot on the credenza, then turned back to the stack of letters on his desk. He'd pulled out the ones that bothered him the most and had gone over them again. He had to be able to do something for these kids.

One caught his eye. The one from the boy whose

twin brother had died. Reid had grown up close to Walker and Cal. His brothers, along with Dani, had meant everything to him. If something had happened to one of them…

He picked up the phone and dialed the number on the letter. A woman answered.

"Mrs. Baker?"

"Yes."

"Good morning. My name is Reid Buchanan. I used to play baseball."

"What? Oh. Really? I know who you are. My son is a huge baseball fan. The sport and the players are his world. Even more so since…well, recently. He hated to see you retire. He talked about it for days."

If the kid knew Reid had screwed up his career himself, he would think a lot less of him.

"Mrs. Baker, your son wrote me about your loss. I'm terribly sorry."

There was a moment of silence followed by a strangled, "Thank you. It's been difficult."

"I can imagine. I was thinking about what I could do for Justin. To take his mind off of things for a little while. I have some friends on the Seattle Mariners and I've been talking to their general manager. How would you and Justin like to spend a long weekend with the team at spring training? You'd be flown down first-class, put up in a nice hotel. You'd have a car and a driver at your disposal, along with money for meals. The hotel has a spa. You'd have free use of the facilities. I'd make sure there was someone to keep an eye on Justin while you were relaxing."

He heard her breath catch. "I don't know what to say," she admitted. "Why would you do this?"

"Because I can. You and Justin have already been through too much."

"You're being incredibly generous," she said quietly. "I don't know what to think."

"I would very much like you to let me do this for you. If you need a little time to think it over, then let me give you my phone number. You can call me back."

She gave a little laugh. "Mr. Buchanan, I might have trouble getting through the day, but I'm not totally crazy. Justin would love this and honestly, so would I. Of course we'll go. Thank you."

"You're welcome. I'm going to have a travel agent call you in a couple of hours. She'll make all the arrangements. But I want you to take my personal number as well. If you have any trouble, anything at all, you call me."

"This is amazing. Thank you."

"Just take your boy and have a good time."

"We will."

They hung up. Reid leaned back in his chair and stared down at the list of arrangements that had to be made. While the travel agent he'd spoken with had promised to stay on top of things, he knew he would be calling around and checking himself. He didn't want another repeat of the no return tickets disaster.

He pulled out a pad of paper and added to the ongoing list. If the foundation wasn't going to have an in-house travel agent, then he wanted to make sure there was someone who would follow up on the arrangements made. There weren't going to be any more screw-ups on his watch.

LORI ARRIVED HOME shortly before five and saw a familiar car in the driveway. She pulled into the garage, closed the door behind her and walked into the kitchen. She could hear Madeline and her mother laughing in the living room and her stomach clenched.

She didn't mind that her sister invited people over—this was Madeline's house, too—but why did it have to be their mother? No matter how the evening went, Lori always ended up feeling like the odd one out.

"Hi, I'm home," she called as she walked into the kitchen and set her purse on the counter.

"We're in the living room," Madeline called. "Come join us."

Lori stood in the kitchen and wished for an excuse to escape to the quiet of her room. If only Reid had wanted to seduce her tonight. But he hadn't been around when her shift had ended and she hadn't been comfortable calling him on his cell to find out his plans. They might be physically involved, but she didn't know or understand the parameters of their relationship. She had a feeling that answers were only a conversation away. But she was afraid to ask.

Talk about dumb, she told herself. She should be willing to ask what he was thinking and explain her own needs and desires. She prided herself on being a take-charge person, and she was. Everywhere but with Reid and her mother.

Evie walked into the kitchen and smiled at her. "Hi, Lori. Did you have a good day?"

"Yes, thanks. Gloria is doing better and better. I'd been concerned about how she would heal, but she's moving forward all the time. She should be back to her regular life in a couple of months."

"That's good."

Her mother linked arms with her and dragged her into the living room, then forced her onto the sofa and settled next to her.

"Your sister and I have a confession," Evie said, then looked at Madeline and they both burst out laughing.

Lori glanced between them, not getting the joke. "What happened?"

Madeline waved her hand in the air. "It's not a bad thing," she said, barely able to speak between gasps of laughter. "Unless you're the chicken."

That set them off again. Lori tried to be patient, even though she felt a powerful need to scream. What was so damn funny?

"We were supposed to have chicken for dinner," Evie said as she wiped at her eyes. "I came over to help Madeline get things started. We were season-ing the chicken. It was wet and slippery and it went flying across the room."

She started to laugh again and couldn't stop. Lori could see how an unruly chicken could be humorous, but this was a little extreme.

"Okay," she said slowly. "And?"

Madeline pressed a hand to her chest. "I picked it up and when we were washing it off, it got away from us again. That chicken was determined not to go in the oven."

"It's true," her mother said. "We dropped it twice more, but we finally got it seasoned and in the pan. We put it in the oven and came in here to recover. Then about five minutes before you got home we realized—" She erupted in laughter.

Madeline joined in, then gasped. "We forgot to turn on the oven."

This set them off again. Lori tried to figure out the humor of forgetting to turn on the oven. Apparently it was one of those moments that had to be experi-enced in real time.

"The thing is," her mother told her. "You would never have forgotten. That's what I was telling Madeline when you came home. You were always the solid one, Lori. Not flaky like your sister and me."

Lori held back an automatic protest that her sister wasn't flaky.

Her mother's laughter faded. "Oh, Lori, you were such a good little girl. I could depend on you to take care of things. In my sober moments, I used to think that wasn't a good thing. Not that I blamed you. You're the only reason we all survived. But with you around, I didn't have to worry about what was happening at home. It was all taken care of."

Lori didn't know what to say to that. Her recollections were similar but she'd never thought of them in the context of holding the family together. She'd done what needed to be done because her mother was always drunk and Madeline was busy with her life.

"I remember Lori nagging me to eat," Madeline said. "Or at least eat better than I was."

"She did the same with me," Evie added. "I can see that sweet little girl, standing in the kitchen, holding a big pot and yelling that we were all going to sit down and eat together, even if she had to physically make us."

Lori felt a rush of memories, most of them bad. She pushed them away, as she always did, but her mother kept talking about how much Lori had done.

"I would have been lost without you," Evie said. "Have I told you that? It's true."

Lori felt incredibly uncomfortable. She and her mother didn't get along. Bonding wasn't allowed. "I didn't do that much."

"Of course you did. Part of recovery is acknowledging what the alcohol did to your family. In your case, Lori, my drinking forced you to grow up too soon. You became the mom. I never wanted that."

Lori squirmed in her seat. "It's fine," she murmured, wishing they could talk about something else. She didn't want to hear any of this.

"It's not fine," her mother said. "I wish things had been different." She frowned. "Where are your glasses? Did you get contacts?"

"She had Lasik surgery," Madeline said, sounding smug. "Isn't she beautiful?"

"She'll never be as pretty as you," her mother said.

The comment made Madeline grimace, but helped put Lori's world back in perspective.

"Eye surgery?" Evie asked. "I didn't think you'd want to do something like that."

"I can't wear contacts," Lori said. "I tried and there's just no way. Now I don't have to worry about glasses."

"Is there a man?" her mother asked bluntly. "Women always do stupid things for a man."

Lori distinctly remembered wishing for a change in topic. Now that it was here, she was having second thoughts.

"I didn't do it for a man," Lori said firmly. "I like being able to see without glasses."

Her mother looked unimpressed.

Lori hated sounding like she'd changed herself for Reid. He'd been the catalyst but not the reason.

"Okay, fine. I am kind of seeing someone. It's nothing."

"It's not nothing," Madeline said. "It's fabulous and so is he. Remember Reid Buchanan? He's that hunky baseball player who blew out his shoulder last year and had to retire."

"I don't remember that," Evie told her. "But wasn't there a mean article about him in the paper recently? Something about him not being…" Her mother's voice trailed off.

Lori didn't know what to say. This was a true definition of damned if you do and damned if you don't. "It wasn't true," she said at last. "Not any of it."

"I see."

Evie and Madeline exchanged a look. Lori didn't want to know what either of them were thinking.

"He's great," Madeline said. "He adores Lori."

"I'm glad." Evie smiled. "It's time you found someone."

Lori supposed life was never all one way and neither were people. Evie was trying. Failing, but trying.

CHAPTER SIXTEEN

LORI SCOOPED some orange chicken onto her plate. "This is really good," she said. "Where's the takeout place?"

"A couple of streets down. I'll show you. It doesn't look like much on the outside, but the food is great."

She and Reid sat on the floor, backs against the sofa in his living room in Gloria's house. The coffee table was covered with open takeout containers. Reid had provided dinner and a chilled bottle of Chardonnay. While Lori was confident they would move into the bedroom later, it felt good just to hang out. More normal, maybe.

"It was strange last night with my mother," she said, returning to their previous topic of conversation. "I know she's trying to reach out and I'm beginning to believe she feels badly for what happened all those years she was drinking. I know forgiving her is the right thing to do."

Reid looked at her. "You will when you're ready."

"Maybe."

Sometimes she wanted to forgive all and get close to her mother and sometimes she was so angry, she wanted the other woman punished forever.

She still remembered being ten years old and breaking her mother's favorite glass. It had been tall and slender, perfect for mixing drinks without too much ice getting in the way of the alcohol.

Lori had been washing the dishes and the glass had slipped, breaking into dozens of sharp shards. Her mother had been drunk and angry. When Lori had confessed, Evie had started screaming.

"You're useless," she'd yelled. "I'm sorry you were born. You're nothing but an accident. An accident I didn't want. I have one perfect daughter—why would I want a horrible girl like you?"

The pain still cut as easily as those pieces of the broken glass.

"I know when Madeline's gone, she'll be the only family I have left. That should mean something. I keep thinking if I tried harder, I could get over everything."

"No one is saying you have to," he told her.

"I know, but I feel guilty for not accepting her changes and moving on. It's weird. We were talking about the past. I realized we all remember different situations or the same incident, but in a different way. I guess that's about perspective. I saw what mattered to me, Madeline saw what mattered to her."

"Maybe everyone has a piece of the truth," he

said. "You can remember the parts you want to remember and let the rest go."

"I wish I could."

He put down his fork. "I want to go public with Madeline's illness. I want to get the story out there so people think about donating. You said she was a rare blood type. I've been doing the research and the odds of finding a donor for her aren't great. I think we can change that."

Lori didn't understand. "Go public as in…"

"Talk to the press. Hold interviews. Talk about the importance of donating. Do you know that here, in the States, you have to opt in to a donation program. That the assumption is you're not interested in donating unless you say otherwise. But in Europe, it's the opposite. The assumption is people want to donate. If you aren't interested, you have to opt out. That makes a whole lot more sense to me. I've been talking to some donation centers. They're willing to help coordinate the process with me. With us." He paused and glanced at her. "Did I get too ahead of myself? Are you pissed?"

Pissed? She leaned over and kissed him. Her eyes burned and she figured the tears weren't all that far behind.

"You'd do that for my sister? You did the research and now you're willing to go out there and face the world?"

She wanted to say he couldn't. That he would be

slaughtered in the press. But Madeline's life was too important. Still, she had to make sure he understood what he was getting into.

"There's still that article," she said. "You know any interviewer is going to bring it up."

Reid shrugged. "The people who matter know the truth about me."

"Meaning me and four hundred other women," she teased.

He didn't smile back. "Meaning you. I'd want to talk to my family. This is going to mean they could be in the spotlight, too."

He touched her face. "It's going to be embarrassing and uncomfortable the first couple of times, but then we'll talk about Madeline and how organ donations save lives. The message will get out. What do I care if a few people make cracks at my expense?"

He was making sense in the best way possible. "I can't believe you've already done research."

"I'm an impressive kind of guy."

"Yes, you are." She leaned in and kissed him again. "More than impressive. You're spectacular. If you ever need a letter of recommendation, let me know."

He wrapped his arms around her and pulled her onto his lap. "I just might take you up on that," he said, before he kissed her back.

REID PARKED in his usual spot, then walked in through the front of the Downtown Sports Bar. A couple of the guys called out to him, he heard a few cracks and kept on moving. Cal, Walker and Dani were already there, in their usual table in the corner. He greeted them.

"I know I'm not late," he said as he made a fist and banged knuckles with both Cal and Walker, then hugged his baby sister.

"We got here early so we could talk about you," Dani said with a grin.

"Great. What did you decide?"

"That you might just turn out okay." She sat back down and pushed his beer toward him. "Actually, we all beat you by about two minutes."

He tugged on a lock of his sister's short hair. "I haven't seen you in a while. What's going on?"

"Still working for Penny while I look for something else. She's hoping I'll change my mind about leaving, but I can't. I need to get going on something of my own."

"Where have you been looking?"

"All over the city. There are some interesting places out there."

"Like where?" Cal asked.

"Valerie's Garden. Fabulous restaurant, great staff, incredibly strange vegan food. Not for me."

Reid had never much been into tofu, either.

"You doing okay otherwise?" he asked.

She nodded. "I'm doing fine. Moving on with my life." She touched his arm. "Don't worry."

"We all worry," Walker said. "It's part of the job description."

"Well, I do need help with one thing," Dani said, looking at Reid. "I want to find out about my father. I have nothing to go on, which means I need to talk to Gloria. What are the odds that her transformation is genuine and that she'll help me?"

Reid looked at Cal and Walker. They both shrugged.

"She's changed," Reid said. "She's trying."

"For you guys," Dani grumbled. "You're family."

"She was great to Penny and the baby," Cal offered. "It's not like she loved the idea of Penny being pregnant with another guy's kid but she was friendly. Almost charming. Honestly? It kind of freaked me out."

"She was good to Elissa and even asked her to bring Zoe on her next visit," Walker said.

"I'm tempted to talk to her," Dani said. "But not quite tempted enough."

"Want me to say something?" Reid asked.

Dani shook her head. "No. This is my dragon. I have to make peace with it or slay it myself. Metaphorically, of course. I'm not advocating killing Gloria…yet."

"No one thinks you are," Cal told her. "We're here for you. You know that, right?"

"I do." She smiled. "So that's me. What's up with you, Reid? You've been lying low these past couple of months."

"With good reason. I do have a couple of things I need to talk to you about." He glanced at Walker. "You got my letter of resignation, right?"

Dani glanced between the two of them, then glared at Reid. "You're quitting your job here? Just like that? Did you know?" she asked Cal.

Cal shifted in his seat. "He might have mentioned it."

Dani grabbed a chip from the pile of nachos and chomped down furiously. She swallowed. "Dammit, I'm *always* the last to know. I swear, the next time I get a great secret, I'm not telling any of you."

"It wasn't a secret," Reid said. "I've been thinking about leaving for a while. I'm not good at running this place, probably because I'm not interested. There are some good managers here."

"I know," Walker said calmly. "Don't sweat it. They'll pick up the slack until I get someone else in here." He looked at Dani. "Are you interested?"

"In working here? No, thanks."

"You'd be in charge. I'd like to keep it in the family. And don't say you're not family because you are."

Dani glanced around. "Not my thing. I want a real restaurant. Not liquor and finger food. But I appreciate the offer."

"I'll find somebody else, then," Walker said. "Let me know if you change your mind."

"I will, but don't expect anything." She turned

back to Reid. "What else do you want to spring on me?"

"I have something, but this time no one else knows."

"Cool."

His brothers looked at him. "What is it?" Cal asked.

"It's a bitch not knowing everything, isn't it?" Dani asked.

Walker glanced at Reid. "Was she always this annoying?"

"Pretty much."

Dani bounced in her seat. "Come on. Enough suspense. Spill."

Reid hadn't figured out exactly how to tell them what he was going to do.

"One of Gloria's nurses is the main reason for her change of heart," he began. "Lori has been great with her. Patient but not a pushover. When Gloria gets her back up, Lori won't take any crap. She's—"

Dani punched him in the arm. "You're dating her. Cal and Walker are nodding knowingly, which means they've probably met her. You're dating this woman and you didn't tell me?"

"It just happened. We're not really dating." He hesitated. "We're involved. I like her, okay? Can I get back to the important part now?"

"You like her?" Dani sounded surprised. "As in 'hey, I really like this girl. Let's see where the relationship goes'?"

"Yes. Do you have a problem with that?"

"No." She looked at Walker and Cal. "You guys should say something."

"You're doing fine messing up on your own," Walker told her.

"I'm not messing up. I'm just happy to find out Reid has a girl."

Reid ignored that. "Her sister, Madeline, is sick. She has Hepatitis C and needs a liver transplant. Because of her blood type, she'll be difficult to match. I've talked to Lori and a couple of donor places. I want to go public and talk about the need for people to donate. That means accepting some of those interview offers I've been getting over the past few weeks. That means having my name in the press, which will impact the three of you. You're family and people will talk."

"You're the one they're going to try to annihilate," Walker said. "There won't be anything they won't ask."

Reid thought about the article in the paper—the one claiming he was lousy in bed. "They're going to take it as far as the censors will let them."

"Are you prepared for that?" Dani asked. "It will be humiliating."

He knew that. He would probably become the butt of a lot of late night comedy jokes.

"This isn't about me," he said. "If something doesn't change, Madeline will die. I don't know any other way to help."

Cal nodded. "Then you do what you have to do. We're fine with it."

Reid looked at each of them. "Are you sure?"

"Of course we're sure," Dani said. "When compared with what Lori and her sister are going through, none of the rest of this matters. We'll be fine."

"We can handle it," Walker said.

Reid had known they were going to say that, but he was still gratified to hear the words. "Then I'll e-mail you and let you know when I'm on *Access Hollywood.*"

Lori had never been inside a television studio before. Reid's *Access Hollywood* interview was being held at a Seattle station.

The set was used for a local morning show. Lori didn't expect it to be so small, or so isolated in a sea of backdrops, lights, cables and cameras.

She and Madeline stood several feet behind the equipment and watched as a woman dabbed Reid's face with a sponge.

"I'm nervous," Lori admitted. "Nothing about this is going to be easy. They're going to ask some awful questions. I know he says he's prepared, but I'm not so sure."

"You think he's going to punch anyone?" Madeline asked.

"No, but I hate to see him humiliated."

"Imagine how I feel," Madeline muttered. "He's

putting himself in the spotlight because I have a sick liver. I'm not even sleeping with him. That hardly seems fair."

"The sex stays in the family," Lori teased as she took her sister's hand. "That's what matters."

"But you're the only one having a good time."

"I'm not going to share," Lori told her with a grin. "Just so we're clear on that."

"It doesn't matter if you're willing or not. Reid is only interested in you. I can see it every time he looks at you."

Lori's insides got all warm. She desperately wanted Madeline's words to be true, but wishing wasn't going to make that happen. Still, a woman could dream.

The reporter, an incredibly beautiful blonde in a tailored suit that emphasized her curves, walked over to Reid and introduced herself. Lori couldn't hear them, but as she watched they shook hands, then the woman leaned over and kissed Reid on the cheek before indicating where he should take a seat.

A man walked over and adjusted the microphone clipped to the front of Reid's shirt, then someone yelled for quiet. Lori and Madeline both put on the headphones they'd been given so they could hear the interview.

"I'm here with Reid Buchanan, a bad-boy baseball player who's been in the news these past few weeks. He's here to talk about something important. Thanks for being with us today, Reid."

"My pleasure."

The woman smiled at him. "I know you have some interesting things going on in your life, but first you know what we have to talk about."

Lori's gaze locked onto Reid's face. Nothing about his expression changed, but she sensed him bracing himself for the assault.

"That last game against the Cubs?" he asked.

"Not exactly. There was a rather insulting article about you in the Seattle paper a few weeks ago. Apparently you and the reporter had a night together and when it was over, she was not a happy camper. Care to comment on that?"

"Are you really asking me a question?" Reid smiled his charming smile—the one that made Lori's toes curl.

"I'm going to be tough and demand an answer."

"She didn't have as good a time as either of us would have liked," he said with a shrug. "I can give you a lot of excuses, but I won't."

The reporter looked disappointed. "That's all? Don't you want to defend your reputation? Several women you've been with have come forward to complain about your…performance, shall we say."

"They didn't complain to me."

"Women seldom do. Is what they say about the fragile male ego true? Do you think your bed partners resisted saying anything because they didn't want to hurt your feelings?"

"If that was the reason, they've gotten over it now." He shifted in his seat. "I love women. Always have. Despite popular opinion, the biggest rush for a guy is pleasing the woman he's with." He held up his hand. "For most guys. Certainly for me. If that didn't happen, I'm sorry. It's always my intent."

"A lot of people, women especially, believe that celebrities aren't very good in bed because they don't have to be. Do you think that's part of your problem?"

Lori groaned. She actually took a step forward, then stopped. Reid didn't need her breaking into his interview so she could tell the world that he was an amazing lover.

"I hate this woman," Lori muttered to her sister.

"I'm not real fond of her myself."

"I don't know what happened with the reporter who started all this," Reid said. "She never talked to me about anything. She came on to me in a bar. For all I know, the whole thing was a setup. It's been uncomfortable. This isn't anything any guy wants to deal with. As you know, I've been avoiding the press."

"I'm aware of that," the reporter purred. "Of all the reporters around, you chose me." She put her hand on Reid's arm. "Are you trying to tell me something?"

Reid looked directly at the camera. "Yes, I am. I'm putting up with these questions because they don't matter to me. Say what you want—I don't care. What's a hell of a lot more important than what anyone thinks about my love life is the fact that every day people are dying when they don't need to be."

The woman sighed, as if aware the juicy portion of the interview was over. "You're talking about those waiting for an organ donation."

"Right. In other countries, organ donation is the norm."

He went on with his pitch, but Lori wasn't listening. She pulled off her headphones and turned to her sister.

"He did it. He got through. I can't believe it. He was great. You saw that. Right?"

"He was a god," Madeline said, then sighed. "Seriously, he was terrific. I'm really grateful."

Lori hugged her. "Me, too. I still can't believe he was willing to go through that for you."

Madeline smiled at her. "No, Lori. He didn't do it for me. Don't you get it? He did it for you."

CHAPTER SEVENTEEN

"BERNARDO IS A GOOD MAN," Mama Giuseppe said as she ladled more pasta sauce onto Dani's plate. "His father started the restaurant nearly fifty years ago. We were so young then, with foolish dreams."

The tiny woman, dressed all in black glanced around the gleaming restaurant kitchen. "Maybe not so foolish." She looked back at Dani's plate. "Eat. Eat!"

Dani cheerfully tasted another forkful of the perfect pasta. The sauce was delicious enough to make her wonder how rude it would be to lick the plate when she was finished. But as she hadn't technically started her interview, she'd probably better remember her table manners.

She'd arrived at three and had immediately been ushered into the kitchen. The prep chefs were hard at work, yelling and insulting each other in Italian. At least she assumed it was Italian. But judging from their expressions and the laughter, she had a good idea what they were saying. Some things about the back of a restaurant were all the same.

Although she'd met Bernardo, the owner of Bella Roma, he'd been called away to take a phone call, leaving Dani alone with his mother. As Mama Giuseppe had been offering incredible food, Dani wasn't complaining.

"I've asked around," Mama said. "I know you are a Buchanan, like the restaurants. Your grandmother, she's not a nice woman."

Dani wasn't sure what to say to that. "Gloria can be a challenge," she admitted.

Mama sniffed. "Is that what we call it? Still, you didn't pick her for family. What can you do? I have four boys. Four. God was good to us. And of the four, only Bernardo wants to go in the family business. One is enough, right? So now my grandchildren are growing up. This one wants to be a lawyer, that one a doctor. Nicholas wants to do hair." She shook her head. "A man who wants to do hair. But he's family, so I love him. The restaurant? Not so much. Alicia, she loved working here, but now she's moving to New York to get married. What? We can't have a wedding in Seattle?"

Mama sighed. "What can you do?" She looked at Dani. "You're not married?"

"Ah, no. I was. My husband and I... He, ah—"

Mama Giuseppe nodded. "I understand. Some men are good men. Some, not so good. My Bernardo, he's a good man. His wife died." She paused, considering. "You're a little young for him. Too bad."

Dani nearly choked on her pasta. Bernie, as he'd asked her to call him, had to be close to fifty.

Just then the man in question hurried into the room.

"Sorry about that," he told Dani. "My daughter's getting married in a month. We're averaging about one crisis every four hours. Has my mother been torturing you?"

Dani glanced at her empty plate. "Not at all. She's been keeping me well fed. I love everything here."

"A girl who eats," Mama said. "Good."

Bernie sighed. "I'm going to take Dani to my office, Mama. We're going to talk business. You'll want to leave us alone for a while."

"I'm an old woman. What do I know about business? I wouldn't want to get in the way of something important. Did I start this place with your father? Did I work all hours of the day while raising four children?"

"Ignore her," Bernie murmured as they left the kitchen and headed down a rear hall. "She can be dramatic."

"I adore her," Dani said and meant it.

"If you're not careful, she'll run your life."

Dani figured she wasn't doing such a great job of it herself, so maybe someone being in charge would be good.

They sat in Bernie's crowded office. He looked at the stack of papers and files lying on his desk and groaned. "I've got to get this organized," he said. "I never have the time. That's why we're hiring a manager. My daughter, Alicia, was working here, but she's moved to New York to be with her fiancé. I was hoping one of the other kids or one of my cousins would be interested, but they're not. They love to eat here, of course, but the work? Not so much."

He sounded a lot like his mother, Dani thought, holding in a grin. She was impressed the two of them could work together day after day and not kill each other.

"We're a close staff," he said. "Most of my servers have worked here for years. Over half the clients are regulars. You know what that means?"

Dani knew he wasn't just making conversation. The interview had officially begun.

"Regulars are a steady cash flow, so you want to keep them happy," she said easily. "They like what they like. Some resist change. They have higher expectations. They want to be remembered and treated as special because they're giving something money can't buy—loyalty."

"Exactly." He sounded pleased. "For a while our customers were mostly older family and retirees. Aging. Then the neighborhood began to change. Suddenly we're hip. Or in. I can't keep up with the right term. Which means I'm neither, right?"

Dani smiled at him. He was terrific. For a second

she wanted to agree with Mama Giuseppe—it's too bad that Bernie wasn't closer to her age.

"So now we're getting a younger crowd. I thought they'd clash with our regulars, but they don't. It's nice to see newlyweds and college kids around."

He passed her a menu. "We're traditional here. Mama sees to that. Our head chef answers to her. Nick has been here ten years and when he and Mama start screaming at each other, it's better to duck and run." He chuckled. "Lucky for you, they argue in Italian, so you'll miss most of it."

He flipped through a couple of papers. "What else? No real staff problems right now, but they come up. The older servers can resent new staff, but they work it out. The restaurant runs fairly smoothly, but there are always hassles."

He paused and Dani sensed he was waiting for her to elaborate on what the hassles could be.

"Late deliveries, missing linens, a batch of bad wine, an off dish that everyone starts sending back," she said. "The party of twenty that booked the private room changes their mind about the menu a half hour before they show up. That sort of thing?"

Bernie nodded. "Right. Good. Okay, then let's talk about your experience."

Over the next hour, she was grilled on everything from her college education to handling the temporary head chef while Penny had been on maternity leave.

When she'd finished, Bernie leaned back in his chair. "We want someone to start right away," he said. "Are you available?"

Dani nodded. "I've given my notice at The Waterfront. I can leave anytime."

"You're clear on the fact that my mother is a big part of the restaurant? She's going to get involved and tell you what to do. She'll swear she won't, but don't believe her for a second."

"I like your mother," Dani admitted with a grin. "We'll work well together."

"Then the job is yours, if you want it." He named an impressive salary. "You'll get a cut of the profits. I'd like you to start out during the day. It's not so crazy then and you can feel your way. Once you're up to speed, we'll split shifts, so neither of us is always working nights."

Dani stared at him. "You're offering me the job? Just like that?"

"Just like that. I go with my gut. You'll do well here, Dani. So what do you think?"

LORI TRIED TO FOCUS on the fact that Reid had asked her out to dinner—like a date. Because worrying about a date was far less scary than thinking about meeting the board that would direct Reid's new foundation.

Nothing was official. The lawyers were still drawing up papers, but everyone was getting together to discuss direction, purpose, a mission statement.

Lori had gone online the previous evening to figure out what a mission statement was. She'd looked at other charities to find out what they were trying to do with their money. In a way it was good she was so scared about the board meeting because it distracted her from what her sister had said a couple of days ago, when they'd watched Reid taping his interview. That he'd put himself in the public eye and had endured humiliation for her. She couldn't seem to get her mind around that.

While it didn't rank as high as Kyle Reese's "I crossed time for you, Sarah Connor" in the first *Terminator* movie, it was damn close. A guy like Reid having to defend his sexual performance on national television was way worse than any punishment she could come up with—and yet he'd done it willingly. It had even been his idea.

Had he really done it for her? Because he cared about her? The possibility made her chest tighten and her eyes burn. She was afraid to believe, because if she believed, she would have to admit she'd fallen in love with him.

They parked in the lot of the Doubletree Hotel in Bellevue and walked into the foyer. Reid took her hand in his and led the way to the conference room he'd rented for the meeting.

"I'm nervous," she admitted.

"Then we can be nervous together."

She looked at him. "Why are you worried? You're doing an incredible thing."

"I'm some dumb jock who's been front page gossip. I picked a hell of a board. Why will important people with expertise in what I want to do take me seriously?"

"Because you have the checkbook."

"I want to be more than just the name on the building," he told her. "I'd rather not use my name at all, but I know I'll be a good front man." He shrugged.

She put her hand on his chest. "You're doing the right thing. I swear you are. I'm impressed. Seriously."

His gaze locked with hers. "That means a lot to me."

"I'm glad, because it's true."

They smiled at each other, then Reid squared his shoulders. "Ready?"

She nodded even though she wasn't and they walked into the conference room.

Eight people already sat there. Five men and three women. They were all over forty, well-dressed and chatting as if they knew each other.

Lori instantly felt out of place. It wasn't her clothes—she'd had Madeline help her pick out a conservative but attractive skirt and jacket, and her shoes were new and more expensive than she wanted to admit. It was that these people were some of the richest and most successful in the country and she was a girl who had grown up in a double-wide.

Reid introduced everyone. There were two CEOs, a founding executive from Microsoft, a woman whose family owned banks and other people who professionally gave away millions.

When they were seated, Reid began.

"I appreciate each of you agreeing to serve on my board. I don't know most of you—my business manager gave me a list of names and I started asking around. You're the best at what you do and I'm going to need that. I have no experience with philanthropy, but that's about to change. I want to improve the world, one kid at a time, through sports. That's my mission statement. It may be as simple as new cleats for football season or as complex as designing and building a stadium after a hurricane. Let the other charities take on diseases, I want us to figure out ways to improve kids' lives through sports of all kinds."

"We have a good financial start," one of the men said.

"I agree." Reid leaned forward. "I'm hoping we'll have more. I've never been one for endorsement deals, but I'm willing to do them now. All the money I earn for speaking for companies willing to pay will go back into the foundation. I'm going to use my name and my former career to get into places most people can't. I want to bring attention to where it's needed. If that means taking a couple of hits from the press, I'm willing to do it."

He stood. "Each of you brings expertise to the table. For some of you, it's managing money. Others have a gift for finding out where that money should go. If you're wondering about Lori's job." He nodded at her. "She's here to keep us grounded. Her professional background is in nursing. She knows how to deal with people going through a rough time. She'll keep us on track."

He smiled at her.

It was one of those melt-your-socks kind of smiles that made her pulse rate double. The woman sitting next to her leaned close.

"Okay, now *I'm* breathing hard and I'm happily married."

"Tell me about it," Lori whispered back.

Reid continued to talk about what he wanted them to accomplish. As she listened she wondered if this was a dream. All her life she'd been too afraid to go for the happy ending. This time she wanted it enough to try. Enough to risk her heart and the possible fall that waited just out of reach.

REID PARKED at the edge of the dock. "I know it's not a restaurant. Is this okay?"

Lori looked around at the lake, the twinkling lights of the houses on the other side, and the tidy row of houseboats at the end of the dock.

"It's great," she said. "Are you cooking?"

He grinned. "Not a chance. Food will be delivered later. Come on. I've been gone long enough that there shouldn't be any press lurking around."

He led the way to the houseboat. As Lori breathed in the damp air and the scent of water and plants, she realized that if the press really had backed off, then Reid didn't have any reason to stay at Gloria's house much longer. Which meant she wouldn't be seeing him as much.

The thought saddened her, so she pushed it away and instead concentrated on the two-story house-boat in front of her.

The structure was dark blue with white trim around the many windows and set away from the neighbors. Planters lined the walkway leading to the front door. Reid unlocked the door, then leaned in and hit a couple of light switches. Lori stepped into a surprisingly open space done in leather and wood.

There was a fireplace and a view of the lights, hardwood floors, warm area rugs and a staircase leading to the second floor.

Beyond the living room was a dining area and a doorway to what looked to be an impressive kitchen. On the other side was a study.

Everything was perfect. Bookshelves lined the angled stairway, taking advantage of unused space. There were trunks in corners, display shelves, wel-coming colors and a real sense of home.

"It's beautiful," she told him. "Really perfect and amazing. I thought you'd be more the high-rise condo type."

He shrugged. "I looked at some, but then I saw this place and I bought it the same day. It was old, so we gutted the place and built new."

"We?" She did her best to hold in a wave of jealousy. "Let me guess. Tall, blond, big boobs and Southern?"

Reid moved toward her and kissed her. "You think you know everything, but you're wrong. My decorator was a guy and I didn't sleep with him."

A guy? She liked that.

"Before you can ask," he said, touching her face, then easing his fingers into her hair. "I don't bring women here. This is my place. It's private. You're the first."

If she hadn't already been in love with him, that single statement probably would have pushed her over the edge. She drew in a breath, not sure what she wanted to say, only to be saved from possibly confessing something she might regret by a knock on the door.

Reid released her and let in a delivery guy. After paying the man, he took the two shopping bags from him and walked into the kitchen.

"Chicken marsala, pasta, a salad and a special decadent cake for dessert," he told her. "I went with chocolate because I know you go crazy for it." He grinned. "I'm trying to seduce you. How am I doing so far?"

He was the best-looking man she'd ever seen, but that didn't seem to matter anymore. While the chemical attraction was still as powerful as ever and probably would be as long as she drew breath, it wasn't the reason she was here.

She was here because of who he was. He hadn't seduced her with his body—he'd seduced her with his soul. The man inside, the heart of him, called to her with a song she couldn't resist.

She crossed to him, took the bags from him and set them on the counter. Then she leaned close and kissed him.

"I don't need chocolate," she whispered against his mouth. "Not when I have you."

"Tonight you get to have both. Pretty close to heaven, huh?"

She smiled. "Closer than you know."

"I'M GOING TO cut your sandwich into tiny bites and then feed them to you," Reid said with a grin. "Later, I'll read to you."

His grandmother glared at him. "You'll do no such thing. I might still be recovering from a broken hip, but I'm strong enough to throw things at your head."

"But can you hit me?" he asked. "I'm not sure about your aim."

"Where do you think you inherited your pitching ability?" Gloria's mouth pulled on the corners, as if she were trying not to smile. "You're in a good mood this morning. Why is that?"

Because, for once, his life was working. Ever since he blew out his shoulder and had to retire from baseball he'd wondered what the hell he was going to do with himself. Baseball had been his world. At last there were possibilities.

"I'm at one with the universe," he joked. "I have a serene spirit."

Gloria rolled her eyes. "You're annoying, but I'm going to put up with it. Starting the foundation was the right decision."

He didn't need her approval, but it was good to hear the words. "I think so."

"I'm not happy about your interviews. You've humiliated the entire family."

No change was perfect, he thought as he pulled up a chair and sat down. "It's necessary and the price of getting my message out."

Gloria lay on her bed. She'd been dressing for the past couple of weeks and getting her hair done. Except for the fact that she wore casual clothing instead of power suits, she looked much as she always had. The frail and broken woman from a couple of months ago had disappeared.

"You're healing," he said. "That's good."

"It was get better or die," his grandmother said. "Lori pushed me, but she was right to do it." Her eyes narrowed. "I know you're seeing her."

Not a surprise. They hadn't been subtle or secretive. "Yes, I am."

"How serious are things?"

"I'm not discussing my personal life with you."

"Why not? I'm your grandmother."

He grinned. "I'm actually clear on our relationship. You've been my grandmother most of my life."

She sighed. "You're tremendously annoying."

"Charming. You meant to say charming."

"I did not. I want to talk about Lori."

"Talk away."

"I want to know what you're doing with her."

He knew she meant in a relationship sense, not a sexual sense, but either way, he wasn't talking. There were a couple of reasons. Keeping Gloria out of his personal business made a lot of sense. Just as important, he didn't know how to answer the question.

He knew Lori mattered. She mattered a lot. He didn't want to think about his feelings or define them, but they were there. Growing. He felt good when he was around her and he missed her when he wasn't. For now, that was enough.

"Reid," his grandmother snapped. "I asked you a question."

"Lori is off-limits."

"I could say the same thing to you."

"I know you care about her. So do I."

"I'm not going to break her heart," Gloria told him. "You very well may."

"I won't," he said and meant it. "Besides, how do you know she won't be the one hurting me?"

His grandmother didn't say anything. Instead she looked out the window, as if she knew something she didn't want to tell him. Had she and Lori talked? But before he could ask, his grandmother said, "I've heard there have been calls about donating. How is that going?"

"Good. No matches yet. Madeline's blood type isn't going to make matching easy, but it's possible. The good news is a guy whose liver was seriously damaged in a car accident in Kansas is getting a new liver. So one life was saved."

"Does that make it worth it?" she asked. "I've seen the interviews. They're not being easy on you."

If being publicly humiliated about his sexual performance on national television counted as "not being easy" then she was right.

"It's worth it," he told her. "Even if no one's life was saved, it would still be worth it. People need to donate and I'm reminding them of that."

His grandmother reached for his hand. He leaned forward and grabbed her fingers.

"I'm proud of you," she told him.

"Thanks," he said, and meant it. For reasons he couldn't begin to explain her words mattered. A lot.

CHAPTER EIGHTEEN

DANI TOSSED her car keys to the valet and then hurried into the restaurant. She saw Gary waiting by the window and rushed up to him.

"I'm late," she said by way of greeting. "I'm sorry. It's only my second day at the restaurant and there's so much to learn. I lost track of time."

Gary smiled at her, then stunned her by leaning in and kissing her cheek. "Hi. I'm not mad. You look happy."

"I am. I love my job. I know it's early and I'm still in the fun part of work, but I love it. I love the staff, the customers. I adore the food. It's amazing. I may actually have to start exercising to keep from gaining weight."

She kept talking—make that babbling—some from excitement, but mostly out of shock. Sure, Gary's light brush across her cheek was hardly newsworthy, but his caress had been unexpected. Nice, but unexpected.

She resisted the need to put her fingers on the spot his mouth had been as she tried to figure out what

SUSAN MALLERY 305

she felt. There hadn't been any kind of *zing* of excitement, but that was okay, right? Sex wasn't everything. Gary might not make her thighs go up in flames, but she liked him.

She smiled at him. "I've probably wound down for now," she said. "How are you? How was your day?"

"Fine." He moved them toward the small desk at the front of the foyer. "We have a reservation."

She glanced around at the crowded restaurant. It was one of those neighborhood places with great food and plenty of regulars. The food smelled good and Dani liked the mix of clientele. There were families, older couples, several large parties and a group of women laughing in a corner.

"This is nice," she said. "I've never been here."

"The food is excellent. The menu has a lot of variety and everything is good."

They followed the hostess to a quiet table in the back.

"How did you find this place?" she asked.

Gary held out her chair, then took the seat opposite hers. "I used to work around here."

They were in an older part of Seattle. She frowned as she tried to place a college. She couldn't think of one in the neighborhood. It was mostly residential.

"Where?" she asked. "At a private school?"

He hesitated. "I wasn't always a teacher."

"Oh. Okay."

It was then she remembered she didn't know very much about her date. She knew he had a sister, that he was kind and a great listener. Embarrassment flooded her body as heat crawled up her cheeks.

"I'm a horrible person," she said, with a groan. "Totally disgusting and self-absorbed."

"What are you talking about?"

"Me. My behavior. How many times have we had coffee together? How many of those conversations have been about my life, my problems, my job search? Me, me, me. It's awful. Why on earth did you want to have dinner with me?"

"Because I like you."

He must or he wouldn't have asked. She pushed aside her menu and leaned forward. "I apologize for my lousy behavior and promise that tonight is just about you. I want to know everything. You can skip the being born part—that's a little too messy for dinner conversation. But feel free to pick up with your first memory after that."

He smiled. "You have nothing to apologize for. I enjoy talking about you."

"Guys like to talk about themselves."

"I'm more comfortable listening. An old habit."

Which made him practically perfect boyfriend material. He was smart and funny and kind. A really decent person.

"So why aren't you married?" she asked. "We've established you're not gay."

He grinned. "But I am thinking of upgrading my wardrobe."

She laughed. "I'm serious, Gary. Are you keeping secrets?"

She'd asked the question lightly, then stiffened when he didn't chuckle or tease in return.

"Not secrets so much as information," he said.

She knew that whatever it was, she was going to hate it. The knowledge formed deep in her gut and sat there like a rock.

"You're married? You killed a man? You used to be a woman? You have a contagious disease and now I have three weeks to live?"

"No." His expression was kind. "Nothing like that."

A woman in her forties walked by the table, paused and backed up a couple of steps. She looked at Gary, her eyes widening in surprise.

"Father Halaran?"

Dani straightened. A thousand thoughts flooded her brain but just one in bright neon letters flashed: Father Halaran? *Father* Halaran? As in...

Oh, dear God.

Gary nodded at the woman. "Hello, Wendy. It's just Gary now. Remember?"

"What? Oh, right." Wendy looked at Dani, then jerked her gaze back to Gary. "How are you? I haven't seen you in a while."

"It's been a couple of years and I'm doing well."

"I'm glad. It's, ah, good to see you, Fa…ah, Gary."

The woman walked away.

Dani blinked several times as her mind slowly cleared. "So," she said, trying to sound casual when in truth she was in the mood to scream. "That was interesting."

"I used to be a priest."

"I kind of figured that out."

He smiled. "Good. I left two years ago. That's when I started teaching. I lived a few blocks from here and always liked this restaurant. I probably should have taken you somewhere else."

Did he really think that was the biggest problem they had? "No. This is lovely. Really."

"Are you all right?" he asked.

"I don't know. I'm trying to absorb the whole priest thing."

"You're not Catholic," he said. "It shouldn't be a big deal."

"You'd think. But it kind of is." Although she couldn't say why.

A priest. As in married to the church. As in celibate. Talk about a springboard to discussion. So had he…been with a woman since? And if he hadn't, did he want to be? Did *she* want to deal with that?

"Say something," he told her. "What are you thinking?"

"No wonder you're a good listener."

"Is this going to be a problem?" He picked up the menu, then put it down. "I wanted to tell you, Dani.

There just wasn't a good time. It's not as if I could introduce myself that way. 'Hey, I'm Gary. An ex-priest. And you are?'"

She smiled. "That would be kind of scary."

She looked at him, at the kindness in his eyes, at the smile that had become familiar to her. She liked him. She trusted him. He was a good man.

"Everything about leaving was scary," he told her. "I'd been on exactly one date in my life before I made my decision to become a priest. I'd never held a job, lived totally alone, been a normal person. I'm still adjusting, but I like it. This is where I'm meant to be. Are you okay with that?"

Was she? She opened her mouth to say she was, but then she couldn't. The knot in her gut hadn't gone away.

"I have the most uncomfortable feeling that God is sending me a really big message. He's telling me I'm not supposed to be with anyone right now," she said. "For once, I think I'm going to listen. I'm sorry, Gary."

She grabbed her purse and stood. He rose, but didn't try to stop her. Disappointment darkened his pale eyes.

"Maybe if you took some time to get used to the idea," he began.

She shook her head. "I don't think so. I'd like to stay friends, but I understand if you don't want to do that. If you expected more."

"I'd hoped," he admitted.

Guilt flooded her. She didn't want to hurt him, but she couldn't ignore how she felt.

"I'm sorry," she said and hurried away.

THE DOWNTOWN SPORTS BAR was crowded for a Thursday night—the Seahawks were playing so the place was busy and loud.

Reid stood behind the bar and leaned toward Mandy, one of the waitresses, to hear her drink order.

He hadn't worked in weeks—not since the article in the paper. His only visits to the bar had been off-hours and low-key. But tonight he was filling in for a guy who'd gotten sick. He was taking a lot of crap from patrons, but he was dealing.

He poured two beers, then grabbed the bottles to make an apple martini. Not his choice for a football game, or anytime, but it wasn't for him. He poured in the right amounts of the various liquors, dumped the ice from the martini glass, filled it up and set it on Mandy's tray.

"Hey, Reid," some guy at the bar yelled.

Reid turned toward the voice, but he couldn't see who had spoken. They were two and three deep at the bar.

"Is it true you're really lousy in bed?"

So far all the comments had been joking and friendly. This was the first direct confrontation.

Despite the fact that the Seahawks had the ball and were inches from a first down, the space around the bar went quiet. He wondered if the guy would have the guts to show himself.

The decision was made for the man when several people moved away, leaving a short, balding guy in his late thirties standing alone.

Reid looked at him, gave a slight smile, then asked, "You want to know for yourself?"

There was a moment of silence followed by an explosion of laughter. The guy shifted uncomfortably, muttered "No," and slunk away.

"Anyone else interested?" Reid asked. "I'm here, I'm working. Take your best shot. I can handle it."

"That's not what that woman in the paper said," another man called.

"Want your wife to give me a recommendation?" Reid asked with a grin. "She will."

The guy grumbled, but didn't show himself.

"Anyone else?" Reid asked. "You've got to have better lines than the ones I've been hearing. Come on. Nail me."

A woman leaning on the bar smiled at him. "Why aren't you mad? Guys I know would want that reporter's blood."

He took another order from one of the servers, then began to pour more beer.

"I was pissed at first," he admitted. "Embarrassed, but then I realized it didn't matter. I was a pitcher for a lot of years. Everybody who watched the game had an opinion about what I did and how I did it. Yet not one of them could come close to doing what I did. I learned there's always some asshole who can do a hell of a job on play-by-play but can't last a second in the game. It's the same with sex."

The woman grinned and several of the guys around him laughed.

"The thing is," Reid continued. "As many women as I've been with, I had to learn something. Right?"

"I know you did, darlin'," the woman said with a smile that told him she was one of the many.

Not that he remembered anything about whatever time he'd spent with her.

Well, hell. What did that say about him? He could only imagine the choice words Lori would have for him if she knew there were women who had been in his bed and he didn't remember anything about them. He couldn't even pick them out of a line-up.

He continued filling drink orders and talking to the customers. No one else made any cracks about him, but he barely noticed. There was only one opinion that mattered. And the only way to keep her coming back was to make sure he was the kind of man she would want to be with for the rest of her life.

FRIDAY AFTERNOON, Reid got back to Gloria's place about four-thirty. He took the stairs two at a time. Lori was working until six, and then she was joining him upstairs. He had big plans for the night. He'd ordered a great dinner, then he was going to seduce Lori three or four times, after which they'd have dessert.

As he'd spent a couple of hours in the gym, he wanted a shower before she showed up. He walked into his bedroom just as he pulled off his sweatshirt. So he didn't see his surprise right away.

"Hi, Reid," an unfamiliar voice said.

He froze in the act of dropping his sweatshirt, swore silently, then shrugged the shirt back into place. He sucked in a breath, then turned to look at the bed.

Two women lay there. Two blond, pretty, young women. They'd pulled back the covers, fluffed the pillows and stretched out naked on his sheets.

Totally naked.

He barely glanced at their bodies before returning his attention to their faces. He recognized the twins. The three of them had had a weekend together and then the twins had gone on CNN to promote some damn book. They'd also taken a couple of pokes at him.

The one on the right sat up then crawled toward the end of the bed.

"Are you mad at us, baby? We were bad. Very, very bad. Do you want to punish us?"

Her large, perfect breasts hung down, swaying gently with each movement. Her skin was pale, her nipples nearly red.

The one on the left smiled. "You could spank us. Wouldn't that be fun?"

Several feelings crashed in on him, but the overriding one was complete and total panic. What if Lori walked in on them right now? What would she think? There was no way in hell he could explain these two. He didn't want to explain them—he wanted them gone.

"Let's have some fun, Reid," the first one said, her blond hair falling over her shoulders. She licked her lips. "Really hot, naked fun. You'll like it. I promise."

"Me, too," her sister said.

He couldn't get out of there fast enough. Not caring if he looked liked an idiot, he turned and ran from the room, then sped along the hall and raced down the stairs. He found Lori in with his grandmother and asked to speak with her.

Lori followed him into the hallway.

"What's wrong?" she asked. "You have the weirdest look on your face. Are you hurt or sick?"

He didn't know what to say to her. How could he tell her the truth? She wouldn't understand. Lori had issues. Some made sense to him and some didn't but he knew they were there.

He touched her cheek. "You matter to me," he said. "You know that, right?"

Her eyes narrowed. "What have you done?"

"I haven't done anything. I swear. It wasn't me. It's not my fault."

"The eternal cry of the irresponsible male."

"It isn't. Dammit, Lori, you know me. You know that I'm a decent guy. I would never hurt you."

She folded her arms across her chest. "Tell me."

"I want you," he said, knowing he was getting it all wrong, but not sure what else to say. "You mean a lot to me. More than a lot. I like what we have together and you like it, too. I would never do anything to mess things up."

She raised her eyebrows. "But?"

He sucked in a breath. "I came home and went upstairs because you're coming up and I wanted to take a shower. I walked into my bedroom and they were just there. I didn't let them in. I've been gone. You know that, right? I've been at the gym. They were just *there*."

He paused and waited, braced for the explosion.

"Who was where?"

"These two women. You don't know them. They're baseball groupies. Twins. I want them to leave, but I don't know how to make them. I'm afraid they'll take anything I say as encouragement."

He couldn't read her expression. Something flashed in her eyes, but it was gone before he could identify it.

"They're upstairs?" she asked.

"In my bed. Naked."

Her eyes widened. "You have two naked women in your bed?"

He nodded frantically, then grabbed her arm. "You have to help me. I swear, I didn't contact them. I don't want them here. I don't want any of this."

One corner of her mouth twitched. "Is the big bad baseball player afraid?"

"Terrified."

"You expect me to go up there and throw them out?"

"That would be great."

"I'm assuming you've slept with them."

He glanced down and shuffled his feet. "It was a long time ago."

"Both of them? At the same time?"

He nodded glumly.

"Impressive."

He looked at her. Okay, maybe he wasn't the best judge of women, but if he had to guess, he would say Lori wasn't totally furious with him.

Her mouth twitched again. "What did you want me to say to them?"

"That we're together. That you don't stand for this sort of thing. Not ever. You could tell them I'm not interested, if you want. Because I'm not. You're the only woman I want in my life."

"All right."

She turned and walked up the stairs. He followed, not sure how this was going to go, but relieved to have Lori take charge.

She walked through the living room and into his bedroom. The twins were still sprawled naked on his bed.

The one on the right smiled when she saw Lori.

"Hi. We've never done a foursome before. This could be fun."

Lori glanced around the room, then walked over to the neatly folded clothing on the dresser and picked it up.

"Aren't you two a little old for games like this?" she asked. "Showing up naked in a guy's bed seems beneath you. You're attractive women. Do something with your lives. Go to college, have a career. Be more than your bust size."

The twins looked at each other, then at Lori. "But we like this."

Lori tossed them their clothes. "Do you? Really? Are you proud of yourselves? Can you tell your grandmother how you spend your day? When you were little, didn't you want more than this?"

The twin on the left blinked. "I always liked working with animals. I thought I'd work in a vet's office, you know?"

"Fine. Do that. Do anything. In about ten years your looks are going to go. Then what? You need to think about your future. Open an IRA, start learning about current events. Grow up. In the meantime, get dressed and get out of here. I'm with Reid and he doesn't cheat on me."

The twins looked at each other again, then shrugged. "Okay," the one on the right said.

They got up and dressed.

"We're sorry about barging in," the spokestwin said. "We didn't know Reid was serious about anyone."

Reid had kept quiet through the conversation,

sensing things would go better if Lori was in charge. Now he walked over to her and put his arm around her.

"I'm serious," he said clearly. "Totally serious. Involved. We're together."

The twins smiled. "That's good. Okay. Well, good luck with everything."

They collected their purses and left.

He waited until their footsteps had faded, then looked at Lori.

"You saved me."

"Apparently. I can't believe you dated those two. They give airheads a bad name."

He stared into her hazel eyes. "I didn't date them, Lori. I had sex with them. That's who I was. A lowlife bastard who accepted every interesting invitation sent my way. I didn't require anything of them and I sure as hell didn't require anything of myself."

It was as honest as he'd ever been in his life.

"I'm not proud of that past. I won't apologize for it, but I'm done with it. I'm not that guy anymore."

He braced himself for a crack or worse, her withdrawal. Instead she leaned in and kissed him.

"I know," she whispered. "You've turned into someone quite amazing."

He liked the sound of that. He put his hands on her waist and pulled her close. "I've always been amazing."

"Okay, maybe. But now it doesn't have anything to do with getting naked."

He cupped her rear and squeezed. "It could."

She laughed softly. "I have to get downstairs to your grandmother, but we're on for later, right?"

"Oh, yeah."

She smiled and he smiled and then it was like someone hit him in the chest with a baseball bat. He felt the impact and the air rushed out of him and he couldn't breathe.

He loved her. Honest to God, he loved her. Everything about her. The way she talked, how her brain worked, the scent of her skin, her sense of humor, her combination of toughness and caring.

She was the best part of his world and she'd made him into a better man. He wanted her and he needed her.

He wanted to be with her always. He wanted to marry her.

"Reid? Are you all right?"

"I'm good."

He wanted to tell her right that second, then he hesitated. Telling Lori he loved her was a big deal and he wanted to say it right. He wanted the moment to be special and powerful. He didn't want her thinking he was just grateful for how she'd handled the twins.

Tonight, he thought. When they were alone. He would confess his feelings and propose. Was there time to go buy a ring?

Her cell phone rang. She pulled it out of her pocket and glanced at the screen.

"It's Madeline," she said, paling slightly. "She would only bother me at work if there was an emergency." She pushed the talk button. "Hello?"

Reid waited while she listened. As he watched, the worry faded and elation took its place.

"Are you sure?" she asked. "For real? When? Oh, my God! I'll be right there. I know. It's amazing. I love you."

She hung up and grinned at him. "She got the call. There's a donor."

CHAPTER NINETEEN

LORI SAT on Madeline's bed and counted socks. "We don't have to worry about you bringing everything," she said. "I can go get anything you need."

"I know." Madeline's lips turned up in a smile, but her eyes looked worried. "I'll feel better when I have my suitcase packed."

Lori suspected her sister's issues weren't about the suitcase. "Are you okay?"

"Sure. I'm scared but excited. Did I mention scared?"

"Scared?" Reid asked as he carried in an empty suitcase and put it on Madeline's bed. "Who's scared?"

"No one," Madeline said with a smile. "Just maybe a little chicken."

"Which beats being a big chicken," Reid said. "Or a duck."

Madeline laughed.

Lori stood and pulled her sister close. "This is a great thing. You know that, right? It's your chance."

"I know. I'm so grateful to find a match. I wasn't

sure we ever would. I'm such a difficult blood type. But we did and now I have a chance again. That's all good. Reid, I don't want you to think I'm not grateful. You put yourself out there for me."

"I delivered an important message," he said. "Nothing more." He patted her arm. "I'll leave you two to your packing."

When he was gone Madeline sighed. "He's a good man. I just wish there'd been more time."

"What do you mean?" Lori asked.

"I'm not ready to do this." Madeline held up her hand before Lori could protest. "I know. Without a transplant, I die. I want the surgery. It's just…"

Lori understood. They were talking about a serious operation. "You have a great doctor. Remember that."

Madeline stepped back and smiled. "I do. Still, it's weird to think about someone else's liver in my body. It sounds so gross."

"It beats being dead."

"You always did have a talent for putting things in perspective." Madeline picked up a nightgown and folded it. "I'm happy, of course. This is a chance for me to live a relatively normal life. But I also can't get my mind around the fact that someone else has to die to make this happen. I don't think I'm worthy of that."

"You didn't kill the person. Even if you don't take their liver, they're still going to die."

"I know, but…" She shook her head. "I guess I

can't explain it. I just feel weird. Happy and grateful, but weird."

"You're not going to change your mind about the surgery, are you?"

Madeline shook her head. "It's too late. Besides, how many people get a second chance like this? I want the operation. I never thought it would happen and yet it's here. But it does make me think. If I don't come back, I want you to be okay with that."

Not come back? Madeline kept on talking, but Lori wasn't listening. Not come back?

Madeline had to come back. She, Lori, refused to accept any other outcome. Coming back was very much a part of the plan.

Until that moment, Lori had never thought of her sister dying in any but the most theoretical sense. Surgery could go badly, but that was for other people. Her sister had always been in her life. They were family. They had always been family.

"You can't die," she blurted without thinking. "I couldn't stand it."

Madeline grabbed her hand, sat on the bed and pulled Lori next to her. "I'm not going to die."

"But you could. I knew that in time your liver could fail, but not now. It wouldn't be fair."

"Life isn't about fair. Odds are, I'm going to pull through and be around for years, driving you crazy."

Lori's eyes filled with tears. "You're my best friend."

Her sister's expression was kind. "I know. You're mine."

"I didn't know," Lori muttered. "I didn't know at all. I've loved you and hated you and all this time you've been my best friend." She blinked back tears. "I'm sorry."

Madeline tucked a strand of Lori's hair behind her ear. "For hating me? Don't be. If I were you, I would have hated me, too."

"Because you're perfect."

"I'm not perfect."

"Hey, I was there. I have the pictures to prove it. I love you despite the fact that you're perfect."

Madeline laughed. "Thanks for being such a generous person, but you have to let go of the perfect thing. Perfect people don't get sick."

"That's not your fault. You were in that car accident and you got a blood transfusion. That's out of your control."

"Fine. My husband left me when I got sick. That doesn't happen to perfect people."

Lori rolled her eyes. "Again, not your fault. He's a jerk."

"I picked him."

"Oh. Yeah. Good point. So you have one flaw. Lousy taste in men."

"It's a big flaw. Which makes me not perfect."

Lori hugged her. "You'll always be perfect to me. I love you. Don't you dare die."

"I won't. I promise. I want to be around long enough to be an embarrassment to you in our old age."

"I'd like that," Lori said as she straightened. Everything would be okay, she told herself. It had to be.

"I want to dance at your wedding to Reid," Madeline added.

Lori sighed. "There's not going to be a wedding."

"I thought you were crazy about him."

"I am, but I have no idea what he's thinking. I know he likes me but liking and marrying are worlds apart. I don't even think about it."

Which was a complete lie. Of course she thought about it. Sometimes it was all she thought about. Being with Reid seemed like an impossible dream. But sometimes she allowed herself the fantasy.

"He's so much more than I thought," she admitted. "He's a terrific man, which wouldn't have been my first guess."

"You're responsible for any changes."

Lori shook her head. "That sounds nice, but he did what he did himself. I…" She swallowed, then confessed. "I'm in love with him."

"Have you told him?"

"No. I'm afraid he'll laugh and point."

"What are the odds of that actually happening?"

"At this moment any odds are too great. I don't need the pain in my life."

Madeline squeezed her hand. "The man is crazy about you."

"Maybe." But was it enough?

"He is," her sister insisted. "Look at it this way—
he's been with enough women to be able to know
what he wants. He wants you. I can see it in his
eyes."

Lori wanted to believe her so much, it hurt.
"Change of subject," she said. "I can't deal with Reid
right now."

"Then let's deal with Mom," Madeline said.
"You're going to have to help her through this."

"I know." Lori didn't want to think about that,
either.

"She's not the devil."

"I never said she was."

"You have to forgive her for what happened
before," Madeline insisted. "She wasn't herself."

Lori wasn't convinced being drunk excused
anything, but she nodded because it was what her
sister wanted.

"In case something happens," her sister continued, "I've listed all my bank account numbers and
other financial information in a folder. It's in the top
dresser drawer. There's also a life insurance policy.
I got it when I got married, but now you and Mom
are the beneficiaries. Help her invest the money,
okay? She won't know what to do."

Once again Lori fought tears. She gently
punched her sister in the arm. "Stop talking like
you're doing to die."

"I need to say this," Madeline told her softly. "Help Mom. She'll have enough to buy a condo or something. It will give her security."

"She'll want to buy a trailer. I just know it."

"Then help her do that. She's getting older, Lori. She's not in great health. All those years of drinking aged her. I want her to be safe and happy."

Lori wiped her eyes. "Fine. I'll help her get settled somewhere. Either a condo or a trailer. If there's any left over, I'll help her invest the money in something safe. I don't want to talk about this."

"I know, but I need you to promise."

"I promise."

"You're sure?"

Lori sniffed. "Why not? We both know nothing's going to happen to you. So I can promise anything."

"I like how you think."

"How much money are we talking about with that life insurance policy?" Lori asked, deciding she would tease them both into a happier state of mind. "Should I get excited?"

Madeline grinned. "You're going to have to wait and see."

"I'm happy to wait forever."

DANI FILED the menus, then turned to face her sister-in-law. Penny had already spent a couple of hours in the kitchen, overseeing the prep work for that night's dinner.

"I love a good reduction," Penny murmured to herself. "If we add a little more Pinot to the sauce, it should broaden the fruit elements. What do you think?"

Dani pushed the file drawer closed and dropped into the chair on the other side of Penny's overflowing desk.

"I miss working with you."

Penny looked up and grimaced. "I hate that you're gone. I know I shouldn't say that. I know you have to go prove yourself out in the world. But I don't have to like it. By the way, you're only proving yourself to yourself. The rest of us are already convinced. Okay?"

"I don't like it, either," Dani admitted. "I mean I'm really excited, but I've loved working with you."

"I am the best chef you'll ever know," Penny said, then grinned. "And the most modest."

"Absolutely."

"You'll love working with Bernie. He's a sweetie. And kind of cute." Penny raised and lowered her eyebrows. "He's a little old for you, but if you like that sort of thing…"

Dani raised her hands and crossed her index fingers. "No way. He seems like a perfectly nice man, but, no. I'm totally and completely finished with romantic relationships. I've heard from the big guy in the sky and the message couldn't have been more clear."

"Just because Gary was an ex-priest does not mean God was telling you to avoid men."

"Okay—so what *was* the message?"

"Avoid that one. Or not. Maybe God was trying to tell you that Gary was a sweetie and you should be gentle with him."

Dani cringed and shook her head. "I don't think so. I feel bad about walking out on Gary, but trust me, I'm the wrong woman to deal with the issues a relationship with him would bring to the table. I don't have the patience."

"I don't know. There's a romantic element to the whole thing. What if you're his first time?"

Dani didn't want to go there. As soon as Gary had confessed his past, the knot in her gut had told her to start running and she'd listened. It wasn't her proudest moment, but she didn't have any regrets.

"It's over," she said. "My budding relationship with Gary and any relationship with any man, ever. I have lived through a series of disasters. It's time to let the romance thing go."

"If you say so. Or you could get into women."

Dani wrinkled her nose. "No thanks."

"Just checking. You don't have to do that," Penny added, pointing at the filing.

"I want to finish what I started."

"You don't work here anymore. You have to let it go."

Dani shrugged. "I have. But I still miss this place, even though I'm totally jazzed about the job."

"If you're giving up on guys, you'll have time to

devote yourself to your work. Lord knows I did that plenty," Penny said.

Dani nodded, then reached for a pen sticking out from under a stack of paperwork. "I've been thinking about getting in touch with my dad."

Penny leaned back in her chair. "That's a big step. Did you find out more about him?"

Dani shook her head. "I don't even know his name. I talked to a private investigator, but she told me what I've already guessed. Without more information, I'm screwed. I need something to go on. I asked my brothers, but they don't know anything, either."

"You know what the next step has to be," Penny said gently.

Dani's stomach tightened. "I'm not giving Gloria another chance to screw with my life. Once was enough."

"She's the only one who knows anything. Just think about it," Penny said. "She's changed. I don't know why or how. Maybe she hit her head when she fell or maybe the day nurse really did work a miracle. I just know she's not the same awful woman you know."

"I don't want to give her the satisfaction of begging. It means she wins."

"Doesn't she also win if you spend your whole life wondering?"

Dani didn't answer—they both already knew Penny was right. But ask Gloria for help?

"I'll think about it," she said slowly. "I hate that she still has control over me."

"She doesn't. Not if you don't let her."

LORI STOOD at the end of the hospital corridor and watched the swinging doors close behind her sister. She sent up a quick prayer that everything would be all right, then walked back to the waiting room where she would spend the day anxious for news.

But as she stepped into the open space, she saw it wasn't the same airy, empty room it had been an hour before. Now the three sofas and dozen or so chairs were overflowing with people and supplies.

Penny looked up and saw her first. She smiled kindly. "We invaded," she announced. "I brought plenty to eat because it's going to be a long day and, hello, hospital food? I don't think so." She motioned to several coolers stacked along the wall. "Drinks, salads, entrees, desserts. Sugar seems mandatory at times like these. How are you holding up?"

Lori felt overwhelmed, but managed to nod. "I'm good."

Reid walked up and hugged her. "Did you tell dirty jokes?" he asked.

"I tried."

It had been his bizarre and yet oddly charming suggestion to fill the few minutes before Madeline was taken to surgery.

"Tried?" he repeated. "I gave you great material."

"I know, but she was already pretty out of it. She laughed, though."

That was the image Lori would hold in her mind. Madeline laughing at the lesbian frog joke.

"So my family is here," he said unnecessarily.

Lori glanced around. Cal held baby Allison in his arms. Walker and Elissa unpacked bags filled with paper plates and glasses. Zoe, Elissa's daughter, lined up several stuffed animals as if she was going to hold class.

"You didn't have to ask them to come," she said, surprised by their willingness to be a part of a very long day.

"I didn't ask them. I told them I was going to be here with you and they came on their own."

Her throat tightened. "You're really good to me," she whispered, staring into his dark eyes. "I want you to know that I'm incredibly grateful. You went on television and let those reporters torture you, all so my sister could have a chance. Now she's getting a new liver and it's all because of you."

He stroked her cheek. "Don't give me too much credit. A donor might have been found regardless."

"I don't think so. You're the best man I know."

He gazed into her eyes. "Lori, I—"

"Hi, everyone."

Lori turned and saw a pretty, petite woman walk into the waiting room. She was in her late twenties, with big eyes and a familiar smile.

"My sister, Dani," Reid told Lori. "Come say hi."

Dani had already greeted her brothers, Elissa and Penny. She turned to Lori.

"Hi. It's great to finally meet you," Dani said. "I'm sorry it has to be like this, with your sister in surgery."

"Thanks for coming."

"Not a problem. We Buchanans hang together." Dani grinned. "Besides, how could I not want to meet the woman who trapped the infamous Reid Buchanan?"

Lori felt herself blush. "I didn't exactly trap him."

"I'm not trapped," Reid grumbled. "I'm here willingly."

"Uh-huh." Dani's expression was knowing. "Call it what you want. You're off the market and hearts are breaking across this great nation."

Lori didn't know what to say to that. Dani excused herself and went to take her niece from Cal. Reid wrapped his arms around Lori.

She let herself relax into his embrace and felt her tension ease away. Funny how being close to him made her feel so safe.

"They don't have to stay," she said quietly. "The operation is going to take all day and maybe into the night. No one has to stay."

"They know," he whispered in her ear. "I told them they're free to leave, but I'm guessing they'll be here for the duration. So you're stuck with us."

If this was stuck, she was all for it, she thought.

Love welled up inside of her. Love and need and a sense of being very lucky. But this wasn't the time and these weren't the right circumstances for her confession. When she knew Madeline had come through she would tell Reid how she felt about him. She would take the step of faith and hope for good news. If he didn't love her back, she would survive. At least she would know. She was done holding back because she was afraid.

She looked around, then frowned. "Where's my mom?"

"In the chapel. She wanted to go pray, but she said she'd be back in a while. Penny showed off some of the food. If nothing else, that should entice her to come back."

Lori didn't think anything could make her or her mother eat today. Despite the distraction the Buchanan clan offered, part of her mind was focused only on the surgery. How far had they progressed? Had the donor liver arrived yet? And what about the other family—the one living with grief instead of hope? How was she ever to thank them for giving her sister a second chance?

An hour later, Lori's mother returned to the waiting room. Lori and Reid introduced her to everyone, then Lori took her aside.

"How are you doing, Mom?" she asked, noting the older woman's dark circles under her eyes and the pain bracketing her mouth.

"Just hanging in there. Everything is in God's hands now. I've prayed until I've run out of words. In a few minutes, I'll go back and pray some more."

"That's all we can do," Lori told her.

Her mother nodded. "I have a good feeling about this. Madeline deserves a second chance." Tears filled her eyes. She reached for Lori's hands. "I know I don't deserve one. I know I hurt you so much, for so long. I'm sorry for that. If you don't believe anything else about me, believe that."

Lori's own eyes blurred as she tried not to cry. "Mom, you don't have to—"

"Yes, I do. I should have said something a long time ago. I know you're angry with me, Lori, and who can blame you? I want to blame the alcohol. I want to blame being drunk, but there's no excuse. I hurt you and you were just a little girl. That's what breaks my heart. You were a sweet, loving child and I never told you that. I never said that I loved you. But I did. I do. The only person I hated was myself. Can you understand that?"

Lori understood the intent behind the message if not the words themselves. She nodded slowly.

Her mother sighed. "I was not a happy drunk. You know that better than anyone. The things I said…" She shuddered. "If I could go back in time, I would take you in my arms and let you know how important and special I thought you were. I still think that. But I'm afraid you believe this is all because of

Madeline. That because I might lose one daughter, I now want a relationship with you."

Pride and old wounds battled with the need to move on. In the end, connection won. Whatever else existed between them, they were family. She reached out and took her mother's hand.

"I know you've been trying to connect with me for a while now," she said quietly. "It's not about Madeline."

"It's not," her mother insisted, fresh tears trickling down her cheeks. "It's about all of us. You always talk about your sister being perfect. She was never that. None of us are. I love you both, so much. I want us to be a family."

Lori swallowed. "I want that, too, Mom."

"Really?"

She nodded.

Her mother brushed away her tears, then glanced around the crowded waiting area. They had a small corner to themselves and the Buchanans talked to each other, as if to give them privacy.

"I like your young man," her mother said. "Oh, dear. That's a horribly old expression my grandmother would have used."

"I know what you mean," Lori told her with a grin. "And I agree. He's very special."

"You should hang on to him."

"I plan to."

They hugged. Her mother's embrace was unfamiliar, but Lori was determined it wouldn't stay that way. Family was too important for them not to connect. All of them getting along would be a great incentive for Madeline to recover even more quickly.

Elissa inched toward them. "Are you two okay?" she asked. "Can I get you anything? Penny was thinking of serving lunch." She looked at her watch. "Make that a late breakfast. There's tons of food. I made pie, which now that I think about it is weird, but Walker loves my pies." She stopped. "Sorry. I'm babbling. I don't know what to say."

Lori hadn't spent much time with Elissa, but in that second, she found she really liked her a lot.

"You don't have to say anything. Just you taking the time to be here means a lot. Mom and I appreciate the support." Lori thought for a second. "You know what? I'd love a slice of pie."

Her mother stared at her. "It's barely nine in the morning."

"I know, and I want pie."

Her mother smiled. "I guess I do, too. Is there whipped cream?"

Elissa laughed. "I'm sure Penny brought some. She thought of everything."

"Your daughter is great," Lori said as Elissa sliced pie. "Really well behaved. At her age I would have been bouncing off the walls."

"She's always been easy," Elissa told Lori. "It

helps that she's hanging out with Walker. She says he's the handsome prince in our lives."

Lori saw the little girl cuddled next to the tall former marine. They seemed lost in their own world. Then Walker looked up and smiled at Elissa. Lori felt the residual heat and despite her worry, smiled. Talk about a couple in love.

SOMEHOW WORD GOT OUT that there was a party going on in the waiting room. Several nurses and orderlies joined them. Lori watched Reid's family embrace her mother, keeping her close, talking to her, distracting her.

Lori rested her head on Reid's shoulder as she curled up next to him on one of the sofas. The minutes crawled by. She could think about something else for a second or two, but then her mind returned to the operating room as she wondered what was happening. How many more hours until they knew the surgery was a success? How much longer after that until Madeline was out of the woods. If she could—

The doctor walked into the waiting room. He was tall, still dressed in scrubs. There were stains on the front of his shirt.

Lori was on her feet in an instant. An initial burst of joy was followed by confusion. It was too soon. The surgery was supposed to take all day.

And then she knew. She didn't even have to look into the doctor's eyes to see the pain there.

The room disappeared into a buzzing blur. There was only the sound of her heartbeat and the doctor's drawn face.

"I'm sorry," he murmured, his voice thick with pain and frustration. "It was her heart. A complication we didn't expect."

He kept on talking and talking, but Lori didn't hear anything else. She didn't have to. Her perfect sister was gone.

CHAPTER TWENTY

LORI DIDN'T REMEMBER anything about leaving the hospital or driving home, but suddenly she found herself standing in the middle of her living room. Reid was next to her, his arm around her waist. He guided her to the sofa and urged her to sit, but she resisted.

She couldn't think, couldn't move, could barely breathe. It was as if her life force had drained away. She ached, but the pain was so all-encompassing that she wasn't even close to tears. It was as if crying were too meager a reaction to what had happened.

Madeline was dead.

The sentence played over and over in her mind, like a song lyric she couldn't escape. With each repetition, her body tightened, as if preparing to be hit. She ached from the inside out and knew nothing would ever be the same.

Madeline was gone. Her funny, beautiful, perfect sister hadn't survived the very surgery that was supposed to save her life.

"What can I get you?" Reid asked.

She shook her head, unable to answer him. Speaking seemed impossible.

The front door opened again and Walker and Cal came in, her mother supported between them. Evie had aged a lifetime in the past hour. Lines pulled her face into a mask of grief.

Lori crossed to her and hugged her close. Her mother's thin arms embraced her.

"I can't believe it," her mother said quietly, her voice thick with grief. "I won't believe it. She can't be gone. She can't."

Lori agreed, but she couldn't defy the truth. It nestled inside of her, a dark, heavy creature that stole her breath. She was cold and shaken and knew there were a thousand things she had to be doing. Only she couldn't think of a single one.

The rest of Reid's family walked into the house. They were quiet and uncomfortable, staying at the fringes of the room. Lori knew she should say something—thank them or give them permission to leave.

Before she could force herself to react, Reid put his arms around her and her mother.

"We'll take care of everything," he said. "Just hang on to each other. That's all you have to do."

Lori nodded.

She led her mother to the sofa where the older woman collapsed. Dani crouched at her feet and took her hands.

"Can I get you a cup of tea?" she asked. "Or coffee?"

"Tea would be nice," Lori's mother said.

"I'll get it." Dani rose. "Lori?"

Lori shook her head.

Reid settled Lori next to her mother. Both women were pale with loss. He'd never seen such a stark expression in Lori's eyes. Her pain was so powerful, it was practically alive.

"Is there a doctor?" he asked. "Someone who can prescribe something for you and your mom?"

"What? I don't know." Lori shook her head and started to stand up. "I don't…"

"My purse," her mother said. "I have medication in there. The doctor's name."

While Dani was off making tea, Reid found Evie's purse and called her doctor. In a matter of minutes, Walker had left for the drugstore to pick up the prescription.

Penny walked out of the kitchen and crossed to him. "She doesn't have anything to eat in the house. I have the stuff I made for our day at the hospital, but that's not going to be enough. I'll write up a shopping list for Cal, then stay long enough to fix a few things. Friends and neighbors might drop off food, but we can't depend on it."

Penny had always believed food was the solution for every problem. It was one of her best qualities.

"Thanks," he said. "That will help."

"Good. Okay, let me get the list going. Cal can shop, then bring the food here. Once that's done, he can pick up Allison. Elissa took her and Zoe home." Penny shook her head. "I'm sorry, Reid. For you, for Lori and her mom. It's so awful."

He nodded, but didn't say anything. There weren't any words that could make what had happened all right. He hated what Lori was going through—what she would keep going through. She and Madeline had been close. The unexpected loss would be devastating.

Dani hung up the phone and waved him over.

"I've talked to the hospital and I have the information on when they're going to release Madeline's body. They need the name of the funeral home. Not right now, but probably by tomorrow. I also called my boss. He's given me today and tomorrow off so I can stay here and make arrangements."

Reid leaned down and kissed the top of his sister's head. Penny was great with food and Dani could organize an army. Together they would all get things done.

"Thanks, kid," he said.

"I want to help."

"Me, too."

He wanted to make things better, but how?

He felt a soft touch on his arm and turned to find Lori standing behind him.

"We should call some people," she said. "Friends and stuff. We have a few relatives."

"I'll do it," Dani said gently. "If you show me where to find the names and numbers, I'll make the calls."

"Okay." Lori was pale and looked as if she weren't quite sure where she was. "There will be a funeral. There has to be."

"We'll all help with that," Reid said. "We can take care of the details. You don't have to do anything."

Her lower lip quivered. He reached out and pulled her against him just as she collapsed. He grabbed her, then lifted her into his arms and carried her into her bedroom. From the corner of his eye, he saw Dani sitting next to Lori's mother and putting an arm around her.

"She's gone," Lori whispered. "I can't believe she's gone. It wasn't supposed to be like this."

"I know. I'm sorry."

He set Lori on the bed and stretched out next to her. She curled up against him. He wrapped his arms around her.

"It hurts," she said, her voice shaking. "It hurts so much. I don't want her to be dead. I don't. It's awful and I can't cry."

"You will," he told her, as he stroked her hair. "You have plenty of time for tears."

A COUPLE OF HOURS LATER, Reid drove back to Gloria's house. Dani and Penny would sit with Lori and her mom for a while, so he could take care of a few things. Then he would return to Lori's house to do what he could there.

Anger grew inside of him. Anger and guilt and the need to fight someone…anyone. But who? The only person to blame was himself.

"You couldn't call?" Gloria said when he walked into her room. "I've been waiting by the phone. It's not as if I had anywhere to go, but I've been worried. It's a complicated surgery and…" She drew in a breath. "What happened? You look terrible."

He sat on the edge of the bed and took Gloria's hand in his. "Madeline died during surgery."

The color fled his grandmother's face. In a matter of seconds she looked old and frail.

"No," she whispered. "No. That can't be. She was supposed to be fine. She was supposed to make it. She can't have died. Poor Lori. And her mother. They must be devastated."

"They are."

"That poor child."

"She won't be coming into work for a while. I'll try to pick up as much of the slack as I can. Sandy said she'd fill in a little extra. Is that enough or do you want me to hire another nurse?"

Gloria's eyes filled with tears. "No one else," she whispered. "I'm fine. Getting stronger every day. I'll be all right."

"I know you will be." He leaned over and kissed her forehead.

"I want to help," Gloria said. "Do they need something?"

"It's all taken care of. Dani is arranging the funeral and making calls to family and friends. Penny's getting food in the house. Walker and Cal are running errands."

"I want to go to the funeral. I can make it," she added before he could say anything.

"Then you should go." He released her. "I'm going upstairs. I have to make some calls, but I'll be back down in an hour or so. You'll be all right?"

"Go. I'm fine."

She waved him away and he left. When he reached his room, he closed the door, walked to the sofa and sank down. Only then did he let his emotions loose. They swept over him, surrounding him, speaking the truth in a volume he couldn't help but hear.

Madeline was dead because of him. He'd killed her as surely as if he'd stopped her heart himself.

He'd been so intent on proving himself by finding her a donor. He'd been so damned proud of himself. He'd wanted to be the hero and instead he was the reason Madeline had lost the last year she was going to live.

She could have still been alive today—living with Lori, talking, laughing, *being*. Maybe there would have been a cure, or a better donor. Maybe she would have been ready.

He'd heard what she'd said the day before the surgery. That she wanted more time. Because she felt responsible for him going on television, she'd gone forward with the surgery.

It was his fault. He had to go and try to fix things. To show off. To try to make up for all the other screw-ups. But look what had happened.

He'd ruined things when he hadn't been trying and he'd made things worse when he'd been doing his best. He couldn't win for losing.

He sat there for a long time, feeling the anger and regret. Knowing that Lori could never forgive him for taking the most precious part of her life and killing it. All he'd wanted was to help the woman he loved and instead he'd destroyed her.

AFTER THE FUNERAL, Madeline's friends poured into Lori's house. The small space overflowed with Madeline's coworkers and girlfriends, people she'd known and touched in her too-short life. Lori greeted them as they came in, accepting their condolences. Evie stood next to her, but after a few minutes, excused herself.

Lori knew the last few days had been incredibly hard on her. Her mother seemed to have shrunk. She hoped that time would help, as it usually did, but as she, too, was still in shock, it was hard to imagine ever feeling better.

"I'm so sorry," Gloria said as she entered. She

leaned heavily on a cane and on Cal. "I don't know what to say."

Lori hugged her. "You don't have to say anything. Thanks for being here. But don't overtire yourself. You're still recovering."

Gloria's eyes filled with tears. "Don't you worry about me, child. I'm fine."

Lori nodded, and Gloria and Cal moved on. A few minutes later, the last of the mourners had arrived and she was able to walk through the crowd.

She was amazed at the number of people who had shown up to celebrate her sister's life. There was an equal number of smiles and tears as friends recounted funny and touching stories about Madeline's life.

She found Penny manning the kitchen, organizing enough food to feed the city for three days.

"We're good," Penny said as she looked up from a tray of corn cakes topped with vegetables and tiny shrimp. "I have the food together and Dani's handling the rest of it. I made some pretty intense desserts. At times like these, sugar always helps, don't you think?"

"It does for me," Lori said. "You've been great. All of you. I don't know how to thank you."

"You don't have to. You're one of us. Of course we want to take care of you."

One of them? If only. But she didn't say that. She thanked Penny again and returned to the living room.

Reid stood by the makeshift bar set up in the corner. She crossed to him and accepted a glass of white wine.

"You okay?" he asked, then shook his head. "Let me rephrase that. Are you able to handle all this?"

"There's not a whole lot for me to handle," she told him. "Your family took care of everything. I want to thank you for that. For being there for me. It means a lot."

She couldn't have gotten through this without him. He'd stepped in with Gloria, staying with his grandmother for much of the day, then showing up here to be with her. He'd spent every night since Madeline had died, holding her until she fell asleep.

Part of her felt guilty for not being able to give him more, but honestly, there was nothing left. Her emotional insides were a gray, empty void. Eventually he would get tired of that and move on, she thought grimly. Which meant she was looking at even more pain.

She wanted to say something to him, something that would keep him around until she'd started to recover, but there weren't any words. Still, she had to try.

But before she could come up with anything, a woman walked over and started talking about Madeline.

"She adored you," the woman said, smiling, but with tears in her eyes. "I still remember how happy and touched she was when you invited her to come live here. She told me she wasn't scared anymore. She knew you'd be with her no matter what. She knew how much you loved her."

Lori nodded. Her eyes burned as her throat tightened. "She was my sister," she managed.

The woman gave a little sob. "Sorry. This has to be ten times harder for you than for me and I'm barely holding it together. I just wanted you to know that Madeline talked about you all the time."

"Thank you."

Others approached her with different stories. There were more kind words until Lori couldn't take anymore. She escaped to her sister's room. After closing the door and leaning against it, she realized she still wasn't alone. Her mother stepped out of the small closet, a red blouse over one arm.

"I remember when Madeline bought this," her mother said, wiping her tears. "She had just filed for divorce and she said she wanted to buy something cheerful. But the blouse looked horrible on her and I couldn't seem to lie about it. I remember us standing in my living room, laughing over the fact that she couldn't even buy the right blouse." Tears fell and she wiped them away. "She was always ready to laugh at herself."

"I remember. She tried to pawn that blouse off on me, but I told her there was no way it could look better on me than on her."

Her mother sighed. "She was always a beautiful girl. Even as a baby, she was lovely."

"I know. She never took a bad picture. Even those horrible school pictures turned out great. I hated that." Emotions swept through her. She sank on the bed and clutched her sister's worn and tattered teddy bear to her chest.

"I hated her," she whispered. "God forgive me, sometimes I hated how beautiful and charming she was. How everyone loved her."

Her mother sat next to her and hugged her tight. "You hush right now. Don't beat yourself up, Lori. You didn't hate your sister. Not ever. You wanted what she had and there's a difference. You never give yourself enough credit. I know I'm to blame for that and I'm sorry."

"Don't be sorry," Lori told her. "It's fine. I'm okay. I just wish…" She swallowed hard. "I wish I'd been nicer or something. I wish she'd known how much she mattered to me."

"She knew. Don't you think she knew? You asked her to come live with you in her time of need. You opened your heart and your life. You were saving money so you wouldn't have to work her last months. She knew all that. She would have loved you anyway, but she loved you for that. She respected and admired you. She told me."

Lori felt her eyes fill and for the first time since hearing that her sister had died, she cried.

Big, fat, hot tears spilled down her cheeks. Sobs shook her body.

"I m-miss her," she said, her voice thick and broken. "I miss her so much. I want her back. I know she had to try with the transplant and I'll always be grateful she died with hope, but, God, I miss her."

"I know you do."

They held on to each other, connected by a grief that seemed endless. Eventually the tears slowed. Lori wiped her face.

"Mom, do you want to come live with me?"

Her mother smiled at her. "I appreciate the offer, but we're both too stubborn for that to ever work. But I would like us to be close. We have each other and I don't want to waste a moment of that."

"Me, either."

BETWEEN HER NEW JOB and helping Lori and her mother through the funeral, Dani hadn't had much free time. So it was another week before she found an empty afternoon and the courage to face Gloria.

She parked in front of the large, old house and stared up at the sparkling windows. As a child, the house had terrified her. As a teenager, it had represented a place to escape from. She'd never been comfortable inside the well-decorated walls and she didn't expect to feel any better at the end of this meeting. But she had to try.

She'd called Gloria and had asked for a meeting, explaining the purpose and, despite the older woman's civilized behavior at the funeral, had expected to be shut down. But the woman she would always think of as her grandmother had agreed.

"It doesn't mean anything," Dani muttered to herself as she climbed out of her car, then walked toward the front door. "She just wants to torture me in person."

There was no other logical explanation for Gloria's agreeing to see her. Still, she couldn't help the spark of hope that burned inside.

She was let in by Reid who gave her a thumbs-up after he led her to Gloria's room. Apparently the accident meant she couldn't climb stairs because Gloria sat in a wing chair in the study. The room had been converted to a comfortable bedroom, complete with an adjustable bed and large television.

"Hello, Dani," Gloria said. "Have a seat."

"Thanks." Dani crossed to the other chair in the room and sank down. "You're doing much better. You seemed to be getting around pretty well at Madeline's funeral."

Gloria shrugged. "I'm healing, but still getting older and older. It sucks, but there we are."

Dani blinked. She'd never heard her grandmother use the word "sucks" before. It was kind of scary to hear it now.

"I understand you went to work for Bella Roma? An interesting choice."

"I'm happy with it. Bernie is great to work for."

"His mother can be a bit of a challenge."

Dani remembered that Mama Giuseppe hadn't

had very much nice to say about Gloria and wondered about a past the two might share.

"I'm enjoying the new place," Dani said, going for a neutral response. "It is challenging, but fun. Great people, great customers and the food is amazing."

Gloria studied her. "I haven't seen much of you lately."

"I know."

"Why is that?"

Dani stared at the other woman, unable to believe the question. "You made it clear I wasn't family in the cruelest way possible. You deliberately hurt me. Why would I want to come back for more and why would you want me to?"

Gloria looked down. "Yes, I suppose when you put it like that…"

There was an uncomfortable silence. Dani found herself feeling almost guilty, which really pissed her off. None of this was her fault. She hadn't done anything wrong. So why did she feel like apologizing?

"I don't want to keep you," Gloria said, pointing to a folder on the bookcase. "That's for you. There's basic information about your father inside. I didn't bother with anything else because you'll be able to find out whatever most interests you yourself."

Dani stared at the folder, but didn't reach for it at once. "You're going to tell me his name?"

"Of course, Dani. I understand why you're doing

this, but please be careful. A man in your father's position…" She sighed. "It won't be easy. You have to understand that."

Dani stood up and grabbed the folder, but didn't open it. "What aren't you telling me? Is he a murderer? Someone I'll hate?"

"Not at all. He's—" She waved at the folder. "Open it, for heaven's sake. Then you'll understand what I mean."

Dani sucked in a breath, then flipped open the folder. The top sheet of paper showed a picture of a man in his early fifties. His face was handsome, smiling and incredibly familiar.

Shock held her frozen. She couldn't read the words underneath or bring herself to turn the page. She looked back at Gloria.

"Mark Canfield?" she asked, her voice breathless. "Senator Canfield?"

"Yes."

"He's my father?"

"Yes."

Dani didn't know what to think. "He's running for president. Of the United States. You're telling me my father is running for president?"

"His campaign is still in the exploratory stage, but that's what I've heard."

Dani sank back into the chair and tried to catch her breath. She couldn't get her mind around this life-altering reality.

"I can't believe it," she murmured. "Mark Canfield? I know who he is. I voted for him."

"I'm sure he'll be delighted to hear that," Gloria said with a smile.

REID WOKE in the middle of the night and found himself alone in the bed. He lay there for a second before getting up and walking into the living room.

Lori sat curled up in a corner of the sofa. Outside, street light spilled through partially opened drapes and allowed him to see she was awake.

"Bad dreams?" he asked as he settled next to her.

She shrugged. "When I can sleep, which isn't often."

"You could take something."

"I'm not ready to resort to medicating myself, although I'm close to giving in on that front." She drew in a breath. "Why are you up?"

"You were gone."

She didn't answer that. He put his arm on her shoulder to draw her close, but there was a stiffness in her body that resisted his attempt to offer comfort. Uneasiness settled in his gut.

She was still deeply mourning the loss of her sister. This was hardly the time to talk about their relationship, yet he felt compelled to say something.

"You've been quiet," he told her. "I know you're going through a lot. I've been hanging around to help. Would you rather I wasn't here?"

She turned to him, her eyes dark and unreadable in the half light. "I think that would be better. I need some space right now."

It was as if she'd crawled inside his chest and drop-kicked his heart. The rejection was as sharp as it was instant. He didn't know what to think, what to say. Lori didn't want him around. Lori didn't want *him*.

"I, ah, okay." He stood. "I'll go."

He paused for a second, but when she didn't say anything else, he had no choice but to leave.

As he got dressed he remembered all the times she'd worried that he would be the one crushing her. Looks like she'd spent too much time worrying and he hadn't spent enough.

CHAPTER TWENTY-ONE

GLORIA THREW DOWN her napkin. "What's wrong with you? You're hanging around the house too much. Frankly, you're starting to get on my nerves."

Reid looked at his grandmother. "I can move out anytime."

She sniffed. "I'm not ready for that, but I want to know why you're so quiet and moody. While Madeline was a perfectly lovely young woman, you hardly knew her. So it can't be that."

It wasn't. "I miss Lori," he said quietly, knowing at this point there was no reason to hide from the truth. It slapped him in the face every single minute of the day. "I finally found the woman I want to be with and we can never have a relationship."

"Why on earth not? The girl's crazy about you. She has been from the beginning. I tried to warn her off, but would she listen? Of course not. Young people today."

"She's not crazy about me anymore. She barely speaks to me. About a week ago I asked her if she'd like me to stop coming around all the time, if she needed space. She said it would be better that way." He stared at his uneaten dinner. "She can't forgive me, which I understand. I can't forgive myself."

"For what?" his grandmother demanded. "What is your horrible crime?"

How could she not know? How could she want him to say it aloud? Unless this was her way of forcing him to take responsibility.

"I'm the reason Madeline died."

"You've always had a flair for the dramatic," Gloria muttered. "Dear God, Reid. You weren't in the operating room. It's not as if you ran her over with a car. How is any of this your fault?"

"I found the donor. I insisted on moving forward with that."

"So she could have a chance. The new liver was supposed to save her life."

"But it didn't," he said, feeling the helpless fury rise up inside of him. "It didn't do a damn thing. If I'd just left things alone, she could have had another year. Do you know what that year would have meant to her? To Lori and her mother?"

"I do know," Gloria told him. "But you're taking your already overdeveloped sense of self-importance a little too far. Be logical for a moment. Madeline wanted a liver transplant. You didn't force this upon her. Lori and her mother wanted it, as well. As far as they're concerned, you made a miracle happen."

"You don't know that."

"I have a good idea about it. Besides, based on what you told me, the doctor said Madeline would never have survived any major surgery. She had a heart condition no one knew about. So regardless of who found the donor, she would never have made it."

"But she wouldn't have died that day," he said heatedly. "Maybe, with time, she would have had a chance."

"Or not. You did the best you could. Reid, you put yourself up for public ridicule in an effort to save someone's life. You acted as you did with the best of intentions. No one blames you. Not even Lori."

"You don't know that."

"Of course I do. Did it ever occur to you that Lori's actions have nothing to do with you? That she and her sister have been close for years and that the loss has devastated her? Did it occur to you that she's withdrawn as a way to deal with the pain? Or maybe because she thinks you don't care enough to deal with her grief. Have you talked to her at all?"

"There's nothing to say."

Her expression tightened. "I don't remember you being this much of an idiot before. If you don't get your act together, go to her and tell her how much you love her, I'll write you out of my will."

That nearly made him smile. "I don't need your money, Gloria. I have plenty of my own."

"Fine. I'll fire you."

"I already quit."

Her eyes narrowed. "Then I'll stop loving you."

That got him. He straightened. "I didn't know you did."

She looked away. "Of course I do. You're my grandson. I've watched you grow up and become, until today, a relatively decent man."

"You've never said the words."

She sighed and returned her gaze to his face. "Fine. I love you. Are you happy?"

It kind of surprised him, but, yeah, he was happy to hear it.

He stood, walked around the table and hugged her. "I love you, too," he said.

"I know. So stop telling me and go say it to someone who matters."

LORI WAS SORRY she'd started crying the day of Madeline's funeral. It had been nearly a week and she couldn't seem to stop. She wasn't eating or sleeping. Instead she lived in a world of pain where she missed her sister in ways she hadn't thought possible.

The pain was made worse by the loss of Reid. She'd known letting him go was the only thing that made sense. He couldn't possibly want to hang out with her while she mourned, so when he'd wanted to leave, she'd let him. But as he'd been her only anchor in a swirling, scary world, now she was alone and it terrified her.

Her mother had gone back to her little trailer. All her friends gathered around her and she seemed to be doing all right. But Madeline had been one of Lori's only friends.

"I'm pathetic," Lori muttered to herself as she walked into the kitchen to make some tea. "I have to pull it all together."

She had a job. Although she'd talked to Gloria a few times, she'd yet to make a commitment on returning. Part of her knew that Gloria was well enough to survive without her. Which meant she, Lori, should start looking for another job. But where? The thought of having to deal with someone else right now, to start over at yet another house with another family, was more than she could stand.

She put a spoonful of tea leaves into the pot while she waited for the water to boil. As she reached for a mug, she almost called out to ask Madeline if she wanted tea, then remembered Madeline was gone.

The wave of agony was sharp and fresh. It cut through her, slicing away her strength until she could only collapse and slide toward the ground.

But instead of falling, she was caught in strong arms. She turned and saw Reid standing there.

Gratitude replaced a little of the pain. She threw herself at him.

"You came back."

"I had to," he said, his eyes dark with emotion.

"To tell you I'm sorry. I know this is all my fault. I know I'm the reason she's gone."

The kettle began to whistle. Lori released him and turned off the burner.

His fault? How could he think that? "You don't have anything to do with Madeline dying."

"I found the donor. I pushed for the surgery. I made it happen. She wasn't ready. She made that clear. If I hadn't pushed, she could have survived another year."

Lori supposed a soft, gentle caring response was in order, but she was too stressed. She folded her arms over her chest and shook her head.

"I've always suspected you had delusions of grandeur, but I never expected this. Madeline died because her heart stopped beating. That's it. Unless you have a direct line to God and put in a request to end my sister's life, you had nothing to do with it."

"But I—"

"Stop," she told him. "Just stop. Madeline was going to die from her disease. One way or the other, she was lost to us. Do you know what it's like to live day after day, knowing the end is coming? Sure, we're all going to die eventually, but most of us get to pretend that moment is a long way off. We get to live normal lives. But that wasn't going to happen for her. She was going to get more and more sick. The liver cleans the body from the inside. So she would get more toxic as time went on. Massive bruises would cover her torso. She would be poisoned to death by her own body."

She dropped her arms to her side, but she didn't touch him. She wanted him to listen, to not be distracted by anything else.

"You gave her what no one else could, Reid. You gave her hope. In fact you gave it to all of us. Don't ever make that less than it is. Hope is everything. Hope is a miracle."

"So if you don't blame me, why did you send me away?"

"What? I didn't," she said. "I thought you *wanted* to be gone. I know I've been caught up mourning Madeline. It just seemed like you would want to be somewhere else."

He glared at her. "Dammit, Lori, why do you always do that? Why do you assume I'm here because it's convenient or easy? Why do you think I'm going to disappear at the first sign of trouble?"

His temper surprised her, as did her reaction to it. She was more than ready to fight. "Because you have a long history of taking the easy way out. We've talked about it. You don't hang around when things get difficult."

"In my past," he said. "When, with you, have I ever flaked out?"

Good question. "You haven't had the chance."

"Oh, great. So you're just waiting around for me to screw up? Because that's what I do, right?"

"No. I don't mean that." She didn't. Not exactly.

"So what did you mean? You dumped me before I could dump you?"

"No," she told him. "I'm in mourning here."

"A convenient excuse."

"You should know—you're the king of them."

He shook his head. "You talk about me. Sure I've spent my life taking the easy way out. Well, you've spent your life not even trying. At least I show up."

The unfairness and the truthfulness of the statement cut her. "You don't know anything about me," she said, her voice getting loud. "You don't know what it's like to live in someone's shadow."

"Bullshit," he said in a low voice. "You called me on using my sad past with Jenny as an excuse to hide. Allow me to return the favor. You stopped hanging out in Madeline's shadow a long time ago. Sure the story worked while you were still a kid, but you've been on your own for a long time now. You have a career, a house, you're more than capable of taking on the world. So why are you so damned afraid to step up and take a chance?"

How could he be hounding her like this? Didn't he know what she was going through?

"Why were you always so convinced that I could never really want you?" he asked when she didn't say anything.

"Because you couldn't," she yelled.

"So this has all just been a game? I'm playing you?"

"Maybe," she muttered.

"Maybe?"

"Yes," she told him. "Yes, this is easy and convenient and fun and when it gets hard, you won't be here."

Then she started to cry because as she said the words aloud, she knew that the last couple of weeks had been hard and he'd been with her every step of the way. He'd never flinched from any of the emotional messiness. She'd been the one hiding, the one afraid to believe she was worth loving.

"If that's what you really think," he said quietly, "then I don't belong here."

He turned to leave.

It was like drowning. In that second, Lori saw her entire life flash before her. But it wasn't the years she'd already lived—it was the years to come. The old, empty years of regret. Years where she would search the local papers for some word of Reid. Where she would waste her life wondering how things could have been different.

She could see herself hiding in a crowd, hoping to catch a glimpse of him, wishing he would look up and see her and give her another chance. She could see years of playing it safe.

"Don't go!"

She ran into the living room and grabbed his arm before he could reach the front door. "Don't go. Please. Don't."

She brushed at the tears in her eyes so she could see him. "Reid, don't go. I love you. I love you so much. I'm terrified you'll leave and I'll never survive that. So I thought it was better to get over you now. To hold back, to push you away. I'm afraid. But that's not fair to either of us. I've always hidden because it was easy and safe. But it's lonely and not how I want to live my life anymore."

"What if I don't love you back?" he asked.

She felt cold all over. "Then you're really stupid," she said, trying for bravado and failing. "It'll hurt, but I'll recover. It's easier to get over a heartbreak than it is to try to heal from regrets. And I would regret pushing you away. I'd regret it for the rest of my life."

She decided to be more honest with him than she'd ever been with anyone…including herself. "I've spent too long not trying. Giving up instead of risking. That stops now. I love you, no matter what. You are a part of who I am."

"I love you, too."

She blinked at him. "You do?"

"I do. I love you in a way I've never loved anyone. You bring out the best in me, Lori. You don't let me get away with anything. You're not easy, but you're the greatest time I've ever had." He grabbed her hands, raised them and kissed her knuckles.

"I love you," he repeated. "Seriously, deeply, forever. I only want to be with you. I want to marry you. I want to have babies with you."

"I love you so much," she said as she threw her arms around him and pressed close. "How could I not? You're everything to me."

He grabbed her upper arms and held her far enough away so that he could see her face. "Yeah?"

She smiled. "Yeah."

"And you'll marry me?"

"Yes."

Something light and warm brushed against her arm. It wasn't Reid and the air wasn't blowing. Still she felt the touch and knew she'd made the right choice. For the first time since her sister died, her heart was at peace.

Thank you, she said silently.

The soft brush came again and with it, a faint whisper: "Be happy."

If she hadn't been saving money to stay home with Madeline, she wouldn't have taken the job with Gloria. If she hadn't taken the job, she would never have met Reid, wouldn't have known what it was like to be loved by this man. She might never have found him, or herself.

For the first time in her life she knew what she wanted and where she belonged. With Reid. She'd finally reached the place where she could not only believe in him…she could believe in both of them.

*Turn the page for a look at Susan Mallery's
next enticing Buchanan family novel...
TEMPTING*

CHAPTER ONE

"LET ME MAKE THIS easy for you," the man in the expensive tailored suit told Dani Buchanan. "You don't get to speak to the senator until you tell me why you're here."

"Amazingly enough, that information doesn't make things easier," Dani murmured. She'd already talked her way through a receptionist and two assistants. She could actually see Mark Canfield's door just down the hall. But standing between her and it was a big, determined-looking guy.

She thought about pushing past him, but he was pretty tall and she wasn't. Not to mention the fact that she'd actually worn a dress and high heels—neither of which were normal for her. The dress was no big deal, but the heels were killing her. She could handle the pain in the balls of her feet and the slight pulling in her arches, but how did anyone stay balanced on these things? If she moved at anything faster than a stroll, she was in danger of snapping an ankle.

"You can trust me," the man said. "I'm a lawyer."

Dani smiled. "A profession designed to inspire trust? I don't think so."

His lips twitched as if he were holding in a smile. *A good sign,* she thought. Maybe she could charm her way past this guy after all. Not that she'd ever been especially good at charming men, but if she could fake it, that would be enough.

She drew in a breath and tossed her head. Of course, her hair was cut short, which meant there was no flip over her shoulder. Which left Dani completely out of charming-men-type tricks. Good thing she'd sworn off dating for the rest of her life.

"Think of me as the dragon at the gate," the man said. "You're not getting past me until I know your business."

"Didn't anyone ever tell you that dragons are extinct?"

Now he did smile. "I'm living proof they're alive and well."

Fine, she thought absently. Which was better than *well.* He had a nice face—handsome enough that you wouldn't turn to stone looking at him, but not so pretty that he wouldn't need to develop a personality. Killer blue eyes. A strong jaw, which meant stubborn.

"I'm here for personal reasons," she said, knowing that wasn't going to be enough, but feeling the need to try.

Dragon-man's face tightened as he crossed his

arms over his chest. Dani had the instant sensation of being shut out and judged, all at the same time.

"I don't think so," the man said sharply. "The senator doesn't play those kind of games. You're wasting your time. Get the hell out of here."

Dani stared at him. "Huh?" What was he... Oh. "You think I'm implying the senator and I—" She grimaced. "Yuck. No! Never. Ew." She took a step back, a dangerous act considering the shoes, but she had no choice. Distance was required. "That is too disgusting for words."

"Why?"

She sighed. "Because there's a chance I'm his daughter." Better than a chance.

Suit-guy didn't even blink. "You'd do better to imply you were sleeping with him. I'd be more inclined to believe you."

"Who are you to pass judgment on what Mark Canfield may or may not have been doing twenty-nine years ago?"

"I'm his son."

That got her attention. "Alex, I presume?"

Dragon-guy nodded.

Interesting. Not that she and the senator's oldest son were related. Mark Canfield and his wife had adopted all their children, including Alex. But it was possible they were *family*.

Dani wasn't sure how she felt about that. Dealing

with her known family was complicated enough. Did she want to take on another one?

The sense of needing to belong by blood burned hot enough to give her the answer. If Mark Canfield really was her father, she wanted to get to know him, and no one was going to get in her way. Not even his oldest and unrelated-to-her son.

"I've been patient through one secretary and two assistants," she said firmly. "I've been polite and understanding. If nothing else, I'm a registered voter in this state and I have every right to see my senator. Now if you'll just step aside, before I'm forced to escalate the situation."

"Are you threatening me?" Alex asked, sounding almost amused.

"Would it work?" she asked.

He slowly looked her up and down. In the past six months she'd learned that male attention was not a positive thing in her life. It inevitably ended in disaster. But even though she'd sworn off men, she still felt a little quiver as his steady gaze drifted across her body.

"No, but it might be fun," he said.

"You are such a *guy*."

"Is that a bad thing?"

"You have no idea. Now step aside, dragon-boy. I'm going to see Mr. Canfield."

"Dragon-boy?"

The amused voice hadn't come from the person

in front of her. Dani turned toward the sound and saw a familiar man standing in front of an open door.

She recognized Senator Mark Canfield because she'd seen him on television. She'd even voted for him. But those acts had been from a distance. She'd never thought of him as more than a political figure. Now he was here and there was a very good chance he was her father.

She opened her mouth, then closed it. Words faded from her brain as if she'd just lost the power of speech.

The senator walked toward them. "Are you Dragon-boy, Alex?" he asked the younger man.

Alex shrugged, looking faintly uncomfortable. "I told her I was the dragon at the gate."

The senator patted his much taller son on the back. "You do a good job, too. So is this young lady a particular threat?" He turned to Dani and smiled. "You don't look especially threatening."

"I'm not," she managed.

"Don't be so sure," Alex told him.

Dani glared. "You're being a little judgmental here."

"You're going to make trouble with your ridiculous claims."

"Why are they ridiculous? You don't know for sure, yet."

"Do you?" Alex asked.

The senator looked at both of them. "Should I come back at a better time?"

Dani ignored Alex. "I'm sorry to barge in like this. I've been trying to make an appointment to see you but every time they ask me why, I can't give them the real reason. I…"

The enormity of what she was about to do crashed in on her. How could she just blurt out what she'd been told? That twenty-nine years ago he'd had an affair with her mother and she was the result? He would never believe her. Why would he?

Mark Canfield frowned at her. "You look familiar. Have we met before?"

"Don't even think about it," Alex told her. "You don't want to mess with me."

She ignored him and turned to the senator. "We haven't, but I believe you knew my mother. Marsha Buchanan. I look a little like her. I'm her daughter. And, I think, maybe yours."